LORD

MONTAGUE

Sons of the Marquess

Book 4

A Regency Romance

by Mary Kingswood

Lord Montague: Sons of the Marquess Book 4

Published by Sutors Publishing

ISBN: 978-1-912167-09-8 (paperback)

Cover design by: Shayne Rutherford of Darkmoon Graphics

About this book: *A traditional Regency romance, drawing room rather than bedroom.*

Lord Montague Marford is looking forward to a quiet life as clergyman of a rural parish where he can hope to do some good. But sometimes his compassionate nature gets him into trouble, and when a bedraggled young woman turns up on the doorstep to call in a long-forgotten debt, Monty's sense of honour compels him to offer to marry her. But he soon begins to wonder if he's made a huge mistake.

Miss Melissa Frost is very grateful, and thrilled to find herself surrounded by luxury. It's just like a fairy tale, and although Monty is an unlikely prince, she'd love to be his princess and make him happy. But she daren't tell him the truth — that she's run away from home and her guardian wants her back. She has to keep Monty at arm's length until she comes of age, or she could lose him altogether.

Book 4 of the 5-book Sons of the Marquess series, each a complete story with a HEA, but read all of them to find out all the secrets of the Marford family!

About Sons of the Marquess: *when the ninth Marquess of Carrbridge finds himself short of funds, his five younger brothers have to make a choice: take up a career to support their lavish lifestyle or marry an heiress. But love has a strange way of appearing when it's least expected…*

Book 0: The Earl of Deveron (a novella, free to mailing list subscribers)

Book 1: Lord Reginald

Book 2: Lord Humphrey

Book 3: Lord Augustus

Book 4: Lord Montague

Book 5: Lord Gilbert

Table of Contents

1: A Debt Of Honour

"Melissa, I hope you have a pretty gown for evening tucked away somewhere," the new earl said. She still thought of him as the new earl, although his father had died more than two years ago.

"My lord?"

"You will be dining with the family tonight, so be sure to look your best."

"With the family? Me?"

"Ah, I see your pleasure," he said smugly. "A rare treat for you. But why not, just this once, eh?"

So rare a treat was it, that Melissa could never remember it happening before, and was mistrustful. The new Lord Bentley was not a man who dispensed largesse, or even kindness, as a rule, and she was quite certain this outburst of generosity had some dark motive.

But still, a dinner in company was a welcome event. She curtsied and thanked him with sincerity, and went to see which of her two evening gowns might manage to rise to the occasion. Neither were worn very often, and both had been cast-offs from the present earl's stepmother, taking pity on Melissa before the annual servants' ball. The pink, she supposed, being the newer and least outdated of the two. The previous Lady Bentley had had a pale prettiness that was well-suited to delicate colours, and the gown had looked charming on her. With Melissa's dark complexion, it looked less well. How she wished the present Lady Bentley would offer her a gown, for the striking colours she liked would suit Melissa admirably.

When the dressing gong sounded, Melissa was already in her little room, half undressed and trying to decide whether the addition of ribbons in her hair made her look even more ridiculous or not, when a tap at the door revealed Miss Thompson, Lady Bentley's maid.

"Milady sent me to help you dress, miss," she said, with an audible sniff of disapproval.

"Oh. How very kind of her ladyship." And how very unexpected. Now Melissa was deeply suspicious. She had a sinking feeling that she was being wrapped up like a gift, to be shown off to someone. Perhaps the countess had found her another position, now that she was no longer wanted at Bentley Hall? Although prospective governesses were not usually paraded at dinner. Well, she would find out soon enough.

Miss Thompson primped and curled and fussed until Melissa hardly recognised herself in the glass.

"There, miss, you look very pretty," Miss Thompson said, and her thin lips almost twitched into a smile.

Was she pretty? She would love to be pretty, or perhaps handsome. Everyone said that the present Lady Bentley was handsome, and it seemed to be a compliment, but Melissa was not quite sure what they meant by it. Lady Bentley was elegant, to be sure, in her exquisite colourful gowns, and her manner of piling her blonde curls on top of her head gave her an imposing height, but her countenance was not pleasing. But perhaps that was because she was always scowling when Melissa saw her.

She was not scowling when Melissa entered the drawing room. When she smiled, however insincerely, she did indeed look quite handsome.

"Ah, here she is at last! How impatiently we have awaited you, Melissa dear, but we do not mind in the least, for see how we are rewarded. I never saw you look better, my dear."

"I did not mean to be late. I beg your pardon."

She tittered. "My dear, I intended no rebuke."

Melissa was silent. Since when had Lady Bentley *not* had a rebuke on her lips? Her first lesson as soon as the new earl had married was to learn to keep out of his wife's way.

The countess rose smoothly from her chair and crossed the room to where her husband and brother-in-law stood with a third man, unknown to Melissa. The earl was shorter than average, with an undistinguished air. His brother tended to foppery, with a complicated and slightly lop-sided cravat, a bright red coat and such an array of rings and pins and fobs as to quite dazzle the eye. The stranger was excessively fat, his coat buttons straining across his vast stomach, and a balding head already shining from the heat.

"Here she is, gentlemen. Mr Pontefract, may I present to you Lord Bentley's ward, Miss Frost?"

"Enchanted, my dear," he murmured, creaking as he inclined very slightly from the vertical in what Melissa supposed was a bow. As she rose from her curtsy, he was licking his lips as if she were a particularly tasty dish presented at the dinner table. "Delightful, quite delightful." His eyes ran slowly down to her shoes and back up again, before settling on her chest. "Charming!" He rubbed his hands together, and leered at her.

Melissa shivered.

Dinner was an awkward affair. The Miss Wilkeses, Lady Bentley's daughters from her first marriage, were late, which put the earl out of countenance. Then they giggled and whispered throughout the meal, which put the earl's brother out of countenance. Melissa was seated beside Mr Pontefract, which would have put her out of countenance if she had only dared. She was beginning to have some inkling of the reason for her invitation, and it turned the food to ash in her mouth. She ate but little, and took no more than two sips of her wine, and tried to make pleasant conversation with Mr Pontefract. It was hard work, for he ate prodigiously, leaving him little opportunity to speak, and when he looked at her, his eyes somehow never rose to her face and his breathing grew heavy. In addition, Melissa soon discovered that he had very few thoughts in his head beyond his plate and wineglass. Fortunately, a casual mention of his dogs led her to enquire further, and he then talked with great animation of his kennels and his numerous dogs, and which of them he had bred from and which others he intended to breed from, and so the meal was got through somehow.

When the ladies withdrew, and the Miss Wilkeses had disappeared in a giggling cloud of sarsenet and spangles, still whispering, Melissa would have retreated to her room, duty done, but Lady Bentley summoned her with a crook of one finger into the drawing room.

"You see how generous Lord Bentley is, my dear? For you could not have expected so handsome a gesture, I am sure. But so it is with my dear husband — no effort spared, even for someone like you. What a fortunate young woman you are, to be sure. You may be quite comfortable now, for your future is assured. If you and Mr

Pontefract see Parson Albright tomorrow to arrange the banns, you may be married within the month."

"Oh, *marriage*," Melissa said, relieved that nothing worse was expected of her, as had happened at midsummer with the pretty under housemaid, who had left in tears the next day. Mr Cornelius Brockenhurst, the earl's brother, had a roving eye and, it was said, roving hands as well, and all the female servants had learnt to keep away from him and his lascivious friends. It had always surprised Melissa that she had never attracted his attention, but she supposed she was not pretty enough.

"Yes, marriage, of course. Mr Pontefract is an admirable man, I am sure, and a better catch than you could have hoped for. I trust you will express your gratitude to Lord Bentley."

"Indeed, I am very grateful to his lordship for all his trouble, but I do not in the least wish to marry Mr Pontefract."

"What you wish is not of the slightest consequence. Lord Bentley is your guardian and—"

"I beg your pardon, but I shall soon be of age, my lady. I shall be one and twenty in three months."

"Oh, very hoity-toity! And what other options do you have? Do you have a better husband in mind?"

"No, but I acted as governess to the late earl's daughters for several years, so—"

"And they are gone, and my own daughters do not need any tuition from a rustic like you. So you see, my dear, you have no place here."

"I am sure I could obtain a position as governess elsewhere, my lady. All I should need is a reference—"

A triumphant expression settled on Lady Bentley's face. "Not from me, and not from my husband's stepmother, either, not while he has control of her jointure."

"I see." Melissa's stomach churned with fear, but she tried not to show it. She found some stitchery to occupy her trembling hands, and when the gentlemen returned and sat down to cards with Lady Bentley, Melissa watched her future husband and tried to imagine herself married to such a man.

Mr Pontefract left in a flurry of creaking bows and smiles, kissing her hand with a smirk Melissa could not misunderstand. Lord Bentley went to the door to show him out, and the two men could be heard laughing together in the most amiable way.

"I congratulate you, Melissa," Lord Bentley said when he returned to the room. "Pontefract is quite charmed by you, and will return in the morning to make his offer in form."

"I am very honoured, my lord, but I shall not accept him."

Lord Bentley exchanged a glance with his wife. "You were always wilful, even as a child, so these flashes of disobliging behaviour are no more than to be expected. However, you *will* marry Pontefract. I am your guardian and you must do as I say."

Melissa jumped to her feet. "I may not marry against your wishes, but you cannot *force* me to marry a man I cannot like."

"No?" He crossed the room in two strides, and caught her wrist in a grip so tight that she cried out in pain. "Remember that your bedchamber has no lock to it. All it would take is for me to invite Pontefract to stay for the night, and show him the way. By morning, you would be happy enough to marry him, I swear. And if even *that* is not enough for you, I know the very place in Portsmouth for you, and once there, no man will ever want to marry you. Think carefully on it, Melissa, before you spew your defiance at me."

When she returned to her room, she found the housekeeper awaiting her, to help her undress, just as she had when Melissa was a little girl.

"Oh, Mrs Clark, what am I to do? He is quite dreadful! Yet I daresay he is respectable enough."

"Perhaps," the housekeeper said. "I've heard rumours... I don't like to think of you in the hands of a man like that."

"I suppose... they mean it kindly?" Melissa said. "Surely they do. It is nothing to their advantage, so they must feel it is to mine. Do you not think?"

Mrs Clark sighed. "I've heard that Mr Cornelius got into some difficulty with gaming debts, and rather than ask the earl for help again, he borrowed money from Mr Pontefract. I suppose this is his way of repaying the debt. Gentlemen regard such debts as a matter of honour."

"Mr Pontefract does not know his danger," Melissa said defiantly, not sure whether to laugh or cry. "If ever I were to marry him, I am sure I should make his life a misery and he should be very sorry he ever thought of me. Luckily for him, he is safe from me, for I have no intention of marrying him."

"But what will you do, Melissa? You have no family, no friends to take you in, no money and no possibility of respectable employment without a reference."

"I shall think of something," Melissa said stoutly.

And she knew precisely what she would do. She still had her letter, and there was another debt of honour to be repaid, but this debt was owed to her. Yes, she would go to Drummoor. As soon as Mrs Clark had gone, she pulled out her purse and began to count her coins.

~~~~~

Lord Montague Marford was bored. After the excitement of his brother agreeing — finally! — that he might become a clergyman, and then the joy of his ordination, and several months spent as assistant to Mr Callimont at York, now he was right back where he had started, at Drummoor. His brother, the Marquess of Carrbridge, had several livings in his gift, but none of them were vacant, nor likely to be soon. He could amuse himself as chaplain at the Drummoor chapel, but that was only one day a week. For the other six, he must sit and wait and wait some more. It was dispiriting. Even the weather was in dreary sympathy with his mood.

He laid down his book of sermons, and looked across the winter morning room at the only other occupants. His sister-in-law, Connie, was bent over the worktable, making a list. Guests to invite, possibly, or chores for the housemaids, or chutneys and preserves for the kitchen to make, or perhaps just one of her endless lists of Things That Must Be Done. Meanwhile she was chattering non-stop to her sister, Mrs Allamont, who was presently visiting. Mrs Allamont was more productively employed in trimming a bonnet, although she seemed to take her full share in the conversation, even though her fingers never stopped moving. Aunt Jane March said nothing, but she nodded and smiled at intervals, while steadily tatting.

Monty could hear Carrbridge and Mr Allamont out in the hall, laughing about something. No doubt Mr Allamont had come up with another of his outlandish schemes of improvement to his land, for he was full of ideas, while Carrbridge was much more conservative in his methods, and teased him unmercifully. It was all rather remote to Monty, the productivity of milking cows being very far from his concerns as a clergyman. His interest would be in the spiritual welfare of his parishioners, and if he kept a few chickens at his parsonage, that would be as near as he would come to agricultural matters.

If ever he had his own parsonage, of course. Eventually, Mishcombe would be his, which was a fine living within half a mile of Drummoor, but the present incumbent, Mr Hay, although elderly, was perfectly hale and likely to live for another twenty years at least. In the meantime, he had to wait with as much patience as he could muster for one of several clergymen to drop down dead so that he might have their place, and it was an uncomfortable feeling. He did not wish any of them dead, but nor did he much like sitting about at home, being bored. Perhaps the Archbishop would have some sudden need for one of the gentlemen, and summon him to York, leaving the way clear for Monty. That was a happier thought, a promotion rather than death.

Connie rang for tea, and that brought everyone into the winter parlour, including the usual array of aunts and uncles who had been invited to visit in the summer and had stayed on for months. For once there were few house guests other than family. Connie loved to have the place full of visitors, but with her confinement fast approaching, even her enthusiasm for entertaining had waned somewhat.

Daniel Merton came in with a note for Carrbridge, and the two whispered together for some time. They were an interesting contrast, Carrbridge every inch the aristocrat, his coat, his trousers, even his hair all of the first style, and his manner patrician. Merton, his secretary, was a gentleman and so there was nothing obsequious in his manner, but he never put himself forward, either, and his plain black coat was just as unobtrusive as the man himself.

Now the two of them came towards Monty. "There is news, my lord," Merton said.

"Good news or bad news?" Monty said. "I do not like to hear bad news, you know."

"It is both, I believe," Merton said, as Carrbridge chuckled. "Mr Whittaker, from Kirby Grosswick, has died."

"Oh."

"The living is vacant now, you see," Carrbridge said, beaming happily at him. "Congratulations, Monty. You will be installed there in time for Christmas."

"Oh." Happiness bubbled up inside him. "That... *is* good news! Not for Mr Whittaker, of course, but..."

And then they were all crowding round him, congratulating him, the gentlemen shaking his hand briskly, the ladies exclaiming in delight, and Connie shedding a tear.

From the door, the butler coughed. "Beg pardon, my lord, my lady, but there is... a person in the hall. A Miss Frost. She is asking to see the Earl of Deveron."

The room fell silent. "The Earl of Deveron?" Connie said, her tone shrill.

"That is what she says, my lady."

Merton cleared his throat. "Is Miss Frost a lady, Crabbe?"

"Hard to say, sir," the butler said in haughty tones. "Not a servant, I should say. She is carrying a portmanteau."

"Shall I investigate?" Merton said. But in the end Connie and Carrbridge and several others went out to the hall too, and Monty drifted along behind them, feeling rather sorry for this Miss Frost who was neither lady nor servant.

She was very young, perhaps twenty, and tall but exceedingly thin, as if she had not eaten properly for a long time. Her boots, travelling gown and pelisse were of reasonable quality, if rather worn, and her bonnet had once been quite stylish. Now it was so sodden that the remains of two feathers trailed listlessly onto her shoulders and dripped steadily.

"Miss Frost?" Carrbridge said. "I am the Marquess of Carrbridge and this is Lady Carrbridge. What is this about the Earl of Deveron?"

The girl lifted her chin defiantly. "I want to talk to him."

"Might one enquire as to the nature of your business with him?"

"I am betrothed to him." She looked Carrbridge right in the eye, as if daring him to disagree with her.

"*Betrothed* to him?" Connie burst out. "Impossible!"

"It is perfectly true," the girl said defiantly. "The engagement is of long standing, and now that I am old enough, I intend to hold Lord Deveron to his commitment."

It was so ridiculous that it had to be a joke, but Monty felt not the least desire to laugh. The girl — Miss Frost — was so sincere, so determined that it almost seemed a shame to unravel her plan, but it had to be done.

"Perhaps," he said carefully, "Miss Frost might care to meet the Earl of Deveron?"

"Oh, yes please," she said at once. "I should very much like to meet him, so that we may... begin making arrangements and so forth."

"This way," Connie said, leading the way towards the stairs. "Crabbe, tell Mrs Compton to prepare the rose room. Miss Frost will want a hot bath as soon as may be. My dear, you are quite soaked. Did you walk up from the village in all this rain?"

"From the village with the big cross in the middle. That was as near as the farmer could bring me."

"Mishmere Cross? Good gracious! That must be... a very long way."

"Close to ten miles," Merton said from behind her.

"Good gracious," Connie said again, faintly. "Here we are."

She threw open a door, and immediately the air was filled with squeals, as several children chased each other round and round the room on hobby horses. In a corner, three nursemaids sat in a gossipy huddle, leaping to their feet and hastily curtsying as soon as they realised they were observed.

Connie made no reprimand. Instead she waded into the mêlée and scooped up a sturdy boy of four, who immediately grinned and tried to grab the ribbons of her cap. Connie carried him back to the door.

"Miss Frost, may I present to you the Earl of Deveron. Dev, say hello to Miss Frost."

The girl's face grew ashen, and at first Monty thought she might faint from shock. Then she turned and stomped back out onto the landing. The others followed her out.

"I am so very sorry," Connie began.

"No, you are not," the girl said, her eyes flashing. "You think it a great joke, I daresay. Some poor deluded woman turns up to marry a child of... how old is he?"

"He will be five next birthday," Connie said, "and I do not think it a joke at all, for you have come all this way... where have you come from?"

Was that a hesitation? She licked her lips. "Cornwall."

"Well, that is a great way indeed. But you may see for yourself that you have been misled. Whatever understanding you have cannot be with Dev. You may stay here until the weather improves and then we will see you on your way back to Cornwall."

"Oh, that is very fine, and no mistake," Miss Frost cried. "So that is the end of it, is it? I was promised a husband, look, it says so here." She pulled a letter from some inner recess of her pelisse, and waved it at them. "The Marquess of Carrbridge — you, sir — promised me to your son, and now you think you can just shrug and walk away, do you? You nobles are supposed to have a sense of honour."

Carrbridge was reading the letter. "It does seem... Merton, read it, will you. My father's hand is very distinctive, so this would have been my father promising you to *me,* Miss Frost. I was the Earl of Deveron when he was alive, you see. But I do not quite see what can be done about it now."

Merton looked up. "Miss Frost, it looks to me as if your father gambled you away to the eighth marquess in some wager that went badly for him. The eighth marquess tells him to keep you for the present, and he will marry you to the Earl of Deveron when you are of age."

"I know what it says!" she spat.

"But you must see that such an offer has no legal force. There is no obligation—"

"Yes, there is!" she said, stamping her foot. "I have been in expectation of the marriage for years. If the Earl of Deveron is not available, then you must find me another husband, that is only fair."

"I do not think—" Carrbridge began, frowning.

Monty raised a hand. "Carrbridge, this a matter of honour, a debt that we must repay."

"No, Monty, no!" Connie cried, realising what he was about.

"A matter of honour," he repeated firmly. "Therefore *I* will marry Miss Frost."

"And who are you?" she said, staring at him unsmiling.

"I am Lord Montague Marford, Lord Carrbridge's brother."

"Then you will do. I accept."

2: *Dinner At Drummoor*

Melissa followed the marchioness along endless corridors. Latticed windows gave views on first one side, then another, but all that could be seen was house — endless house, with more latticed windows, steeply inclined roofs and tall chimneys. Drummoor must be enormous. Here and there footmen stopped to bow as they passed by, before continuing with their tasks of tray-carrying or lamp-lighting. Already it was growing dusk.

The rose room was huge, the furniture heavily ornate in the style of some fifty years ago. The paint and paper were fresh, however, and pleasingly light. The housekeeper was already in the room, supervising the footmen who were manoeuvring a bath tub, and several maids who were making up the bed, drawing curtains, placing lamps on every surface and coaxing the fire to life. The room was still chilled, and Melissa shivered.

"You poor thing, you must be frozen!" Lady Carrbridge exclaimed. "Do come and stand in front of the fire for a while. Here, let me take your pelisse. Mrs Compton, send for Harker, if you please. There, Miss Frost, there is a good blaze now. We shall soon have you warm. When did you last eat?"

"I... am not sure. Stamford, perhaps." After that she had saved her few remaining coins for hot coffee. Who would have thought the stage coach would be so expensive? She had but a few shillings left, and if Lord Carrbridge were to throw her out she would be destitute, and what would she do then? She shivered again, and not solely from cold.

Lady Carrbridge blinked. "Stamford. Good gracious. Mrs Compton, some hot soup for Miss Frost. Are you feeling some benefit from the fire now, Miss Frost?"

"Thank you, yes." She gestured vaguely towards the marchioness's swelling stomach. "When—?"

Lady Carrbridge dimpled. "Oh... two more months, I believe. Perhaps three."

"This will be your fifth or sixth?"

She looked startled, then laughed. "Oh, the nursery! No, only two of those are mine. Mrs Pembroke's daughter is visiting her — in the village, you know — and her three are much of an age with my two, so they play together often. Or riot together, perhaps one should say. Ah, here is my lady's maid. Harker, Miss Frost will be staying for a while. Pray unpack her portmanteau, and prepare something for her to wear this evening. If..." She glanced at Melissa's travel-stained clothes. "If there is nothing suitable, borrow a gown from my wardrobe until Miss Frost's boxes arrive. For this evening, I suggest the green figured silk would be an admirable choice. You will not mind wearing one of my gowns, Miss Frost? For I cannot wear much of my wardrobe just now anyway, and the colour would suit you so charmingly, it might almost have been chosen with you in mind."

Melissa nodded, and for a moment was almost overcome. Nothing here was as she had expected. Drummoor was far grander than she had ever imagined. Bentley Hall, for all the earl's airs, had been very modest by comparison. Nor had she expected to receive such kindness. Anger, hostility, disbelief — certainly. Perhaps a purse of money to rid themselves of such a disagreeable situation.

Or they might have known of a suitable position as governess for her. But an instant offer of marriage from the younger brother! And now she was to be dressed in the marchioness's own clothes. That was beyond her expectations, and guilt almost overwhelmed her. What would they say when they realised that she had no boxes to arrive, that all she had in the world was contained in that portmanteau? She wanted nothing but to crawl into a corner somewhere and weep.

But she must not weaken! The moment she showed how afraid she was, they would pounce on her and throw her out. So she lifted her chin defiantly, and reminded herself that she was entitled to be there. Had her father not *given* her to the previous marquess? So now they had an obligation towards her. Yes, she must keep reminding herself of the obligation, for a noble family would not walk away from that, surely. She must show no softness or doubt, and never, ever admit to the terror crouching inside her, like a cat ready to spring out of hiding.

~~~~~

"Monty, you are *insane!*" the marquess cried, running his hands through his hair in distraction. "You cannot do this, you *must* not! I forbid it. It is one thing to be handing out coins to anyone who gives you some Banbury tale of bad luck and poor investments, but you cannot marry a complete stranger who turns up on the doorstep. You know nothing about this girl."

The men had all retreated to the ship room, so called because of the paintings of ships adorning it, which was both the marquess's office and a male sanctuary. Merton had taken his usual seat at one end of the huge desk, and Uncle Lucius and Uncle Joshua sat side by side on two chairs against the wall. Hugo Allamont lurked by the door, scooped up in the general exodus from the drawing room, but looking as if he half-expected to be turfed out, excluded from Marford family business as an outsider.

Monty himself was perfectly composed. His offer had arisen on the spur of the moment, but he was entirely satisfied with it. As a clergyman, he was expected to marry, and this way relieved him of the tedious and time-consuming business of courtship, and also gave him the very great satisfaction of offering Christian charity to a young lady in distress. Yes, it was perfect.

"The offer is made now, Carrbridge," he said mildly. "I could hardly withdraw, even if I wished to. Which I don't. *'Remember them which suffer adversity'*."

"But it is madness!" Carrbridge cried again. "You are not thinking clearly."

"On the contrary, it makes perfect sense. Father made a promise, and here is an excellent way of honouring that promise with the least inconvenience to anyone. I must marry sometime, you know, and this is as good a way of going about the business as any."

"But you know nothing about her."

"And how much would I know about a lady met only in ballrooms during the season? That she dances well, perhaps, and can talk about the weather while dancing the quadrille, but not a great deal else. That is not much of a foundation for marriage."

"But you would know who her family is," the marquess said. "You would know her history."

"Which would be no guarantee of happiness in matrimony," Monty said gently. "There are innumerable examples of perfectly matched society marriages which brought misery to both parties. Happiness in the married state is a matter of temperament, not family history. *'Marriage is honourable in all.'*"

"But she could be… an opera dancer, for all you know. Or some man's rejected mistress. Think of the family name, Monty!"

"My dear brother, I am going to be a country clergyman, not parading around town. If we find we dine with half a dozen families, I shall be surprised. She will be perfectly acceptable in such a setting."

"But you do not know that!"

Merton cleared his throat. "We could, perhaps, ask the lady for details of her family, and then make enquiries, if that would set your mind at rest, my lord?"

"No, no, no," Monty said firmly. "I will not have Miss Frost interrogated or investigated like a common criminal. *'Ask no question for conscience sake.'* We have the letter from Father which lays a very clear charge upon us to help her, and even without that we must, as Christians, offer her the hand of charitable kindness. I am perfectly content to do this, Carrbridge, and no amount of striding up and down will change my mind."

"Merton, pray enumerate the reasons why he should not."

"You have already given the primary reason, that Miss Frost is a stranger to us," Merton said. "However, Lord Montague has made it clear that that will not weigh with him. Besides… I am inclined to agree that there is *some* family obligation towards Miss Frost. It need not involve marriage, but it does seem to me that honour demands some recompense, especially as her father, this…" He scanned the letter again, which he still held. "…this Thomas Frost was obviously a friend of the eighth marquess."

"Why do you say that?" Uncle Lucius said. "I never heard of the fellow before, and I thought I knew everyone that Charles ran with."

"Perhaps Frost is not his name," Merton said. "But he must have been close to the eighth marquess, because he is addressed by his Christian name. There is no direction on the letter, it was never sent through the mail, or through servants, so the marquess must have given it to Mr Frost himself. That strongly suggests a close acquaintanceship."

"I remember something of the business," Uncle Joshua said. "It was the talk of the town for a while, that some fellow had wagered his daughter. Charles put up his famous Arabian filly, a splendid horse, and someone said to the fellow with the daughter, *'Have you no filly of your own to set against Charles?'*, and the fellow said, *'Bless me, so I have! You can have my daughter, for I am sure I do not want her!'*. But I thought it was an earl who had the daughter. Just goes to show how these stories get muddled in one's mind over the years."

"But the central point of the story is not in dispute, I take it?" Merton said. "There really was a wager, and the daughter was the sum wagered, the bet was lost and she belonged to the marquess in some sense. He would perhaps have seen himself like a guardian. He does seem to have been very protective of everything of substance he won over the years. When it was property, he kept it separate from his inherited properties, so that the original owner might have the opportunity to buy it back later. The letter does seem rather remorseful about the bet. *'We both drank far too much of Dunmorton's claret last night, but we must make the best of it, and do right by the girl'*, he says."

"Would Father truly have expected me to marry Miss Frost?" Carrbridge said, suddenly bleak. "For an arranged marriage must be the very devil. A man should love his wife, in my opinion. That is the only proper foundation for a happy marriage."

"I daresay he would merely have introduced the two of you, to see if anything took," Uncle Lucius said. "If not, he would have hauled the girl off to London and got her fixed up there. But his own marriage was arranged, so you can hardly expect him to disapprove of the idea on principle."

"No!" Carrbridge cried. "Father loved Mama, I know he did."

"Oh, certainly. A man can grow very fond of his wife over the years, but it was no love match originally, I assure you. Arranged marriages can work very well."

Allamont said, "That is very true. This is a point on which I can speak with some authority, for my wife and I married for purely pragmatic reasons, to save Allamont Hall from being given away to the church under the terms of her father's will. But it worked out very well for us, and Hope and I could not be happier."

"Thank you, Allamont. You encourage me," Monty said. "'*We have done that which was our duty to do.*'"

"Just be sure to give yourselves plenty of time," Allamont said. "Do not rush things, and get to know each other, and I am sure everything will work out well for you."

~~~~~

Melissa hardly knew herself. The rail-thin child in the worn gown who had arrived at Drummoor had been magically transformed into a fairy-tale princess. The gown took her breath away, for it was exactly what she would have chosen herself. Its sea green underskirt and paler tunic with a silver net overskirt suited her so perfectly that she could not speak a word. Several ladies' maids crawled about her with pins and needles to fit it to her thin shoulders. Then her hair was pulled into a fashionable topknot and wrapped about with silver bands, in such a simple but elegant manner. She supposed there must be some grand function that evening, to require such a fine gown, but when she suggested this to the maids, they giggled and told her that it was just a family dinner. She supposed that this was a family that always dressed in its finery for the evening.

Lord Montague was waiting for her at the bottom of the stairs. Her betrothed, she supposed, although it was a strange idea. And if she were a fairy-tale princess now, then he must be her prince. He was certainly handsome enough, which she had been too nervous to notice before. He was as unlike the hideous and vulgar Mr Pontefract as it was possible to be. His clothes were sombre black, it was true, and she would have preferred a little colour about him, but everything was of the finest, his manners were impeccable and his face had a great deal of countenance, with dark eyes that shimmered with compassion, and full lips that betokened a passionate interior. He was very restrained in his public manner, but she had read enough novels to hope for a man of passion.

He bowed and complimented her on her appearance and asked was she rested now after her journey? His voice was so quiet and solicitous that again she was close to tears. No, she must be strong!

"I am perfectly well, I thank you, my lord."

He offered her his arm and led her through to the drawing room. She had never in her life walked about on a man's arm, and she had to mind her steps, to measure her pace to his. It was not so easy as she had thought.

As they entered the drawing room, every conversation died away, and every face turned to watch them. She was so unused to being looked at that she could not stop herself blushing. But she must not be demure, that would be fatal. They were a rich, powerful family — lions pacing around their prey. She must not give them any opportunity to pounce. She raised her chin and gazed around as if she belonged there. She *did* belong there! Was she not about to marry one of the family?

Lord Montague led her across the room to Lord Carrbridge, who rose and bowed and told her that he was glad to see her looking so refreshed. He was very civil, but unsmiling. Then she was introduced to everyone in the room and given all their names — Lord This and Lady That, and just a handful who had no title. And they all made polite noises about what dreadful weather to be travelling, and hoped she would enjoy her stay at Drummoor. But there was no warmth in any of it, and not one of them congratulated her on her engagement, which she felt very much that they ought to have done.

"Shall you stay long, Miss... er, Frost?" enquired one very elderly lady in puce bombazine, raising a quizzing glass to one eye.

"Just until I marry Lord Montague, my lady," Melissa said robustly.

"Oh!" The lady swivelled the quizzing glass onto Lord Montague, who smiled benignly.

"Miss Frost and I are betrothed, Aunt Ruth," he said in his quiet way.

"Oh!" she said again. Then, "Oh. I did not know. Nobody tells me anything."

"It is not widely known, as yet," he said. "Miss Frost, this is my Uncle Ambrose — Lord Ambrose, for he is a Marford. He is married to Aunt Beatrice — you met her a few moments ago. And this is Uncle Joshua — Mr Thornton. He is married to Aunt Theodosia, Lady Theodosia, that is, although she has a cold and is not dining with us tonight. And Uncle Lucius is from the March side of the family, and here is his sister-in-law, Aunt Jane March."

Her head was spinning, and it was a relief when they went into dinner. She had Lord Montague on one side of her and one of the many uncles on the other. The food was exactly as she had expected it to be, elaborate, exotic and plentiful. Vast numbers of footmen moved silently about the room, overseen by the fearsome butler.

The room was perhaps four or five times the size of the dining room at Bentley Hall.

When she made some comment to this effect, Lord Montague smiled. "Ah, but this is only the green dining room, which we use for just the family. In the summer or at Christmas, when the place is full, we use the pink dining room, and for special occasions we dine in the great hall."

"The great hall?" she said faintly.

His eyes twinkled. "Naturally there is a great hall. What self-respecting medieval house would be without one? Tomorrow, if you wish it, I shall take you all over Drummoor, and tell you something about the family. And you may tell me about yours, of course."

Her heart sank like a stone. She had her story prepared, of course, and some of it was even true, but it was one thing to sit in her attic room at Bentley Hall rehearsing the details in her mind, and quite another to tell bare-faced lies to so trusting a man as Lord Montague. Well, it might all go wrong yet, but until then she would eat and drink and enjoy herself, and hope for the best. And as dish after dish was removed and replaced with another even more delectable, and she gazed about at the candles lighting the room as bright as day, the many silent footmen, the heavy silver knives and forks, and sparkling cut glass goblets, she felt that living at Drummoor would be a wonderful thing. This truly was a fairy-tale and she a princess! But was Lord Montague really her prince?

As the meal drew to a close, the marquess rose and rapped on the table to quieten the conversations.

"Pray indulge me, everyone, with your attention for a few moments, for I have a piece—" He threw a glance at Monty. "—*two* pieces of good news to impart to you all, concerning Monty. Firstly, he is this day betrothed to Miss Frost, of Cornwall. And secondly, the living of Kirby Grosswick has fallen vacant, and it will be my very great pleasure to bestow it upon my brother."

There was a murmur of pleasure around the table, and Lord Montague rose and bowed, then sat down with a little smile.

"You are a *clergyman?*" Melissa said, aghast.

"Oh, yes! I was ordained earlier this year, but I had no hope of an early living, you know, so this is a piece of great good fortune. Not for the previous incumbent, of course, who is now dead, but it is wonderful news for me. For *us*. It is only a small country parish, but a very good living. We shall have almost two hundred pounds a year to live upon. Such a sum will keep us very comfortable, I am sure. Do you know how to look after chickens? I believe we shall be obliged to keep chickens."

Melissa stared at him, stunned, as all her pleasant dreams of a life of luxury at Drummoor trickled into dust.

3: Lady Harriet Arrives

When the ladies withdrew, Monty was again the focus of attention.

"Not really planning to marry the chit, m'boy?" Uncle Ambrose said.

"Certainly I am."

"She looks a great deal better in one of Connie's gowns than she did when she arrived," Carrbridge said. "Not that I am reconciled to this, Monty, but at least she has decent manners."

That was very true, and Monty had been pleased to see that Miss Frost did nothing that might startle the company. She was not forthcoming, but she answered readily enough when addressed on unexceptional subjects, like any well-bred young lady.

"But she is not accustomed to formal dinners," Merton said. "She was watching carefully to see how to go on."

"I noticed that myself," Uncle Lucius said. "And any woman would look well after Connie has taken an interest in her. I cannot forget the girl's appearance when she arrived here — everything patched and faded, and nothing but a portmanteau with her. Not a maid or chaperon to be seen. And how did she get here? She had a lift on a farmer's cart to Mishmere Cross, but she must have come by stage or mail coach to Sagborough, and all alone. That is not the behaviour of a proper lady."

Monty's temper rose, and he had to take a deep breath and remember his calling before he was able to suppress it. "This is not helpful, uncle. *'He that is without sin among you, let him first cast a stone at her.'* Miss Frost is my future wife, and I will not have aspersions cast on her behaviour. We do not know the circumstances of her journey."

"Then let us enquire into them," Uncle Lucius said.

"It is of no interest to me how she came to Drummoor," Monty said firmly. "Therefore it cannot be fruitful to enquire further. Let us offer the hand of friendship to Miss Frost, as a stranger in our midst, and do nothing which might make her uncomfortable. *'Be not forgetful to entertain strangers: for thereby some have entertained angels unawares.'*"

"Oh, by all means let her not be uncomfortable," Uncle Ambrose said testily. "Let her walk in here from who knows where, and sit at Carrbridge's table eating his turkey and drinking his claret and wearing his wife's gowns and enjoying herself thoroughly, and heaven forbid we should enquire into who on earth she is, or whether she is a proper wife for the son of a marquess. You are a fool, Monty, but you will not be guided in this matter, I can see."

"I have seen nothing in her behaviour to suggest that she is anything other than a gently-brought-up lady who has fallen into some financial difficulties," Monty said calmly. "That makes her a perfectly proper wife for a clergyman with a modest income. My mind is made up, and further discussion will not alter my resolution. I am going to join the ladies, so you may discuss the matter as much as you please without me."

When he entered the drawing room, he searched for Miss Frost, finding her seated between two of the aunts. They were both talking at once, and Miss Frost had such a glazed expression her face that Monty almost smiled. The poor girl was exhausted, and quite incapable of withstanding the onslaught.

"Miss Frost?"

She looked up at him so hopefully that he could not help smiling. "My lord?"

"Aunt Theresa, Aunt Juliana, you will not mind if I steal Miss Frost away from you?"

"Very well, very well," Aunt Juliana said, then added ominously, "We shall talk again tomorrow, Miss Frost."

He gave Miss Frost his arm and led her out of the room.

"Where are you taking me?" she said, eyes narrowed in suspicion.

"Away from my aunts who would talk you half to death," he said. "I thought you might have had enough of the Marfords for one day. The card tables will be coming out soon, and then you would never escape. Should you like to go to your room now?"

"Oh... thank you. I *am* tired."

"You have had a long journey," he said, shepherding her towards the stairs.

"Indeed, and the stage coach is very uncomfortable. I had no idea. It seems so romantic, the idea of travel, but the reality is not in the least romantic. Bad inns, broken wheels, and every bump in the road shakes one's bones."

"I can imagine," he said sympathetically. "Fortunately, you will never have to travel by public coach again, Miss Frost."

She fell silent, so he kept up a patter of conversation about the house and the various rooms they were passing until they reached the door of her room.

"Your maid will be waiting to help you undress," he said. "She will bring you your morning chocolate, too. We breakfast at ten, but there is always a fire in the winter morning room before that, if you rise early. Have the maid show you the way, or else you will get horribly lost. Everybody does, just at first. Good night, Miss Frost."

He bowed, she bobbed a hasty curtsy, and he turned to go.

"Thank you, my lord," she called after him.

"You had better call me Monty," he said. "Everybody does."

A half smile, then she turned the doorknob and disappeared into her room.

~~~~~

Melissa woke abruptly from dreams of formless terror, not quite sure where she was. She had fallen asleep instantly, exhausted, but the softness of the bed and the warmth of the blankets were unusual enough to drag her back from deep slumber. With the curtains drawn all round the bed, she was in darkness, but there was no sound in the house, and she guessed that it was still the middle of the night. After some fumbling, for she was unused to such things, she pulled the bed curtains apart, and slipped out of bed, still shaky from her dreams. The remains of the fire glowed in the grate, and oh glory be, there was coal in a scuttle beside it. She soon had a good blaze going, then lit a candle — wax! In the bedrooms! The indulgence of it.

Prowling around the room, she found decanters of sherry, port and brandy, and a jar of macaroons. Sipping port and nibbling a macaroon, she opened drawers and closets, found several delicious gowns she did not recognise in the wardrobe as well as her own four, and discovered a cache of books in the bedside cabinet. With a smile of anticipation, she closed the door again. Tomorrow would be time enough for reading, and somewhere in this great monstrosity of a house there must be a library. Her whole body quivered in delight.

She fetched a pillow and curled up on the rug in front of the fire, savouring the unaccustomed warmth. Oh, what joy to have a fire in her bedroom again! In recent winters she had never been able to get warm. She stretched like a cat, rolled over, curled up again and was asleep within moments. This time the dreams were more vivid, of someone rattling the door of her attic bedroom, trying repeatedly to get in. She screamed, but no sound would come.

The next time she woke, rain was clattering against the window, and somewhere nearby a loose shutter was banging. The fire had died down again, and she had used all the coal, so, shivering, she dived back into bed, pulling the layers of soft blankets around her. So much luxury was almost overwhelming. Her whole life had been one of restraint, hoarding candle ends so she could read in bed, mending and remaking her gowns to save money, even before the old earl had died, but the last two years had been little less than penury. She could hardly believe the plenty that now surrounded her. A corner of her mind nudged her conscience, but she suppressed it. She was entitled to be there, after all, for had the late marquess not promised her... well, *something*. His son, except that he was already married. But something, certainly.

Ever since she had crept out of Bentley Hall in the cold and dark, she had tried not to think of Lord and Lady Bentley, but the dreams brought them back to her mind. What had they made of her disappearance? Were they even now trying to find out what had become of her? Were they following her trail northwards, asking at every coaching inn along the road? A young woman of just such a height and colouring, wearing a pelisse of this colour and a hat with two feathers... and the innkeeper, keen to help so fine a gentleman, and an earl too, would say, yes, my lord, she took the London coach. And then it would not take long to find that she had later taken the York stage. Oh God, they could be in Yorkshire already!

What would she do if they found her? Lord Montague would learn that she was under age, and not free to marry without Lord Bentley's consent. He would learn that she was betrothed to Mr Pontefract, his offer accepted with her best attempt to smile and appear complaisant, to give herself time to escape. Mr Pontefract, so keen to secure her hand that he had raced off to London to obtain a special licence. There had been no time left to think or to plan or to cover her tracks. She had crept out of the house that very night and fled. And now she sat at Drummoor, waiting to be found, waiting to be dragged back to the nightmare.

Then the tears came, the tears she had been fending off ever since that dreadful night when Mr Pontefract had leered at her, and she had learnt her fate. No, before that, ever since the old earl had died, and the new earl had sent away his step-mother and her children. Melissa's only friends. For two years she had been stalwart and obedient, smiling even as she patched her gowns and hoped the servants would sneak her an extra chicken leg. For two years she had kept her feelings at bay. But there in the quiet of the night, wrapped around with the softest wool blankets and smooth linen sheets, she wept and wept unstoppably.

~~~~~

The morning passed pleasantly enough. First came the chambermaid to get the fire blazing again. Then, later, a cup of chocolate, a treat which she had not enjoyed for a long time but which was just as delicious as memory made it. Then a maid of her own, Margaret, helping her dress and showing her the way to the winter parlour, where she read a newspaper until Monty found her and took her to the breakfast parlour. Happily, the room was devoid of aunts and uncles, and everyone was terribly polite to her, while she stuffed herself with the vast array of breads and pastries on offer, tasting everything. Then Monty took her all over the house, which was a warren of odd wings and courtyards and abrupt corners and dead ends, until her head was spinning.

The great hall was indeed medieval in appearance, with its soaring wooden beams and the minstrels' gallery, but there were paintings on the wall by previous guests, of a style which suggested more enthusiasm than talent, and a collection of misshapen arrows, made by Lord This or Lord That as children, which gave the place an intimate feel. Drummoor might be one of the great houses of England, but it was also a family home.

As they walked down the length of the gallery, gazing at portraits of long dead Marfords, Monty asked once or twice about her own family, but after telling him that her parents were dead, her guardian was dead — which was true in a way — and that she was entirely alone in the world, he stopped asking. Perhaps he noticed the wobble in her voice when she spoke of such things.

"Perhaps you would care to have this returned to you, Miss Frost?" he said, producing a paper from his pocket. Her letter!

"Oh... thank you."

"I daresay you have few reminders of your papa, and you must have had this for a great many years."

"Only four," she said. "My foster family gave it to me when I was... um, when they considered me old enough."

"Your foster family?"

"My nurse and her sister. They looked after me until I was five, when my guardian came for me."

"So you never knew your parents? How horrid for you."

She bowed her head, for the tears were very close.

"He must have been a man of some importance, your father," Monty went on casually. "For my father to have agreed to marry you to my brother, I mean."

She said nothing, only gripping her letter rather tightly. She had wondered so much about him, what had happened to him and why he had chosen Lord Bentley as her guardian. Yes, he must have been a man of some standing! But it did no good to think about it. He had not wanted her to know who he was, so it was best left alone.

"Is there a library here?" she said brightly.

Late in the morning, as Melissa was gazing in awe at the endless rows of books in the vast library, a carriage rattled up the drive.

"Ah, Harriet is home," Monty said. "My sister."

The Lady Harriet Marford was thirty years of age, with a head of dark curls, mischievous eyes and a warm smile. Within two minutes of arriving in the house, she was peeping round the library door, her smile widening when she saw them.

"There you are, Monty! What is this I hear about a betrothal? Normally when I arrive home and ask Crabbe what has been happening, all I hear is *'Lady Hester is a little better'* or *'Lady Hester is a little worse'*, but *'Lord Montague is betrothed'* is a new experience. And is this the lady? Oh, yes, yes, Mrs Compton, do take my bonnet if you please, and help me off with this pelisse. Crabbe, be so good as to send in some tea. You will like some tea, Miss Frost, I am sure. Thank you, Mrs Compton. Oh, Fitch, yes, that box is full of cheese for the kitchen, something quite special from France, as I understand it, although it is rather fresh, I am afraid, so it may be necessary to keep it in the cellar. Goodness, I can smell it from here! I could not keep it in the carriage with me, for Martingale felt quite faint with it so close, so John Coachman had to have it under the box, which was quite all right, for he cannot smell anything since that accident when he was a beater. There, my dear, do let us sit down and have a comfortable coze. And Monty, you are not at all wanted in a female conversation so you may go away."

Melissa was quite dizzy by this time, and could do nothing but sit in the chair opposite Lady Harriet, and try not to let her mouth flap open in amazement.

Monty smiled fondly at his sister. "And did Crabbe also tell you that I have a living, Hatty?"

"No! Truly? Where?"

"Kirby Grosswick."

"Mr Whittaker? Well, he must have been ninety if he was a day, and a dry old stick, but I am very sorry for it, all the same. He used to ride around everywhere on a donkey, do you remember? He said if it was good enough for Our Lord, it was good enough for him. Such an eccentric old gentleman! Well, that is sooner than we had expected, but it is not a terribly good living, Monty. What is it, two or three hundred a year? But now, go away, do, for I want to talk to Miss Frost."

He laughed, and made her an ironic bow before quitting the room.

"Now we may be comfortable, Miss Frost. I do beg your pardon, but I have not introduced myself properly. One tends to assume everyone knows one, does one not? I am Lady Harriet Marford, as I am sure you have worked out already."

Melissa laughed. "Indeed I have. Melissa Frost. From... Falmouth."

"Oh! You are a long way from home, Miss Frost. And how long have you known Monty?"

"About..." She did the sums in her head. "...twenty hours."

For the first time, Lady Harriet was silenced, her eyes wide with astonishment. Then she chortled. "There is a story here, I see. Do enlighten me."

So Melissa explained about the bet and the letter, and how she had travelled north to marry the Earl of Deveron, only to find him a child of four. "And so Lord Montague offered to marry me instead, for he felt it was a matter of honour."

"Oh, I can well believe it," Lady Harriet said. "Monty has the most delicate sense of honour in the world. If he sees a single creature in distress, he must needs rescue it at once. When he was very small, he rescued some young ducklings that had become separated from their mother. They were newly hatched, and so they thought *he* was their mother and followed him everywhere, until Luther, the butler then, got cross and dispatched them all. Monty cried for days. Such a sensitive soul, and naturally he would feel obliged to offer for you. But you have accepted him?"

"Oh yes. I have no family, and nowhere else to go," she said, quite truthfully. "I am very grateful to him."

The tea arrived just then, and for a few minutes conversation was suspended while the little ceremony of pouring was carried out. But when the butler and footman had withdrawn, Lady Harriet said, "So how were you managing before you came here, Miss Frost? Have you been alone in the world for long?"

Now she was called upon to tell her little story. "No, only a month or so. My parents both died many years ago, and then I lived with my guardian, Mr Knatchbull and his sister in Falmouth. But he died two years ago, and his sister died a month ago. Finding myself without a friend in the world to call my own, I spent my last coins to take the stage coach north to find the husband who was promised to me." It had sounded much better in the silence of her own room at Bentley Hall. Now, over the teacups, she saw the disbelief on Lady Harriet's face.

"You had no friends at all in Falmouth?"

"No one. Mr and Miss Knatchbull lived very quiet and never went into society, so I knew no one."

"Which way did you come on the stage coach?"

That was tricky. "To... to Devizes, and then north to... to Oxford."

"Really. You did not come through London?"

Melissa licked her lips nervously. "Um... no."

Lady Harriet rose and opened one of the many cases of books. After a few moments of searching, she pulled out a battered book. "Now then, Miss Frost, here is the timetable of stage coaches throughout England. It is not the most recent edition, but I daresay it will serve the purpose. Do, pray, show me how you got from Falmouth to Sagborough by way of Devizes and Oxford. For I assure you, there is no way that it may be done."

4: Brothers And Sisters And Cousins

Monty was quite calm. No matter what was said about Miss Frost, he was perfectly content with his decision, and had no cause to regret it.

"She is *not* from Falmouth," Harriet said, lips pursed in disapproval. "She will not say where she has been living until now, or anything about her circumstances, except that her parents and her guardian are dead, and she is quite alone in the world. So she has come here to try her luck with us, and happened upon the very person to fall for her schemes."

"It is really too bad," Carrbridge said. "I will not have you taken advantage of in this way, Monty."

They were gathered in the ship room in the gathering winter gloom of late afternoon, the lamps already lit, the rain still lashing down outside.

"No one is taking advantage of me," Monty said mildly. "Hatty, you did not see Miss Frost when she first arrived, completely soaked through, for she had walked all the way from Mishmere Cross. You must have sympathised with her plight if you had seen her."

"I am sure I am very sorry for her, but being wet does not give anyone the right to marry you. We should give her the coach fare and send her on her way back to… wherever she came from."

"And she would not go," Monty said. "If she has no family and friends, and was so destitute that she left there in the first place, she will hardly go back there of her own accord."

"I do not like being misled," Carrbridge said fretfully. "She may be as poor and wet as she likes, but she should not try to bamboozle us. Lady Carrbridge, what is your opinion of Miss Frost?"

Connie smoothed her skirts, twisting her lips as she thought. "I rather like her," she said at length. "She came here on the stage coach, all alone, with nothing but a portmanteau, which I suspect contains all that she owns. Her clothes are of good quality but have been mended a great deal, which gives me a very poor opinion of her guardian, whoever he may be. And yet she is well educated, speaks with a good accent, and her manners cannot be faulted, so she has been brought up in a good family. You have seen how well she looks and behaves when she is properly dressed. I truly believe she is escaping from some dire situation, and deserves our sympathy, not condemnation."

"And there is still the letter from Father," Monty said gently. "That alone gives her the right to our compassion."

"One might be very compassionate without marrying the girl," said Uncle Lucius.

"Yes, indeed," Carrbridge said. "You do not need to marry Miss Frost. Something else may be done for her, perhaps."

Merton cleared his throat. "If she is indeed well-educated, perhaps a position as governess may be arranged for her?"

"No," Monty said quietly. "The question of what to do with Miss Frost is already settled. She is to become my wife, and for myself, I have no great desire to know any more of her history. No doubt she will tell us as much as she wishes us to know."

Carrbridge threw his hands into the air. "You are determined to be a martyr, I see."

Monty smiled, shaking his head in bemusement. "It is hardly martyrdom to marry a pretty and amiable young lady, brother. The impulse to marry her may have been compassionate, but that does not make it a penance. It will suit me very well to have a wife to provide me with a comfortable home to return to when my spiritual duties are finished each day."

"Hmpf. At least wait a while before the banns are called, Monty, for who knows what else we may discover about her?"

"I see little point in waiting, but it shall be for Miss Frost to determine the date," he said.

"But you will not object, my lord, if I make some discreet enquiries?" Merton said.

"Excellent idea," Carrbridge said. "And if you can find out something about her father, Merton, that would be helpful, for how can one put a notice in the paper as things stand? One cannot say, *'Miss Frost, daughter of Mr Thomas Frost, deceased, who did not live at Falmouth'*. If indeed he is deceased, or even called Frost, for who knows what stories she may be telling us? Monty's ancestors are known almost back to the Conquest, whereas Miss Frost..."

"Quite so," Merton said. "I shall see what may be found out. If Lord Montague has no objection?"

"As you please," Monty said calmly. "It is of no consequence to me."

"In any event, you must get your parsonage ready before you can marry," Connie said brightly. "I daresay that will take some time.

And while that is being done, we may all get to know Miss Frost a little better."

~~~~~

As the days passed, Melissa began to grow accustomed to the grandeur of Drummoor, and could find her way about without getting lost more than once or twice a day. She still could not quite believe she lived in such a wonderful place. Every meal was a glorious feast, in the evenings she was surrounded by interesting conversations or could stretch her mind with cards, and during the day she could hide away in the library and read as much as she wanted. Nothing was said about her non-existent boxes, but her wardrobe gradually filled with an array of delicious gowns and shoes and bonnets, while the chest of drawers held fans and silk stockings and soft kidskin gloves.

"I shall not need this again," Lady Carrbridge would say, "and the colour is perfect for you", as she brought yet another confection for Melissa.

Monty, bless him, had taken himself to York one day and returned, smiling shyly, with some small packages from a jeweller.

"A betrothal present," he said, fastening an enchanting garnet bracelet around her wrist and a drop pendant around her throat. "Once we are married, I shall buy you some proper jewellery."

Proper jewellery. Melissa could not shake off the feeling that she was dreaming. Surely soon she would wake up, and there would be the usual pile of curtains or sheets to sew, and Mr Pontefract's heavy breathing as he ogled her. Or worse than heavy breathing. In her darker moments, she remembered the earl's threat to show Mr Pontefract to her bedroom.

She was introduced to two more Marford brothers, Lord Reginald and Lord Humphrey, who lived nearby with their wives, and discovered that there were another two, Lord Augustus, who had settled in Northumberland and was shortly to be married, and Lord Gilbert, who was in the Hussars, and was presently in Kent recovering from an injury. She got to know Mr and Mrs Allamont, who were sister and brother-in-law to Lady Carrbridge, and then a cousin arrived, a Lady Hardy, who was a widow. Melissa began to feel a quite unaccustomed degree of happiness in having so many congenial people around her.

Lord Carrbridge and his brothers went off in the heavy skies of early December to support Lord Augustus through the ordeal of matrimony. Lady Harriet rolled her eyes and declared it a great piece of nonsense to be travelling about at such a dark time of year, and all for such a foolish reason as to see their brother married.

"It would be more sensible to send Connie, for she at least would be able to report faithfully on the fashions pertaining in the frozen north, and whether the bride blushed to the requisite degree, and if the new carriage be large or small, whereas the men will be hard put to it to remember whether Gus wore a blue coat or a red. They will no doubt tell us all about these horses he is to manage up there, and we shall hear nothing else for weeks and weeks."

"I think it very touching that they should go so far for their brother," Lady Hardy said. "It shows a very proper family feeling."

"They have always been close," Lady Harriet said. "It was like having an army in the house when they were boys. Always on the rampage."

"But how lovely to have so many brothers!" Mrs Allamont said. "You are so lucky, Lady Harriet. They have grown up into such splendid young men, too. Not like mine, who are not at all the thing."

"Two of mine are not much better," Lady Hardy said. "But Hugo turned out well, did he not, Hope?"

And Mrs Allamont blushed and agreed that her husband had indeed turned out well. "And Miss Frost is marrying just such an excellent man. Lord Montague is such a *good* person, do you not agree?"

"Oh, terribly good," Lady Harriet said impatiently. "What could be more dispiriting than a worthy clergyman? And he gets so preachy if one wants to read a novel on a Sunday, or do anything other than read sermons. You will have a very dull time of it, Miss Frost, I am sure."

Melissa kept silent during any discussion of families. She had neither brothers nor sisters nor cousins, and although she had watched the previous Lady Bentley's four children growing up, and had been close enough for them to call her their friend, it was not the same as being part of the family. She had always been an outsider. But for the first time, she felt the warmth of a family wrapping itself around her in the comforting manner of a warm shawl. The aunts were covertly hostile, and most of the uncles treated her with distant coolness, but the younger members of the family, even Lady Harriet, were beginning to feel perilously close to friends. What would she do if all this were snatched away from her now? What if Lord Bentley should find her and drag her back to her dank little attic room, and the terrible prospect of marriage to Mr Pontefract? She could not bear it. It would be better to be dead, she was quite sure.

Of the younger ladies, it was Lady Hardy she saw most. She was the widow of a baronet, although only in half mourning now, a handsome woman of perhaps a little above thirty. She was engaged in cataloguing the books in the library, a task which Melissa suspected would last her a lifetime, for the room was as big as a ballroom and lined from floor to ceiling with books. At first, Melissa sat in a big chair beside one of the fires, absorbed in her reading, but from time to time Lady Hardy asked her opinion of one or other book, in the most flattering manner, and gradually she became interested in the project. Not many days had passed before they were working together, one reading out the titles and names of the authors, while the other wrote the information down on a small card, which was then filed away in a drawer in a special cabinet.

Each morning, they spent two or three hours thus employed, and in the afternoons one or other of them would read to Lady Hester, the very frail old lady who kept to her bed and hardly seemed aware of anyone, but who was, her nurse said, more tranquil when she had company.

One day, Crabbe, the butler, entered with a silver salver. "Two letters for you, my lady," he said to Lady Hardy. "And one for Miss Frost."

"For me?" Melissa was so startled that she almost dropped the book she was holding. Who could possibly be writing to her? No one knew where she was. It was impossible. For an instant, panic swept over her. Had the earl found her? Or Mr Pontefract?

The butler's eyes twinkled. "I believe it is from Lord Montague, madam."

"Lord Montague! Oh. Of course." She took it from the salver, but her hands were shaking so much that she dropped it, and the butler had to bend down to retrieve it for her. She broke the seal impatiently — how wonderful of him to write her a letter! It was perfectly unexceptional, hoping she was well, telling her that they had arrived safely at Castle Morton despite some sleet and very bad roads, looking forward to the two weddings, for the Duke of Dunmorton was to marry at the same time. A duke! She was marrying the son of a marquess who was attending the wedding of a duke. It all seemed so improbable for Miss Melissa Frost, daughter of who knows whom.

When Crabbe had withdrawn, Lady Hardy said, "Forgive me if I am impertinent, Miss Frost, but you looked quite frightened for a moment. Is there perhaps a letter that you do not wish to receive?"

Melissa chewed her lip, not knowing how to respond.

Lady Hardy went on, "I do not know the circumstances you left behind when you came here, my dear, nor do I mean to invite confidences you are unwilling to give, but you may be assured that you are quite safe here. Lord Carrbridge is a powerful man, and can protect you from a great deal of unpleasantness. However, it is easier for him to do that if he knows what sort of unpleasantness might arise."

"Oh, there is nothing... unpleasant," Melissa said hastily. "I have done nothing wrong, nothing at all."

"I am sure you have not!" Lady Hardy said at once. "Who could ever suspect such a thing! You are too sensible and resourceful a girl to find yourself embroiled in any wrongdoing. And because you are so sensible, I know you will not take it amiss if I offer you a little advice. Here you are, all alone in the world, your only hope a letter written to your father years ago promising you marriage, and perhaps you are grasping at the prospect as the only future open to you. It would distress me greatly to see you rush into a situation which might not promote your greatest happiness. Now, do not imagine me as advocate for the idea that every marriage must be founded on romantic love, for I could hardly do so, given that my own marriage was not."

"You did not love your husband?" Melissa whispered.

"It was not in the least a love match, for I was escaping from a vindictive step-mother, and Sir Osborne Hardy was being hounded by his own mother to wed. But I had known him for years, and had always held him in high regard. His character was in no doubt, and he knew mine, and so we realised that we were well-suited. Indeed, we got along in the most amiable manner, for Sir Osborne was always the perfect gentleman, and his behaviour was ever designed to enhance my comfort. He was a most agreeable husband."

She sighed, while Melissa kept respectfully silent at such a panegyric.

After a few moments, Lady Hardy went on, "Perhaps you and Lord Montague may be just as fortunate, but you do not yet know each other, and it would be advisable not to rush into marriage until you are quite sure of each other's habits and temper. There is much to be said for a match founded on practicality, rather than romantic love, Miss Frost, but one must be very sure of one's husband before entering into such an arrangement."

~~~~~

One day at breakfast, Mr Merton, the marquess's secretary, came through with something approaching a smile on his face. He was a solemn, not to say dour, man above thirty, who took his responsibilities very seriously, and Melissa knew he was investigating her background and therefore saw him as an enemy. Today, however, he seemed pleased.

"There is a letter from York, Miss Frost," he said with a bow. "His Grace the Archbishop is pleased to approve Lord Montague to the living of Kirby Grosswick."

"Oh. Thank you, Mr Merton." Melissa felt she should be pleased at this development, but her feelings were mixed. It meant the marriage need not be delayed beyond the wait for the banns to be called, and she would have her own establishment and her own servants, and that must be an agreeable situation for her. But still, she would be very sorry to quit Drummoor and all the comforts to be found therein.

Other doubts gnawed at the back of her mind. She was technically betrothed to another man, and, what was worse, she was still under age and could not marry officially without Lord Bentley's approval, which he would never give. What would be the situation if she were to marry Monty? Would the marriage even be legal? Could Mr Pontefract still claim her? Would Monty renounce her when he learnt the truth? God help her, what a mess she was in! Yet she could hardly tell anyone the truth, for that would delay the marriage until she was of age, and surely the earl would find her long before that. If only she could have hidden away somewhere until she reached her majority. But she tried to smile, all the same. No one must guess at her turmoil.

"Oh, that is excellent news," Lady Carrbridge said. "Now we may look at your house, dear Miss Frost. Shall we go today?"

It was the first time Melissa had ventured outside since her arrival, and she was aware of a flutter of excitement. Oh, to be free, to *go* somewhere, to not be tied to the house. She was so unused to any kind of freedom that it had never occurred to her to go for a walk in the grounds of Drummoor. She could even have asked for the carriage, if she had thought of it. If she had dared!

But now she was to go to Kirby Grosswick with Lady Carrbridge, Lady Harriet and Mrs Allamont. Lady Hardy smiled and said that she would continue her efforts in the library.

"However, I shall expect a full report when you return," she added.

The carriage was summoned and Melissa had her first opportunity to wear one of the two new pelisses in her wardrobe, with the most ravishing little hat to match. She was so warm and snug, with a little fur muff and tippet, and although Mrs Allamont grumbled a little about the cold, and worried that the road was so rutted that they might be overturned, Melissa found not the least thing to trouble her. She gazed out of the window as the bare trees and empty fields passed by, admired a succession of little villages and then the town of Sagborough before they climbed onto open moorland, with a wild beauty in every direction.

"Do you ride, Miss Frost?" said Lady Carrbridge.

"No, not at all."

"You must get Monty to teach you. Kirby Grosswick is almost twelve miles from Drummoor by road, but no more than three miles away as the crow flies, and you will find it very pleasant to be able to ride over whenever you wish. We are just coming to the turning for Great Mellingham, where Reggie and Robinia live. We may call on them for tea on our way home. And just a few miles beyond Kirby Grosswick is Silsby Vale, where Humphrey and Hortensia have settled." She sighed. "It is the most comfortable thing in the world to have them so close by, and now you and Monty will be very near, too, and we shall be calling on each other very often. How delightful it is. I wish my sisters were closer to me. They come and stay with me, or else we meet in London, but it is not enough, and Dulcie is far, far away in Scotland and I have only seen her once since she married."

"Perhaps we should all go to Scotland to visit her," said Mrs Allamont.

"Oh yes!" cried Lady Carrbridge, clapping her hands in glee. "Oh, what a charming idea. I shall tell Lord Carrbridge this evening that we must go."

Melissa smiled at her certainty that he would agree to the scheme, but she felt a pang of envy too. How wonderful it would be to have such a large and loving family, to be connected to others in the world by the unbreakable bonds of blood. Perhaps one day, when she and Monty had a horde of little Marfords at their feet she would finally feel that she belonged somewhere.

5: The Parsonage

Kirby Grosswick was an unprepossessing village which sprawled along the road in an uncoordinated fashion, as if all its houses and cottages had been shaken up and then scattered randomly about. A rushing stream alongside the road clattered noisily over stones and under simple plank bridges. There was no obvious centre to the village, no cross or pond or green, although they passed a small inn and a sprinkle of shops, as well as a blacksmith and an apothecary. A wagon road crossed the stream by means of a sturdy stone bridge, and wound into the wooded hills to the south. At the far end of the village, where the land began to rise, were a few better houses and the church and parsonage.

The parsonage would possibly have been a fine house, if they could have seen it, but the walls were completely covered with thick ivy which obscured most of the windows, and the drive was so choked with weeds that the carriage could not get along it.

"Never mind," Lady Carrbridge said briskly. "We will walk up to the house. It is not far."

It was indeed not far from the gateposts, the gate long missing, to the front door, but only a narrow path led through the weeds and brambles. Here and there, self-seeded shrubs towered over their heads, and fallen branches from nearby trees almost blocked their way.

"Dear me," Lady Carrbridge said. "Monty's first job will be to engage a gardener."

The peeling paint on the front door and the ivy reaching out its rattling tendrils suggested a similar level of neglect applied to the house. The doorbell was missing but a sturdy knocker announced their arrival in echoing terms. Then they waited. And waited. Lady Harriet knocked twice more before bolts could be heard sliding back, and the door slowly opened.

The white-haired head of a very elderly man peered round the door at them. "He be dead and gorn. Can't help. Good day."

He was about to close the door again, but Lady Harriet stepped forward to prevent him. "We are not here for Mr Whittaker. We are here on behalf of your new parson, Lord Montague Marford."

"Never heard of him."

Again he would have closed the door, but Lady Harriet, with a cluck of annoyance, pushed it wider and stalked into the hall. "Now, my good man, I am Lady Harriet Marford and this is Lady Carrbridge. You have heard of Lord Carrbridge, I take it? Good. Well, this is his wife. And here is Mrs Allamont, and this lady is Miss Frost who is to marry Lord Montague and so will be mistress here. This is her house, you see."

The old man looked at her through eyes so pale they were almost colourless. He swayed slightly on his feet. "Mr Whittaker's house. He be in the churchyard, but 'tis his house."

"Not any longer," Lady Harriet said crisply. "We shall just have a look around, you know. We shall not be here long, I am sure, for there is a very queer smell in here and I do not suppose any of us will want to linger. Come along, ladies. Let us get on."

They followed her into the dark hall, lit only by a single lamp standing on a table. Opening the first door, a foul smell filled the hall. The room was completely dark. Picking up the lamp, Lady Harriet strode forwards then stopped.

"Hmm. Do not come in, ladies. The floor is... not clean."

Peering over her shoulder, Melissa felt the understatement was commendable. There may perhaps have been a rug on the floor, and furnishings here and there, but they were buried under mounds of—

Mrs Allamont screamed. "Rats! *Rats!"* She turned and fled.

They were indeed rats, scuttling about in the darkness, heaps of their droppings littering every surface. Lady Harriet slammed the door shut.

"Connie, you should not be in here, not in your condition," Lady Harriet said. "Perhaps you and Hope may wait for us in the carriage? Miss Frost, are you strong enough to venture further? The hallway is relatively clean, and we do not have to enter any room, but you will want to get an idea of their number and size."

Melissa trembled with shock. "I do not know how it is to be cleaned," she whispered. "I can beat rugs and lay a fire, if I have to, but this is beyond my experience."

Lady Harriet smiled, her face softening. "I should hope it is beyond the experience of any of us. But you need not do anything yourself. Tomorrow, Mrs Compton will come with an army of housemaids and footmen and grooms to clear it out, and have a great bonfire, for I do not suppose there will be anything to be saved. We shall need Ben Gartmore with the dogs, too, to deal with the rats and whatever else is living here. Then we shall be able to see what needs to be done to make the place habitable, for no one can live here as it is at the moment. But I must see the rest of the house to determine how large an army Mrs Compton must bring. It is just the one room infested, or is it the whole house? Do you see?

But you need not come with me if you do not like it. You may wait in the carriage."

"Oh, no, I will come with you," Melissa said. "I am not afraid of rats and mice. We used to have them in the stables at... where I lived, so I am used to them."

"You are a brave girl for one so young. How old are you?"

"Twenty... one and twenty," she amended quickly.

Lady Harriet looked at her thoughtfully. "Very well. Let us get on."

All the while, the elderly manservant had been standing behind them, wringing his hands, and muttering, "'Tis Mr Whittaker's house, so it is."

"What is your name, my good man?" Lady Harriet said, but he gave no coherent answer.

With a sigh, she picked up the lamp and began her inspection of the house. Melissa followed her dutifully as she opened door after door, climbed stairs, prodded walls and peered up at ceilings, while the strange servant walked behind them, muttering to himself. The rats were only in one room on the ground floor, but the mice and spiders were everywhere, and only one room in the house was even partly habitable, the kitchen, where the late Mr Whittaker and his manservant had apparently been living for some time. The cellar doors were locked, but neither lady was inclined to ask for the keys.

"Goodness, fresh air is most welcome," Lady Harriet said, as they emerged from the house, the manservant slamming the door behind them. "Well, it will be quite a task to clean up, but I do think the house is sound enough. Getting rid of the rats and mice will be the biggest problem, but the dogs will deal with them. We should go down into the village to spread the word that Monty will be coming here, and find out who that poor soul inside is, and whether he has any relatives to take care of him or else he must go to the work house."

"Oh, no!" Melissa said, shocked. "I daresay he has lived there for decades. He would hate to move now, and the house is big enough that room may be found for him. He will be no bother, I am sure."

Lady Harriet spun on her heel to gaze at Melissa in great amusement. "My dear, you and Monty are better matched than I had supposed. That is exactly what he would say, for he can no more resist a charitable case than the sun can resist rising each morning. But it is likely that the old man is half mad, and will be a great nuisance to you. Much better to let him go to the work house."

"No one should have to leave their home, if it can possibly be avoided," Melissa said in a low voice. "It is too distressing."

"Well, well, the decision is for you and Monty to make," Lady Harriet said equably. "I shall walk down the road, I think, but you may go in the carriage if you wish."

Melissa relished the clean air after the close confinement of the house, so after a brief discussion with Lady Carrbridge, the carriage rolled away to await them at the inn, and Melissa and Lady Harriet walked on down the hill. From their higher position, the whole valley was laid out before them, its fields and woods edging up onto the moors, while the houses clustered along the stream. Two tributaries gave it strength, one bouncing precipitously down from the moors in a series of cascades, while the other descended more circumspectly, and fed a couple of mills nestling amidst trees. Now that she was looking more carefully, Melissa noticed that the more important buildings all stood on the good ground along the road, while most of the labourers' cottages sat on boggy land bordering the stream, and their winter vegetables looked pallid and yellow.

"Why do they build in such a bad position?" she asked Lady Harriet.

"I daresay they can get no other place," Lady Harriet said with a shrug. "Poor people must live where they can afford."

"But it must be so damp and unpleasant. I daresay they suffer terribly."

Lady Harriet turned surprised eyes to her. "Why, working folk are much stronger than people like us, you know. They have to be to work all day in the fields. The educated classes are born to rule, and the lower classes to do physical labour, and so it has always been. It is a good system, on the whole, and one may offer a little help now and then for those who fall into occasional difficulties, or are ill. But it is not healthy for them to be given everything they need without effort, or else they will grow lazy and not do their work at all, and then where would we be? Ah, here is the apothecary. Let us enquire regarding the mysterious servant at the parsonage."

The apothecary was out, but his daughter, a buxom girl of about Melissa's age, came out to attend to them, and bounced with delight when she heard who they were and the reason for their errand.

"Ooh, that's so excitin'," she said. "Best news all year, I'd reckon. We did wonder, when poor Mr Whittaker were buried, and knowin' it's Lord Carrbridge what says who comes in, and knowin' his brother be ordained... well, we did wonder. And he'll be marryin', too. Bad news for us village girls, I'd reckon. There were some thinkin'... but that'd never work, him bein' a lord an' all. So excitin', and maybe he'll be in by Christmas, d'ye reckon?"

"Maybe," Lady Harriet said. "The house needs a great deal of work before anyone will be moving in. And who is that poor soul still living there?"

"Oh, that'd be Callum. Don't know his other name. He's from Scotland... or was it Ireland? Don't know. Been here for ever, though."

"Does he have family nearby? Nearer than Scotland. Or Ireland."

"Oh no, no one. Never married, that I ever heard. But so excitin', to have a new parson!"

They left the apothecary's daughter still bouncing at the thrilling news that a vacant living might soon be vacant no more, and walked on to the inn. Lady Carrbridge and Mrs Allamont were settled in the best parlour, or rather the only parlour, for it was a very small inn, drinking sherry.

"There seems to be nothing else on offer except varieties of ale, and one does not quite like to offend the innkeeper by refusing all refreshment, when they have lit the fire specially for us," Lady Carrbridge said.

"One does not have to drink the stuff, however," Lady Harriet said, sniffing the jug disapprovingly. "It does not resemble any sherry I have ever seen."

"What is the rest of the house like? Is it quite dreadful?" Mrs Allamont said. "I was never so shocked in my life! Rats!"

"The ground floor is quite infested with wildlife of one sort or another, and one dares not imagine the state of the cellar," Lady Harriet said. "The upstairs is not so bad, but still, everything will have to be stripped out and burned. Connie, may I borrow Ben Gartmore? His terriers will make short work of the livestock, and then perhaps Mrs Compton...?"

"Oh, of course. Naturally. And the library attic is full of furniture removed from Marford House during the renovations, so there will be plenty of—"

A commotion could be heard outside the parlour door, shouting from at least one female voice and several males ones.

"Whatever is going—" Lady Harriet began.

The door crashed open and a young woman half fell into the room. Behind her were the innkeeper and the potboy, arms waving.

"So sorry, milady," the innkeeper said. "Come along, Bridget, don't be troubling her ladyship and her friends."

"I won't keep them long," Bridget said. "I'm sure you ladies can spare a few coins for those less fortunate than yourselves."

"Bridget!" the innkeeper said, grabbing hold of one of her arms, started to drag her away.

"No, let her stay," Lady Harriet said. "I for one should like to hear what she has to say."

Bridget grinned triumphantly.

The innkeeper froze. "It ain't suitable, milady," he said firmly. "Bridget is... she ain't respectable enough to mix with the likes of you ladies."

"I shall be the judge of that," Lady Harriet said firmly. "Come in and sit down, Bridget. My good fellow, do you not have some tea? Or coffee? Anything but this horrid stuff. Lady Carrbridge is too polite to refuse it, but I am not so kind-hearted."

The innkeeper promised coffee and went away, shaking his head at the odd ways of the nobility.

Bridget was a good looking woman approaching thirty, dressed in rather better clothes than might have been expected from a person of questionable respectability, and with a very fetching bonnet. From beneath it, blonde curls peeped out.

"Now, Bridget, tell us about your mother," Lady Harriet said.

"My *mother?*" Bridget said, the smile wiped from her face. Her eyes narrowed in suspicion. "Why do you want to know about your mother?"

"Or your father. What did your mother tell you about him?"

Bridget flushed scarlet. "What are my parents to you?"

"You do not know, then, who your father is?" Lady Harriet went on relentlessly.

Melissa held her breath. Lady Harriet was always forthright, but this interrogation seemed too personal, too intrusive. "My lady, it may be that Miss... er..."

"Kelly. Bridget Kelly."

"It may be that Miss Kelly would prefer not to discuss her parents. Not with a stranger. I know I should not at all like to be asked such questions by one wholly unrelated to me."

Bridget looked at her in surprise. "Why, thank you, my lady."

"I am not a lady. My name is Miss Frost."

"Then thank you, Miss Frost. You're quite right, I don't like people prying into such matters. Not when they have no right." She lifted her chin defiantly and glared at Lady Harriet. But that lady was not at all deterred, and was smiling, seeming greatly amused.

"Oh, Miss Kelly!" Lady Carrbridge said, her eyes wide. "Then you do not know! And yet it must be so, I am quite sure of it, and you see it too, Harriet, clearly."

"Oh yes," Lady Harriet said. "The most obvious signs imaginable."

Bridget got to her feet, her chair scraping noisily on the wooden floor. "Now you're just making fun of me! I won't stay here to be talked about in riddles." And she stalked towards the door.

"Oh, please, do stay!" Lady Carrbridge cried. "I beg your pardon, but it is your *nose*, you see, Miss Kelly. You have the Marford nose, there is no mistaking it. Which means, I fear, that your father must very likely have been the eighth Marquess of Carrbridge."

6: Chickens And Stipends

"What?" Bridget flopped back into the chair abruptly, as if her legs had given way. "The *marquess?* Your husband?"

"Oh, no, no, no!" Lady Carrbridge looked shocked at the idea. "My husband is the *ninth* marquess, and he would *certainly* not... No, indeed! It would have been his father. He left such little reminders all over the place. You are the third... no, the fourth that we know about. And you were not aware? Your mama did not tell you?"

Bridget laughed. "She didn't, no, because she never knew herself. Got drunk at the harvest home one year at Great Mellingham, got a little too friendly with one of the guests behind the big barn, never did know his name. Stupid woman," she added, affectionately. "Lost her place there, of course. Can't have a chambermaid with a bairn, can we? She's lived hand to mouth ever since, until I grew up enough to bring in some money."

"By begging," Lady Harriet said, with pursed lips.

"Asking for a little Christian charity from the fortunate to help the less fortunate," Bridget said, eyes flashing. "Do none of you ladies wish to help those who have fallen into hardship?"

"It depends upon how they came to fall into hardship," Lady Harriet said. "I will not give a penny piece to the feckless or lazy or drunken idle."

"How about those in trouble through no fault of their own, who just need a hand to start them off right?" Bridget said.

"If you mean your mother—"

"No, no," Bridget said, her face lighting up with laughter. "She was a fool, but it was her own fault, right enough, and she's managed to survive without turning to—" She stopped, blushing, with a quick glance at Melissa, then went on hastily, "She's all right, now. But it was hard for her for a long time, and there's plenty of girls end up the same way where it wasn't their fault at all. Forced by the master of the house, or one of the sons, or a guest, and then thrown out when they get big. It's not right, my lady, and so I tell you. I'm trying to help some of them that can sew a bit by providing material and thread and fashion journals, and selling the finished gowns."

"Gowns already made up?" Lady Carrbridge said. "Why would anyone want such a thing? Why, it might not fit!"

"We make them a little on the large size, so that they can be taken in to fit," Bridget said. "We can sell them a lot cheaper than you'd pay for one made specially. Lots of women don't have much money for clothes and would be happy to have something stylish at a very good price. It's easier to adjust a gown that's already made than to create one from nothing." She frowned. "But it's hard to find somewhere to sell them. The shops in York only want work for their own seamstresses."

"You need your own shop to sell them," Lady Harriet said. "How many women do you have at present?"

"Only six. Can't fit any more in ma's little house," Bridget said, with a wide smile.

"But if you had larger premises…" Lady Harriet grew thoughtful. "I like the idea. I like it very much, and no doubt there is no shortage of such women as you describe. What you need is somewhere big… a good sized house where the women could live, with their unfortunate offspring, and do all the stitchery. Then there would be a shop selling the finished products. Yes, it could be done. And it *should* be done. This is exactly the sort of project that I must approve of, for it puts these women into gainful employment and prevents them from falling into further sin."

Bridget stared at her. "I'm very glad you approve, my lady, but… it would take a lot of money to do something like that."

"Which my brother has," Lady Harriet said briskly. "He will be happy to help out, given your connection to the family. Let me have your direction, Miss Kelly, and I shall call on you very soon, and we shall begin making plans. How glad I am that we met you today!"

And so, when the rather dreadful coffee finally arrived, the bemused innkeeper found Bridget deep in conversation with Lady Harriet Marford.

After leaving Kirby Grosswick, they made the small detour to Great Mellingham to call on Lady Reginald. Melissa had met her once, briefly, and found her a pleasant if not very interesting person, but now she had a chance to see her in her own home. The house itself was about the same size as Bentley Hall, having only five rooms on the ground floor, none with the grandeur of Drummoor. But the furnishings and decorations were all brand new, and the talk was all of plans for new wings to be added, with a library, a ballroom and a larger music room. A butler and two footmen served tea and cakes. There was a great deal of wealth on display, even though the house was not large, and she could not help comparing it with the shabby interior of Bentley Hall. She had never realised before just how little money the earl spent on his home.

The drive back to Drummoor was enlivened by Lady Harriet's enthusiastic monologue on all the steps necessary to put her plans for fallen women into action. She did not seem to require an audience, but Mrs Allamont took it upon herself to say, "Yes, Lady Harriet" and "No, indeed, Lady Harriet" at suitable intervals, so Melissa was able to retreat into her own thoughts. But when the carriage slowed to avoid some obstruction in Sagborough, Lady Carrbridge turned to her.

"You are very quiet, Miss Frost. I hope you do not repine too much on the dreadful state of the parsonage. Everything can be set right, in time, and you will have the most delightful home eventually."

"You are very kind, my lady, but I am… disappointed, that is all. I had hoped there would be nothing to stop the banns being called as soon as Lord Montague returns."

"Oh, you *are* in a hurry! I did not realise. As to that, you may marry whenever you please, for there is room enough for you at Drummoor. You may have a whole wing to yourselves, you know, should you wish to. So *that* need not be a consideration. But you do not look any happier. Is there some other matter weighing with you?"

"I have been trying to work out how it may be possible to manage at the parsonage with just two hundred pounds a year. I cannot see that we will be able to have more than a couple of servants, and I daresay I will have to cook and I do not know how to. And as to looking after chickens—"

"Chickens!" Lady Carrbridge exclaimed. "Shall you keep chickens? What fun! Now that I think about it, the Miss Hays keep chickens, so it does seem to be the sort of thing a clergyman's wife might do. But you will not need a French chef, as we have. A good plain cook would serve, and that cannot be terribly expensive, can it? And a kitchen maid, parlour maid and chamber maid would be all you would need living in, for you can get a woman from the village to come in for the spring cleaning, and do the laundry. And you must have a manservant or two — to act as footman, but also as groom and coachman. Then, in time, you will want nursery maids and a governess, and so forth. That will not cost much, for servants are so cheap, to be sure."

Melissa said no more, finding herself unequal to the task of explaining the realities of eking out a small income to a marchioness who spent a fortune on gloves and stockings alone every year.

~~~~~

For Monty, the journey to Northumberland was no hardship. The carriage was comfortable, and as long as there was light enough to read by, he was content. Even when it grew too dark to see the pages of his book, he could sit quite happily pondering the last sermon he had read, and contemplating its meaning.

For his brothers, however, whole days confined to a swaying coach were pure torture. Carrbridge grumbled at every lurch in the road, Reggie fretted over delays in case they might not reach their overnight inn before night fell and Humphrey... Humphrey was too big and active a fellow to be squeezed into anything so small as a travelling coach for more than five minutes at a time. Monty being the smallest of them, it fell to his lot to sit beside Humphrey, trying not to crowd him or bump against him when the coach plunged into a hole in the road and out again. Humphrey, for his part, tried not to exclaim more than ten times an hour, "Oh, if only I had brought my horse!"

"I wish you had brought your horse, too," Carrbridge said crossly. "At least then we would be spared so much complaint."

"Think how wet and cold he would be," Reggie said. "Look, it is snowing again. How miserable to be riding in such foul weather. I do not know how John Coachman contrives to see the road. Have we much further to go, do you suppose? Surely we must be within sight of the next inn by now."

Monty kept his thoughts on his sermons, and ignored them.

But they arrived without mishap, and there was Gus to greet them, and show them to their rooms in Castle Morton, and all was laughter and good-humour again. Gus's lady was a charming young woman, a widow with a boy of four who was heir to the Duke of Dunmorton, and so she and Gus must make their home at the castle. He seemed quite contented about it, and he had a whole stud farm to manage, enough horses even for Gus, who was never happier than when he could spend his days lurking in the stables.

Yet the prospect of marriage had changed him, as became most apparent when the brothers gathered for a final brandy before bed at the end of their first day at the castle.

"Humphrey, I have a commission for you, if you will, for I cannot spare the time to go south just now. Will you sell all my horses at Drummoor, and in London? I shall keep only Jupiter and the bays for my curricle. And you may sell my other curricle, and the phaeton too. The hunters you may keep, Carrbridge, if you will, or sell if you prefer, for I am sure you paid for most of them, one way or another, and have kept all my mounts in hay and oats for years."

The brothers stared at him. "*Sell your horses,* Gus?" Humphrey said at last. "Are you addle-pated? Or has love gone so far to your head as to change your character altogether?"

Gus laughed. "Perhaps it has, or at least it has brought me to the realisation — rather belatedly, I am sure you will agree — that I have far too many horses, more than any sensible man needs, and that there are in this life things of more importance than horseflesh. Like my soon-to-be wife, for instance, and her son, and… well, family generally. You fellows, for example."

"I will not argue on your latter points," Humphrey said. "None of us would, I am sure, but you hardly need to sacrifice your horses to demonstrate your love for your wife. You can well afford to keep them now, after all."

"It is not about demonstrating anything, or about the money," Gus said firmly. "My good lady is a very modest, quiet-living person, and I greatly esteem her for it. Her gentle ways have made me realise how ostentatiously I have lived up until now, and yet I was dissatisfied with my life in many ways. I have discovered that the simplest activities can bring the greatest joy, like a walk through the woods or a game of toy soldiers with a child. I no longer want or need so many horses."

Monty could not but approve of such sentiments. "Have I not always said that a simple life is one of great satisfaction? *'It is easier for a camel to go through the eye of a needle, than for a rich man to enter into the kingdom of God.'*"

Humphrey rolled his eyes. "Sometimes, Monty, you are the most sanctimonious prig. You live very well on Carrbridge's money, so there is no need to be so self-righteous about it."

"Only because I have had to, having no other income," Monty said calmly. "Once I am settled at Kirby Grosswick, I shall live on my stipend."

"I shall enjoy watching you try," Humphrey said. "What is the living worth? Three hundred a year?"

"Two."

"Two hundred! Ha! You will never manage it. You never stayed within your allowance, and that had only to cover your clothes and a few oddments, for Carrbridge fed and housed you. With a wife and a whole household to manage — ha! A monkey says you will be asking Carrbridge for help within a month."

"I shall not accept the wager," Monty said with dignity.

"But I will," Gus said. "Monty is perfectly sensible, Humphrey, and has never spent to excess on himself, only to help others. If he can resist the urge to give his money away, he will do very well, even on two hundred a year. Many people live respectably enough on twenty pounds a year. So long as his wife is frugal... Tell me all about her, Monty, for this is such a delightful surprise, to hear that you are entering the married state too, yet Connie's letters are so garbled, I can make nothing of the business at all. She says Miss Frost just appeared at the door one day, and... something about little Dev, which I could not make out, and before the day was over you were betrothed to her. Which makes my efforts look quite dawdling by comparison."

And so the story had to be told again, and the letter from their father explained and worried over. But what worried Gus most was that Monty knew so little of his betrothed.

"It is all very well to do the honourable thing and offer for her, and no doubt she is very glad to accept you, but who is she? And who was her father? No one has no history at all, Monty."

"We have been telling him so from the start," Carrbridge said. "But will he listen? Monty always thinks he knows best and goes his own way."

Monty stood up. "It is tiresome to have everyone telling me what a fool I am to marry a woman so little known to me. Father knew *her* father well enough to make wagers with him, so she is a lady, and that is good enough for me. I am going to bed."

"Now, you must not get in high dudgeon, Monty," Gus said. "You know we only have your best interests at heart. But it does seem to me that if a lady will not tell even her future husband all about herself, then it is most likely because she has something to hide. Now it may be nothing bad," he added hastily, as Monty turned and stalked to the door, "but whatever it is, you ought to know about it before you become a tenant for life. Far too late to find out afterwards."

"How much did any of *you* know about your wives when you married them? Or they about you? Carrbridge was pretending to be in love with someone else. Lady Reggie neglected to tell him she was in love with a militia man. Lady Humphrey was pretending she was a penniless companion. And Gus's lady has been masquerading as a nobody with a natural son, when in truth the boy was the Duke's heir. I really do not think any of you are in a position to lecture me on this subject."

And into the resulting silence, he strode out, head high.

But there was one aspect of his brothers' marriages that Monty found himself pondering a great deal in quiet moments. For all the convoluted paths they had taken to reach the altar, every one of them was head over ears in love with his wife. Carrbridge's adoration for Connie was now of several years' standing, and the rest of them had chaffed him good-naturedly over it many times. Carrbridge had never minded. He was so happy, he said, that nothing could dent his pleasure in life, so long as he had his Connie by his side. And it was true, they were seldom apart, and he grew fretful without her.

Monty had grown accustomed to it, and considered it a quirk of Carrbridge's character, to dote on his wife so. But now, in very short order, Reggie, Humphrey and even Gus, who had never looked at a woman if there was a horse to be fussed over instead, had gone the same way. All of them exhibited the same broad smiles, the same transfixed light in their eyes when they gazed at the beloved creature. None of them had gone looking for love, or expected to find it, yet they had tripped over it none the less, and fallen headlong.

And Monty had to accept that he was giving up all possibility of the same happy chance in his own life. There would be no meeting of eyes across a crowded room, followed by some distinct physical symptoms — he was hazy about this part, but he was quite sure he would feel *something*, some quickening of pulse or breathing — and an overwhelming certainty that this enchanting creature was the one, the very one to claim his heart for ever. And what if he married and later encountered this happy chance with a woman not his wife? What grief would then be his.

Yet he had to admit that he had not the least doubt of what he was doing. He was not in love with Miss Frost, nor she with him, and they knew nothing of each other, but who can say that they truly know their life's partner before they leave the church as man and wife? Not any of his brothers, that much was certain.

Above all, he was happy at the prospect of having a wife. How pleasant it would be to sit writing his sermon for the week, knowing that his wife was busy ensuring that his dinner would be on the table promptly, and it would be to his taste. And after dinner, they would sit either side of the fire in the drawing room with their books, for Miss Frost loved to read almost as much as he did, or else he might gently instruct her in the meaning of a theological point, or perhaps they would play cribbage or chess together. How delightful the prospect was! And then later there would be the intimacy of the bedchamber, and delights of another kind.

So it was that, as he sat through the interminable formal dinners in the castle, and the two weddings, and the ball which followed, his thoughts were seldom where they ought to be, and very often with a certain young lady with dark hair and green eyes and the most charming pair of dimples when she smiled. He could not wait to return to Drummoor.

7: Just Impediments

Monty endured the drive home to Drummoor stoically, and even his brothers' grumbling could not dent his calm demeanour. His book of sermons lay open much of the time, but it had to be admitted that he was not pondering the intricacies of Scriptures quite as much as before. His thoughts were more pleasurably engaged in thinking about Miss Frost, and wondering just how much she might smile when she saw him again. Had she missed him? He hoped she had, for he had certainly missed her.

He had no intention of enquiring too deeply into her history, or prying from her secrets she preferred to keep buried, but there were certain details that must be established before the banns were called, to ensure that the marriage would be valid. So he determined to have a serious talk to her, and encourage her, if she were so minded, to confide in him. And if she were not so minded, he would accept her word that there was no impediment to the marriage.

Descending from the carriage in a lather of impatience to see his betrothed, Crabbe's first words to him were, "Welcome home, my lord. Miss Frost is at Kirby Grosswick today."

He was aware that his face had fallen in a ludicrous and childish manner. "Ah. Well, never mind. She will be home tonight, I take it? She is not staying overnight at the parsonage?"

"Oh no, my lord. The parsonage is, as I understand it, requiring some work to make it habitable."

"To make it *habitable*? Oh, that sounds bad, Crabbe. Exactly how uninhabitable is it? Leaky roof? Rising damp? Flooded cellars?"

"I do not believe anyone has yet penetrated to the cellars, my lord, but Ben Gartmore is there now with the dogs, so once the rats are disposed of—"

"Rats! Oh dear. That is indeed uninhabitable."

Monty was thrown into unaccustomed gloom. All his brothers were wreathed in smiles, greeting their wives, for both Lady Humphrey and Lady Reggie were there to meet them, whereas he was all alone, abandoned by Miss Frost for the presumably greater delight of watching Ben Gartmore's dogs chasing rats.

Not an hour later, he heard a carriage on the drive, and looked down from an upper window to see Harriet entering the house, and just behind her, Miss Frost, looking rather charming in a maroon pelisse and matching bonnet. But she did not come into the winter parlour before the dressing gong, and so he did not see her until he entered the drawing room before dinner. She smiled when she saw him, but otherwise she showed no sign of great delight in his return, continuing her conversation with Aunt Juliana most composedly. Disappointment nudged him. Should she not show some enthusiasm at his return? Somewhere in a corner of his mind had lurked the hope that she would leap up and run across the room towards him. Or at least come to greet him. Was that so much to ask? He knew he should not be irritated by her restraint, for what could be more proper after all? Yet he was.

He crossed the room and made his bow to the ladies. "Aunt Juliana. Miss Frost... you are well?"

The smile on her face slipped a bit. Perhaps she detected his annoyance, for she said coolly, "Thank you, yes. Did you have a tolerable journey, my lord?"

So formal. "As tolerable as any journey in December."

Aunt Juliana being drawn away at that moment, he sat down beside her. "You have been to Kirby Grosswick, I understand?"

"Yes. It was Lady Carrbridge's idea, since the Archbishop had approved your appointment to the living. I hope you do not mind?"

"Well, if Connie gets a bee in her bonnet, there is no stopping her." Again he was conscious of disappointment. It was *his* living, *his* parsonage, and surely he should have been the first to see it? "It is in poor condition, I hear."

"Very bad, yes. There are… rats, mice, all sorts of infestations. Ben was there yesterday with the dogs, and again today. He is staying at the inn so that he may continue the work each day. Mrs Compton took some of the servants in today to begin clearing the spoilt furnishings."

"I hope she will save what she can. I cannot afford to replace every last chair, you know."

"Oh, but I think Lady Carrbridge means to give us some furniture," she said. "There is a great deal in the attics, she said. And Lord Carrbridge is to pay for the work that needs doing — painting, wood panels, that sort of thing."

"I do not want my brother's charity," he said stiffly. "We will live within our income, and if we cannot afford new furniture, we must make do with the old."

"Oh," she said, her voice low. "I did not know you felt that way."

"Well, you would have done if you had waited to ask me." Then, thinking that perhaps he was being harsh, he added, "But I daresay Connie was the one who rushed in, and swept you up in her enthusiasm. In future, it would be better to talk to me about it first. I shall drive over tomorrow and see for myself what is going on."

"May I come with you?"

"Of course, if you wish it," he said, absurdly pleased at this sign of wifely interest in his company. "We can take your maid as chaperon."

"Monty, I travelled for three days alone on the stage coach," she said, with a sudden smile. "I hardly need a chaperon to drive to Kirby Grosswick."

"You were not then betrothed to me," he said coldly. "We will take a chaperon."

She subsided at once, and he hardly got a word out of her throughout dinner. Fortunately, the talk was so animated that no one noticed that the betrothed couple were silent. Harriet was regaling one end of the table with her plans for a home for fallen women, and grumbling loudly that Carrbridge refused to help fund it.

At the other end of the table, and after the ladies had withdrawn, Carrbridge was telling the company of all that had been discovered of Mr Sharp, the marquess's former agent. He had, it seemed, taken hold of numerous properties of their father, won at the card tables or through one of his eccentric wagers, and kept all the rentals for himself. It was a prodigious sum, hardly to be believed. Every once in a while, Carrbridge would stop and say, "And how much was that worth, Merton?" and Merton would mention some outrageous sum. And all that had gone into Sharp's pockets, or been stashed away in various banks around Yorkshire and the northern counties, and was gradually being recovered. Sharp was now on the run, and the Bow Street Runners informed.

"He held an entire town as his own," Carrbridge said indignantly. "A mill town called Drifford, and had a second wife there and a family, living openly as gentry, if you please. But Gus found it all out, and the Duke of Dunmorton went in there with the army and constables and rooted out the last of Sharp's family and took control of the place. And do you know, the population came out onto the streets to cheer the duke. He was very moved, and there was a great feast afterwards with bunting and music and revelry and so forth."

"And a great deal of ale," Humphrey said, grinning. "The common labourer likes nothing so much as an excuse to get drunk, especially when someone else is providing the barrels. The duke was very generous, and now the good people of Drifford think he is the finest fellow in Christendom."

Monty had heard the tale before, and knew that Gus told it rather differently, giving credit to Merton for finding out much of what was going on in Drifford. Merton, for his part, ate his dinner steadily, and contributed nothing to the conversation, talking composedly to Lady Hardy, who sat beside him. Monty rather approved of Merton, a quiet, self-effacing man with abstemious habits and upright behaviour. Some of his brothers found him dull, he knew, but for himself he could only approve such a man.

Once the dinner had concluded, Monty felt it best to address some niggling matters with Miss Frost which had begun to prey on his mind rather. He had no wish to pry, but as a clergyman it was incumbent upon him to adhere to sound principles in all aspects of his life. When he rejoined the ladies, therefore, he went straight to her side.

"May we talk more privately, Miss Frost? There are one or two matters we must discuss."

She nodded, but she looked pale, and he wondered just what she was so worried about. A newly betrothed woman ought to be happy, ought to want to spend time alone with her future husband. Even without a little affection in the case, surely there must be some uplifting emotion? Gratitude, perhaps. Was she having second thoughts?

He took her through to the winter parlour, still warm since there had been a fire burning there all day. Even now the embers in the hearth glowed, casting an eerie orange light over the room and their faces. He lit a couple of lamps and invited her to sit at the worktable, still littered with pieces of fabric, and a half-made bonnet.

How to begin? Best to be open, he supposed.

"Miss Frost, now that we have spent some time apart, and you have had an opportunity to consider your position, it may be that you have thought better of this marriage."

She jumped to her feet, her cheeks two angry spots of colour. "Oh, I see how it is! Your brothers have been talking to you about me and—"

Politely, he rose, too. "No, I assure you," he said, startled by her vehemence.

"—now you wish to back away from your promise, is that it?"

"Not at all, I—"

"You think because you are so grand and so rich, you may do just as you please! Just because I am nobody, it is perfectly acceptable to toss me aside like a used pair of boots. Does your word mean so little to you?"

"Miss Frost, you mistake me. I have neither the wish nor the intent to break our engagement. I look forward to our marriage with pleasure, you must believe me. But our engagement was... rather precipitate, and it may be that *you* are less certain than before."

"And have I ever given you cause to think so? Have I said or done anything to suggest such a thing?"

"I beg your pardon, Miss Frost. Pray forgive me." Although he was not sure what he was asking forgiveness for, but she was upset, and one never liked to see a lady in distress. "But I must ask you a question which..." He stopped, wondering whether it might be better to abandon any idea of discussing such awkward subjects. But he had to know, and truly, why should she not be happy to answer? "I must enquire just a little into matters which you have not so far seen fit to share with me."

"Nor shall I," she said, almost hissing the words. "My life until now is quite irrelevant."

"But that is all I wish to know," he said, in his calmest tones. "Far be it from me to force confidences which you are unwilling to give, but when we stand before Parson Hay, we must both be sure that there is no unknown obstacle to the marriage, for if it transpires later that there *is* such an obstacle, then the marriage would be illegal, you see, and we should both be in deep trouble."

Now the anger in her drained away, and she looked as white as chalk.

He went on, "So if you have a husband already—"

"Oh!" She laughed then, rather louder than the words justified.

"—or are somehow related to me by blood or marriage, then you must tell me at once."

"No, no! There is no husband lurking in my history, nor am I related to you in any way. *Of course* I would not agree to marry you in either case."

"And you are not known by any other name but Melissa Frost?"

"Oh no! That is indeed my name."

"And you know of nothing else that might be… difficult, should it be discovered later?"

"No, nothing," she said quickly. "Is that all? Are you satisfied?"

"Perfectly," he said, although he recalled Gus's words, *'But it does seem to me that if a lady will not tell even her future husband all about herself, then it is most likely because she has something to hide.'* What could a young lady like Miss Frost, outwardly so respectable, have to hide? Was she, as Carrbridge had once suggested, an opera dancer? Or worse? "Be assured, Miss Frost," he said carefully, "that I have no interest in what you may have been or have done in the past. My only concern is regarding legal barriers to the marriage, for marriage washes away all stains."

The spots of bright colour were back, and her eyes narrowed. "Oh, now you are suggesting that I am terribly disreputable, and you are rescuing me from a life of sin or crime or… or something of the sort. How generous you are, Lord Montague!"

"No, I did not mean—" he began helplessly, but she had already spun around and stalked to the door in a swirl of silk and shimmering net.

"I am going to bed. Pray convey my apologies to Lady Carrbridge. Tell her that I have the headache. Good night, my lord."

So saying, she swept out of the room, leaving Monty in a muddle of regret and bewilderment. How had his simple and reasonable questions brought out such a violent response? For the first time he began to wonder if he were doing a very foolish thing by marrying Miss Frost.

~~~~~

Melissa stamped up and down her room for some time before she was calm enough to consider the interview with Monty dispassionately. She knew perfectly well that he had every right to make such enquiries of her, in fact he had been so forbearing with her that she was tempted to weep on his shoulder with gratitude. He had not asked the really difficult questions, and had, in a roundabout way, told her that he never would. He would not insist on knowing who her family was... although that was a question she could not answer, even if she wished to. But her guardian... if he had asked about *him*...

No, he would not. He knew she would not answer. But the rest of it... the legal barriers to the marriage... she ought to tell him, she knew she ought. What would he do if he knew that she were only twenty, and must have her guardian's permission to marry? He would insist on writing to ask for that permission, of course — good, honest Monty! Naturally he would. And Lord Bentley would arrive, with his evil dandy of a brother, and Mr Pontefract claiming her as his betrothed and then— No, it was unthinkable.

The only way out of it was to get herself safely married to Monty, and then the prior betrothal would carry no weight. But if the marriage were illegal because she was underage... would Monty stand aside and let her be taken away by another man? Surely he would fight for her, and then Lord Bentley would have to give his permission... Yet she could not quite believe it.

So her thoughts ran, round and round, and she could make but little sense of it. The only certainty in her mind was that she must marry, and at once! It was the only way to be safe from Mr Pontefract and his special licence. A prior marriage must override every other consideration, must it not? If only she knew the law better! Yet there was no one she could trust to ask.

How she wished that she could talk to Monty about it sensibly, telling him everything, but she dared not. Besides, already he was wishing he had not committed himself so rashly. He denied it of course — so gentlemanly! — but she could see behind the polite words and she must not give him the least excuse to abandon her. Oh Lord, she had been so rude to him! Fear had risen up inside her, and broken free in snappish words and anger. Whatever must he think of her? Poor Monty! He had looked so bewildered, so lost, and she had so much wanted to smooth his forehead and kiss away the hurt look that he tried so manfully to hide. What a wicked girl she was, using him so shamefully to protect herself.

If only she had had more time to think before she left Bentley Hall. If she could have but planned her escape, she could have found some way to hide, to cover her tracks... but her only thought had been to get away, to run to the one person who might help her. The Earl of Deveron — it would be amusing, if only she were not so terrified of discovery. She must not weaken, she must not!

Even now Lord Bentley might be nearby, following her trail to Drummoor. Every day brought the possibility of disaster a little closer. She kept her portmanteau packed with her old clothes, and her few remaining coins.

8: A Day At Kirby Grosswick

Harriet laughed at the idea of a chaperon for Miss Frost.

"Good gracious, Monty, are we living in the dark ages? I shall be travelling with you as far as Sagborough, and you will have the carriage of Reggie and Lady Reggie with you as far as the Great Mellingham road. It is no distance from there. Besides, you *are* betrothed."

Monty made no further protest. If neither of the ladies objected, it was not for him to insist. He was a little nervous about being in a closed carriage with Miss Frost, even for a few miles, after her manner towards him the previous evening, but he supposed they could maintain the civilities for such a short time. But when Harriet left them at Sagborough, bound on a visit to Bridget Kelly, she took all conversation with her and they sat in silence the rest of the way to Kirby Grosswick.

When the village came into sight, however, he grew excited. He had passed through it many times, but had never taken much notice of such a nondescript place. Now his interest was fully awakened, for this was to be his new home. He remarked on every feature which caught his eye, and Miss Frost, her attention likewise caught, told him what little she had discovered of the place.

They saw the parsonage long before they arrived, for a giant plume of smoke rose vertically in the still air.

"Is the house burning?" he said in wonder.

"Only the rat-eaten furnishings," Miss Frost said, smiling at last. "The men built a giant bonfire on an unused part of the garden. I believe the house itself is sound, apart from a few missing shutters and the like."

The Drummoor servants' wagon was parked outside the gates, the horses contentedly cropping the overgrown garden. Two men could be seen on their knees, weeding the drive, and a man with a scythe was progressing through another part of the garden, with several dogs running around him.

"Ben Gartmore," Miss Frost said, as she descended from the carriage. "Halloo, Ben! Halloo there!" She waved vigorously at him and he waved cheerfully back, and began to walk towards them.

"Morning, my lord. Morning, Miss Frost. Got the worst of the rats and mice out now, but it'll take a while to clear them all. Once you've got permanent servants in place, you can get a couple of cats in to finish off the last of them. Just taking off the grass on what used to be the eastern lawn, then I'll do some more of the ivy. Did you enjoy the pheasant, Miss Frost?"

"Oh yes, it was delicious, thank you, Ben. Goodness, Will and Martin have cleared so much of the drive already, and there is Mrs Compton. Come along, Lord Montague."

And she was away up the drive, leaving a bemused Monty in her wake. Nodding at the gardeners as he passed, and wondering why Miss Frost, who had been at Drummoor for five minutes, knew their names when he did not, he made his way slowly up the drive. The prospect was a good one, for the house was a fair size and of goodly proportions, although the bricks or stone of which it was built were obscured by ivy. But as he walked, and left the trees around the gate behind, another vista opened up to one side — the church. *His* church, he thought, with a burst of pride.

As he drew level with it, he stopped, gazing at it with such joy that he could not suppress a wide grin. How beautiful it looked, its golden stone mellow in the low winter sun, the windows sparkling. Above it, a spire rose to the heavens, a cross at the pinnacle. His church.

Across the gardens lay a broad path, much choked with weeds, but clearly designed to allow the clergyman to stroll from his house to his church on a Sunday. How pleasant to walk that short distance, to meet his congregation, to join his voices to theirs in praise and to teach them the ways of the Lord each week. And there would be marriages to sanctify, babies to admit to the church and faithful souls to lay to their rest. What joy to devote his life to such work! And after every service, every baptism or burial, his wife would be waiting for him at home, his dinner ready, the fires burning merrily, his children smiling up at him, if they were so blessed.

Forgetting the house altogether, Monty's feet turned and walked slowly towards the church, the weeds reaching his knees in places. At the far side, a small wicket gate led to the churchyard and another path, this one free of weeds. The churchyard was in excellent order, the graves tidy, the grass neatly trimmed, the yew trees standing to attention either side of the lych gate. From somewhere out of sight could be heard the rhythmic swish of a broom sweeping leaves. The sexton, no doubt.

He walked round the building until he came to the great wooden door, then lifted the latch and went in. Ah, the familiar scent of the church, of beeswax and dust and candle smoke and, very faintly, incense. The floor was clean, the wooden pews shone, and the stained glass windows threw vivid splashes of colour onto the stone pillars.

Monty made his obeisance and then sat in one of the pews — belonging to the Martin family, from the label. He sat mesmerised, delighting in his good fortune. He had everything he had ever desired from life — his holy orders, his own parish, soon he would even have a wife, which he had always hoped for, in a nebulous way, but never enough to seek for it. But now Melissa had fallen into his hand, by the merest chance, and he was glad of it. God had certainly smiled upon him.

In this mellow mood, he heard the door open and close, and footsteps approaching. Melissa.

"Do you wish to be left alone, or may I sit with you?"

For answer, he slid further along the pew bench and patted the space beside him. She opened the pew door, and sat down.

"This has not been neglected, anyway," she said. "I suppose the villagers keep it clean."

He had not even thought of that. To him, the church was exactly as it ought to be, and so he had seen nothing odd in it.

"It is beautiful," he said.

"I went to Winchester Cathedral once," she said. "It has vast pillars stretching up to the most intricately constructed roof far above, and carvings everywhere. The rood screen, the choir, the patterned floor… everything of the most magnificent. That is my idea of a beautiful church. This is… plain."

"But peaceful," he said. "One may hear the voice of God here very clearly. A cathedral… York Minster, for instance… all is bustle and busyness. But in an empty church, like this one, where it is quiet, or in the woods or a corner of a garden… that is when I talk to God."

"Does he listen?"

"Yes, of course!" He turned to her in surprise. "God always listens."

"And He always forgives, does He not? Whatever we do, He forgives us."

"For those who truly repent. Miss Frost... Melissa... if there is anything... you wish to tell me..."

"No." She sighed, and picked up one of his hands in both of hers. "You are a good man, Monty, and I do not deserve you. I shall go back to the house, and leave you to talk to God."

But when she rose to leave, he did likewise, following her back across the gardens and wondering why she might feel the need for forgiveness, and whether Winchester Cathedral was near the home she never talked about.

The house was considerably worse than Monty had imagined. He had thought there might be a few holes in the wood panelling, shutters broken and smoking chimneys. He was not prepared for rooms with nothing left but bare walls.

"Should have seen this room before we started work on it," Mrs Compton said. "Never seen anything like it in all my born days. Rats everywhere, droppings, nests... we had to clear out everything. This room is the worst... half the floorboards gone. The others are not so bad, but still... there's a lot to do. A *lot* to do. There's an empty house just next door — the agent was here yesterday to ask if you wanted to lease it until this place is fitted up properly. It's furnished and ready to use."

"We can stay at Drummoor until this house is ready," Monty said. "I cannot see the need to move into one house and then another."

"That is as I thought, my lord. Let me show you the kitchen next."

The kitchen was better. A good clean had left it looking shabby, but intact. The store rooms and closets were in the process of being cleared of mouldy grains and fossilised meat and cheese, and would be usable soon. An elderly man stood watching, wringing his hands and muttering under his breath.

"Callum," whispered Melissa. "He lives here. He was Mr Whittaker's manservant. Mrs Compton has set up a bedroom for him off the kitchen, but he is very confused."

"Poor soul," Monty said. "Has he no family to take care of him?"

"No one. This is the only home he knows, so we cannot throw him out, can we?"

She looked up at him pleadingly, but Monty was not hard-hearted. "No, indeed. He may stay here if he wishes."

"Thank you!" she cried, and threw her arms around him in a hug which took him completely by surprise.

With virtually no usable rooms beyond the kitchen, the servants involved in the cleaning work were staying at the inn in the village.

"Is the inn satisfactory?" Monty asked Mrs Compton.

"It does well enough for the men," she said. "I can't leave any of the women there overnight, though, so they have to be driven over every morning. We'd get on faster if they could stay in the village."

"Is there a woman who might take two or three of them in?"

"Not that I know of."

"This empty house…"

"Oakdown House, my lord?"

"Why not lease the place for the female servants? Would that work?"

"It would be a lot bigger than they'd need, but... yes, that would work. I shall send the agent to Drummoor, then."

The kitchen was sufficiently restored to provide a hot dinner for all the workers, indoor and outdoor, who sat around the big kitchen table in a noisy group, not at all abashed by having Monty and Melissa in their number. Monty now realised how Melissa knew everyone so well, for she chattered away happily to them, called them all by name, and even knew the names of Ben's dogs, lolling in front of the range, so stuffed with rats they could hardly move.

Today, it seemed, she wanted to know how long everyone had been working at Drummoor, and where they had been before that. A surprising number had been born on the estate, or one of the many other estates the marquess held. Others had come from smaller great houses, and a good number from Mishcombe or Sagborough. One of the gardeners had walked all the way from York at the age of fourteen to ask for a job, because he had heard how fine the gardens were and wanted to work in such a place.

Ben's story was the oddest, as Monty had guessed it would be.

"I grew up in Ottenham, not far from York," he said. "My ma took in washing and did bits of cleaning jobs around the village. The parson taught me my letters and got me gardening work at a couple of houses in the village. I came to Drummoor earlier this year, and now I work with Mr Gaffney, the gamekeeper. Still do a bit of gardening, though." He grinned.

"Gaffney is one of the footmen, I thought," Melissa said.

"Aye, Mr Gaffney's son," Ben said. "Lily and Sally there are two of his daughters. Molly's married now, and Katy looks after Mr Gaffney."

"But why did you come to Drummoor?" Melissa said.

Ben chewed his lip, and some of the others exchanged glances. Without looking at Melissa, Ben said, "Because of my father. He was from Drummoor."

"Oh, you did not mention your father! What does he do for a living?"

Ben laughed. "Nothing!" Helplessly, he turned to Monty. "What should I say, my lord? How.. how should I describe him?"

Monty smiled gently at him. "It is no secret, Ben, and I am sure Miss Frost will understand the situation if you name him."

"Oh. My father was the eighth Marquess of Carrbridge."

Melissa's eyes widened. "Oh." Then she looked at Monty. "Oh," she said again.

Monty nodded. "Yes, Ben is my half-brother. When you have known us all longer, you will learn to recognise the Marford nose at forty paces."

One of the young kitchen maids gazed at Ben wide-eyed. "Do that mean you's a lord, Ben?"

Everyone laughed, even Monty. "That would be lovely, but unfortunately only the sons of the legal marriage are lords."

"But just think," one of the older women said thoughtfully, "if things had turned out different, Ben might've been a marquess and his lordship the one with the dogs."

There was some uneasy laughter at this upturning of the social order.

Ben raised his hands in protest. "Oh no! I can't hardly think of a worse fate."

"What, bein' rich and bein' waited on by all of us?" said one of the younger maids to another ripple of laughter.

"That part would be fine, but think of the responsibilities," Ben said. "So many people to take care of — his lordship looks quite worn down with it, sometimes. And imagine me in the House of Lords! No, it's fine as it is, as far as I'm concerned."

"We did think, at one time, that Ben might be the legitimate heir," Monty said quietly. "There was some suspicion that my father had married his mother. But it turned out to be nothing after all."

"Thank God for that!" Ben said. "I'm happy to be just a bastard son."

"Don't you mind havin' bastards in the family, milord?" one of the gardeners said. "Bein' a vicar, an' all."

"Why should I?" he said. "It happens in a great many families."

"Even in the Royal Family," someone said, and that set them all off on an affectionate rampage through the illegitimate offspring of the various princes.

Monty listened with amusement, but also with an eye to Miss Frost's countenance. Had she shown the least agitation with the subject matter he would have shut the conversation down at once, but she seemed quite at her ease, not at all discomfited. He could not fail to notice that she was very comfortable in such company, and far more forthcoming than she was in the drawing room at Drummoor.

When they got into the carriage later to begin the journey home, he said, "You have the common touch, Miss Frost. It is a great gift, to mingle comfortably with those much lower in station than yourself."

She turned a worried face to him. "Was I too forward?"

"No, not at all. I merely observed that you were easy in such company, whereas at Drummoor, you often seem... less relaxed."

"Your family is very grand," she said, with disarming simplicity. "I am not at all used to mingling with quite so many members of the nobility at once. There is always the fear of saying entirely the wrong thing, and Lady Juliana or Lady Ruth raising a quizzing glass at me, and looking *so*." She pulled a face redolent of aristocratic disapproval.

Monty laughed. "You need only be your charming self, Miss Frost. And take no notice of the aunts. No one does, I assure you."

"How did you like the house?" she said, as they rolled slowly out of the village.

He sighed. "It is in far worse condition than I had supposed. When you talked of rats and so forth… well, I could not quite imagine it, but now that I have seen all, there is so much to be done. There is hardly a room that is usable at present. I very much fear that we will not be able to contemplate getting married before Easter."

She turned to him with horrified eyes, gripping his arm with both hands. "Oh, Monty, *no!* Surely we do not need the house perfect before we move in? A few rooms… that would be enough."

"Melissa, it is inconceivable that any lady should be expected to live in such conditions. A few rooms? No, I want everything to be right for you. Besides, you will want to take your time to choose furnishings, curtains, that sort of thing. I have a little money set by, so you will be able to indulge your good taste."

"You are very kind to me, but I do not care about any of that," she said, her eyes huge. "Please let us get married at once, Monty. I cannot see the point in waiting. If you get a special licence—"

"No, no!" he said, laughing. "You will not get me haring off to London for a special licence. I do not see the need for any sort of licence. What is wrong with the banns, in the time-honoured way?"

"But that takes weeks!" she cried. "Please, please, let us not wait a moment longer than we have to."

"Why the rush?" he said gently. "Do you not want to choose wedding clothes, and furniture and new sheets and servants? Why not wait for the better weather?"

Her eyes flashed with anger. "Oh, I see how it is! You think to put it off and put it off, and maybe I will give up and go away and you can go on in your own way without troublesome Melissa!"

"No..." he began, dismayed by the violence of her response.

"You are too cowardly to break it off directly, so you think to persuade *me* to do it. You do not want a wife at all, I see how it is. You are a lord and a marquess's son, and I am *nobody* and you only offered for me from obligation and you really want some grand society wife—"

"No!" Monty said, stung.

"Well, I shall *not* go away, and I expect you to keep to your pledged word and... and you are so *unkind* to me and... and..."

Her anger trickling into silence, she laid her head on his shoulder, trembling, and he patted her awkwardly on the arm. "There, there! Do not get upset. It shall be as you wish, but *not* by licence," he added hastily, as her head shot up, her face wreathed in smiles. "We shall have the banns called in the regular way, and Parson Hay shall marry us before the year is out, if that is truly what you want."

Her face fell, but she managed a wobbly smile. "Thank you, Monty. You are very good."

"You ask for so little that it is no hardship to oblige you," he said gently.

But as they continued on the road home, he wondered at her sudden fiery temper, and his pleasurable anticipation of the day when he might call her his wife was tinged with anxiety. Was he allying himself with a termagant?

9: *Secrets*

When Monty arrived back at Drummoor, Merton was waiting for him. "Lord Carrbridge would be grateful if you would wait on him in the ship room as soon as convenient."

"Ah. What is up now, Merton? Another family crisis?"

Merton gave one of his thin smiles. "Nothing of the sort, my lord."

And indeed, Carrbridge also was smiling and relaxed. "Monty, we must talk about your allowance, you know. I shall increase it to a thousand a year to begin with, but if you need more—"

"Brother, I shall not need any allowance. My stipend will support us."

"No brother of mine is going to live on two hundred pounds a year. Do think of my position, Monty, and allow me to be the best judge of this. I will not have you living hand to mouth, and Miss Frost obliged to turn sheets. Whatever it means to turn sheets, for I have not the least idea, except that it is something that very poor people do."

"It means cutting a thinning sheet down the middle and resewing the thicker, outer parts together," Merton said with a little smile. "It makes the sheets last longer."

"You are a fount of knowledge, Merton," Carrbridge said. "It sounds somewhat less horrid than I had supposed. Still, I will not have Miss Frost doing such a thing, and she must have a carriage and a lady's maid and all the other necessities of life for the sister-in-law of a marquess, and you must not argue about it, Monty, or talk to me about this wager between Humphrey and Gus, for I will put a stop to all that nonsense, and so I tell you. Merton has explained to me how much you will need to live properly, as a gentleman, and when you have the living at Mishcombe you will be very well set up, but until then, you will have an allowance from me, and that is an end to it."

"Heavens, Carrbridge, how imperious you are getting," Monty said mildly, amused. "It shall be as you wish, although I daresay I shall not spend the half of it."

"Then you may set it aside to settle on your wife, or on your children," Merton said.

"Excellent idea," Carrbridge said. "So you see, Monty, although I am not at all reconciled to you marrying this girl, for where would we all be if one married a girl just because one felt sorry for her, you will not find me creating obstacles."

"But can you afford it?" Monty said, frowning. "Only last winter we were practically reduced to turning sheets ourselves, or so it seemed. Yet now you think nothing of splashing money around. I heard Connie talking about her new orangery only the other day."

Carrbridge looked smug. "Everything is looking much better, thankfully. Merton has found all these properties that Sharp was hiding from me, and if ever I get my hands on him, I will set the constables on him, I swear it. An agent is supposed to be working on my behalf, and not lining his own pockets and living like a lord at my expense. Heaven only knows how much he has taken from me over the years."

Monty smiled. "Only heaven may *know*, but I am sure Mr Merton has a rough idea too."

Merton's face for once creased into a smile of genuine amusement. "Naturally I do. Two hundred thousand pounds in all, as a very loose estimate."

"Good God!" Monty said, appalled. "And how much of that may be recovered?"

"Some. The properties, if we can find proof of ownership. Some money has already been found, but there is much still missing. We have found several banks where money was deposited from rentals and so forth, but most were emptied. Mr Sharp tried in vain to retrieve money stored in a hidden safe in his house here. However, there may be other safes in other houses. But with what has been recovered so far, and some improved management of his estates, his lordship's income has more than doubled."

"You are a miracle worker, Merton," Carrbridge said.

"No miracle, my lord, merely close examination of documents. Much may be achieved, merely by arranging papers in order and scrutinising them methodically."

"You make it sound so easy, Merton, as if anyone may do such a thing, yet I could not. No, no, do not tell me that indeed I could, if I set my mind to it, for I am perfectly sure that I could not. But you see how it is, Monty. My income is increased, and with Reggie, Humphrey and Gus all settled independently, my expenses are greatly reduced as well, so I can well afford to increase your allowance to honour your married state. Have you fixed a date for the wedding yet, or is it too soon to be thought of?"

Monty grunted. "Miss Frost is very keen to marry quickly. Surprisingly keen. A special licence was talked of."

"I do not like the sound of that," Carrbridge said, with a frown. "Merton, what is your opinion?"

Merton brushed an imaginary speck of dirt from one immaculately-clad leg. "A lady who betroths herself to a stranger and wishes to marry at once *may* be suspected of harbouring a secret," he said carefully. "Such secrets tend to result in the unexpectedly early arrival of the first child of the marriage. Are you prepared for such an eventuality, my lord?"

The same thought had occurred to Monty, too. "I should not mind it," he said. "My purpose in offering for Miss Frost, after all, was in part to rescue a lady in need of help, and such a situation would only make me pity her the more. It would be better, however, if she were to tell me of her trouble, whatever it is. I have no wish to insist, but there is something amiss that frightens her, and it concerns me that she will not confide in me. Merton..." He hesitated, not sure if he wanted an answer to the question he was about to ask.

"You wish to know if I uncovered anything suspect in her background? You may be easy, my lord, for I have not. In fact, I have not discovered anything at all about her. I have written to several of the eighth marquess's close friends enquiring after a Thomas Frost, and no one remembers anyone by that name. The only Thomas anyone can recall moving in the late Lord Carrbridge's circle was the Earl of Bentley. The two were at school together, and were such old friends that they called each other by their Christian names."

"I do not know Bentley at all," Carrbridge mused. "He is seldom in town, I think."

"There have been money difficulties, I believe," Merton said. "The earl sold a couple of minor estates last year. His main estate is in Hampshire, near Winchester."

"Winchester..." Monty said thoughtfully.

"Does that mean something to you, my lord?" Merton said.

"Just something Miss Frost mentioned. But there can be no connection. The letter was written to Thomas Frost, not Thomas, Earl of Bentley."

Merton coughed discreetly. "Forgive me, my lord, but that is not quite true. The salutation was simply to *'Thomas'*, there is no mention of Frost, or any family name."

"But it mentions Melissa," Monty said sharply. "And it was given to her by the woman who raised her, then it *must* be—" He broke off, seeing all the inconsistencies of it. "You have a copy of the letter, Merton?"

Merton nodded and retrieved a paper from a drawer in the large desk.

'My dear Thomas, What fools we are! We both drank far too much of Dunmorton's claret last night, but we must make the best of it, and do right by the girl, for I am sure you did not mean all that you said. It is surely best that you keep her for now, so that she grows up amongst her family, and when she is old enough to be in society then she may come to Drummoor. And you need have no fears or cause to regret your actions, for here is my pledge to you, my old friend: when they are both old enough and wise enough, your daughter, Melissa, shall marry my son, the Earl of Deveron, and no one shall say we did a bad thing last night. I go north tomorrow, but we shall meet again soon. My regards to R, and do not let C forget me, or I shall be most disappointed. I hope the play fulfils <u>all</u> your expectations. Charles.'

Monty read it twice, once assuming it was written to Thomas Frost, and once as if it were Lord Bentley. "It is not entirely clear," he said at last. "This Earl of Bentley — does he have a daughter called Melissa?"

"No. He has several daughters, but none called Melissa," Merton said promptly, tapping one finger on the opened copy of Debrett's Peerage on the desk in front of him. "I have already looked him up. And the family name is Brockenhurst, not Frost."

Monty scanned the page, and then, more carefully, looking for any sign of a connection to Melissa, but there was none. Three wives — Anne, Emilia and Patience. Four daughters — Emily, Alice, Charlotte and Delia. No Melissa anywhere to be found.

"Then it must be intended for Thomas Frost, and refer to Miss Frost," Monty said firmly. Merton nodded politely, but Monty had the unnerving conviction that he was not persuaded. "Dunmorton... Would that be the present Duke of Dunmorton, or his father?"

Merton reached for Debrett's and thumbed through it. "The present one." He looked up thoughtfully. "I wonder if Lord Augustus might ask him? His grace might remember more of those times than some of the others."

"I shall write to Gus myself," Monty said. "I do not feel that Miss Frost is concealing anything material, but I should like to know something of her father, if only for the notice in the paper."

~~~~~

Melissa found another new gown laid out for her that evening, the silk so feather-light it rippled under her fingers like water. She sighed with pleasure.

"Lady Carrbridge is so kind to me," she said to Margaret, her maid.

"That one came from Lady Harriet," Margaret said with a smile. "From Miss Kelly's seamstresses, she said."

"Oh. But this is beautiful. I had no idea they made anything like this. I imagined... worsted or fustian, or something of the sort, not this delicate silk, and so elegant."

"Lady Harriet said that it's very plain at the moment, but suitable for you. When you marry, she said, you can add a coloured tunic over the top and a matching bandeau, and it will be very stylish. So she said, miss, and I'm sure she's right."

"I am sure she is," Melissa said, striking poses before the long glass. "Will you get out the garnets for me, Margaret?"

"Not tonight, miss. Lord Montague's man came to tell me that his lordship will be…" She lowered her voice to a conspiratorial whisper, although they were quite alone. "…bringing you some jewellery."

"Oh." Melissa blushed, although she was not quite sure why. If her betrothed wished to bring her jewellery, why should that be in any way awkward?

Sure enough, just as Margaret was finishing her hair, there came a timid knock on the door, and Monty's face appeared around it, looking rather conscious.

"May I come in? Or should I wait outside?" he said shyly, then, catching sight of her, "Oh, Melissa, you look lovely."

What lady could resist such a spontaneous compliment? Certainly not Melissa, who had never been complimented in her life before she had come to Drummoor. She jumped up excitedly, and raced towards the door in a most unladylike manner.

"Oh, Monty, you say the most charming things!"

He smiled, but lowered his head self-consciously. "I… I have some of my mother's jewellery. If you would like to have it. Connie helped me choose, but if you do not like it…"

"I am sure I shall," she said hastily.

"Here." He put a wooden box on her dressing table. "There are some lovely pieces in here," he said, opening the box, and pulling out a shimmering diamond necklace. "There are ear drops somewhere in here too. This is by way of celebration, since Carrbridge is insisting on increasing my allowance, so we need not scrimp and use tallow candles and turn sheets after all."

The diamonds dripped from his fingers like sparkling rain, shimmering and dancing in the candlelight. Melissa's eyes were wide. She was so close to tears that she could not speak.

Monty must have noticed her silence. "Do you not like it? I can find you something else if—"

"Oh, no, no! It is…" She stopped, overwhelmed.

Monty looked at her, then said, "Margaret, will you leave us for a moment?" When the door had closed behind her, he said softly, "Are you all right? You may speak freely… I shall not be hurt or angry or anything of the sort."

"No one ever gave me jewellery before," she blurted, and then the tears came, and she could not stop them. His arms wrapped themselves round her tightly, and she buried her face in his shoulder.

"Hush now," he murmured. "There, there. Hush…"

So comforting, to rest in his arms. She felt so *safe*, so protected. But she was not safe at all, not yet. Not until they were married. She had to marry him *at once*, for only then would she begin to feel that she had escaped. Lord Bentley could arrive at any moment…

With a great sob, she pushed him away. "Oh, how I wish—!"

"What do you wish?" he said softly, his face so open, so guileless, so innocent.

"I wish we could marry tomorrow! I hate this waiting, Monty. I feel I am caught in the middle, neither spinster nor wife. *Please* will you get a licence so we can marry at once?"

Monty stepped back, frowning. "It is better not to."

"*Why* is it better? It is not better for me! Oh, you are a hateful man! Go away and take your mother's jewellery with you, for you are just showering me with gifts so that I will be quiet and not pester you any more."

He was incapable of concealing his hurt. "I beg your pardon if I have offended you, Miss Frost. I will leave the jewellery box there, for Connie would be distressed if you reject her choices altogether."

"Will you get a licence?"

A long silence, then, "Only if you will tell me everything about yourself and your family, without prevarication."

With a cry of frustration, she balled her fists and thumped his chest, pushing him away. "What, must I talk about my nursemaids and the time I fell in the pond and had to be dragged out by my hair? Or the Italian tutor who spoke with a lisp? You want every detail of my life? It is gone, Monty, gone for ever and there is nothing I care to remember. Do not make me remember."

"Very well," he said, and there was a dead tone in his voice that chilled her to the bone. "But in that case, I cannot agree to a licence. We will have the banns called, and be married in three weeks, and you must contain your impatience until then."

And so saying, he swept out of the room.

10: Of Marriage

Monty was horribly unsettled by this exchange. One minute Melissa was in tears, quite overcome because he was the first person ever to give her jewellery, then next she was spitting at him to marry her immediately. What could it possibly mean? And how was he to live with such a person? His mind was in turmoil.

How he longed to oblige her. He could be at York tomorrow, get a common licence, and be back before dinner, then they could be married the day after, and he would have his wife — he paused here, his breath catching at the thought of it. A wife! A gentle companion to warm his heart, and bring him comfort. He quailed a little at this point, wondering whether fiery Melissa was an aberration, brought on by the uncertainty of her situation, who would vanish for all time once she was safely wed, or whether that was a glimpse of her true nature. For it would not enhance his comfort to face little scenes like that on a daily basis. No, surely she would settle once they were married. In two days, if he were to yield. In two days he would have his wife, and she would have... whatever it was she needed so badly.

Yet what could that be? It puzzled him as he made his way down to the drawing room, and it puzzled him as he stood in a corner of the room, not in the least mindful of what was going on around him. It was only when Harriet touched him on the arm and spoke to him that he was recalled to an awareness of where he was.

"She looks well, does she not? All the work of Bridget's girls."

"What? Oh, Miss Frost?" He had not even noticed her enter the room, but now he realised that she must have been there for some time, for she had already made her greetings to Carrbridge and Connie, had moved past the aunts who sat in a line near the fire, and was smiling shyly at some joke of Uncle Lucius', who was at his station near the decanters. "She does look well, it is true."

"Do not sound so surprised! She is a pretty little thing, and it is a pleasure to dress her. You were miles away! Planning your first sermon for Kirby Grosswick, I daresay. When is it to be?"

"Next Sunday," he said absently, realising that he had been so distracted by Melissa that he had not given his sermon a single thought. That would never do! The first preaching of his career as a proper clergyman must be something special, something the villagers would remember for a long time. Something inspiring and uplifting, while yet reminding the parishioners of the need to work hard and avoid sin. It was hard to be uplifting while talking about sin. He must—

"Just remember the golden rule of sermons," Harriet whispered.

"What is that?"

"Keep it short!"

Monty smiled and shook his head affectionately at her levity. He liked Hatty very much, despite her sometimes frivolous nature. She was a reassuring and constant presence in his life. Which was odd in itself, now that he thought about it.

"Hatty, why did you never marry? For you must have had offers enough."

"Oh, I had offers," she said, eyes twinkling. "Some of them very ardently expressed. But I never needed to marry, Monty. Grandfather's provisions left me very well established — a house of my own, and enough money to be independent. What would a man add to that?"

Monty raised his eyebrows. "Children, perhaps? Rank? A grander home than Westbury House? Companionship? Love?"

"Love…" She pondered the word, almost as if she had never heard it before. "Perhaps love would do it, but I have never had the misfortune to fall in love, you see. And without that, I cannot see a reason why I should surrender my independence, and put myself into the power of a man, who would take all my fortune for his own and give me pin money in exchange. And then the constant production of children, and the associated risks. Of my five greatest friends from my coming out season, two are dead, and another is so worn down she is a shadow of her former self. Monty, women marry because they have to, because they have nothing of their own and they must be subservient to a father or brother or husband all their lives, and at least with a husband they will have an establishment of their own, and be mistress of the house, with all the respectability that entails. And some of them are happy enough, I daresay. But I never met a man yet who could tempt me to marry. I daresay I shall die a dried-up old spinster like Aunt Ruth or Aunt Hester. Ah, here is Crabbe. Dinner at last. I am so hungry! I hope there is goose tonight. I am so fond of a stuffed goose."

Monty was too slow to take Miss Frost into dinner, and had to watch her talking animatedly to Uncle Lucius. There was no doubt that she looked very well this evening. The gown was very plain, but that only emphasised her abundant charms, and she had, after all, chosen to wear the diamond necklace. That pleased him inordinately. Despite her passionate outburst, common sense had reasserted itself and now she was as composed as he had ever seen her. And how had Uncle Lucius managed to coax such lively conversation from her? Monty had never seen her so chatty in company.

When the ladies withdrew and the gentlemen regrouped, he contrived to sit by his uncle.

"Nice little thing, your Miss Frost," Uncle Lucius said, twinkling at him, his big, round face wearing its customary bland expression. Monty was not fooled, for Lucius, despite never marrying, was an acute observer of the female sex.

"But?" he hazarded.

"No buts. I avoided contentious subjects — like who on earth she is, and what she is running away from — and talked to her of books. She is a great reader of novels of a romantic and perhaps melodramatic turn, some of which she described to me in sufficiently graphic terms as to make me desirous of reading them. Have you read *Cecilia*, Monty? No, I thought not. It sounds very lively, far too lively for your serious mind, I should have thought. Miss Frost also enjoys reading books about foreign parts. History she is less enamoured of, and sermons, I regret to say, not at all."

Monty smiled, but did not rise to the bait.

"Then we talked about the parsonage, which she spoke of as *'my house'* more than once."

"And so it is... or very soon will be."

"Indeed. She is very excited about it, and told me the exact number of rooms and how each will be employed, and how she hopes to furnish them, if the attics here can provide her with castoffs enough."

"It pleases me to hear that," Monty said. Then, nervously, for he knew his uncle would answer him honestly, "Do you truly think she is running away from something?"

"Naturally," his uncle said. "Why else would she come haring up here from... somewhere or other, all alone, on the stage coach? Give Ambrose a nudge, will you, Monty? He has been holding onto the port for an age. Ah, my thanks." He poured himself a good measure, and sipped it with a sigh of satisfaction. "I will say one thing for your brother, he always keeps a good table. I did wonder when he married the Allamont chit... but there, she likes to entertain as lavishly as he does, bless the girl. Where was I? Miss Frost, yes. Here is my thinking, Monty. Her parents are dead — so she says, so let us suppose it true. And the guardian, too. She is quite alone, with no one to protect her, and no fortune to attract an honourable offer. Such a girl is... very vulnerable. She could easily become prey to the wrong sort of man. But, being a spirited and virtuous young lady, she runs away and comes here, where she wants to marry you at once, if you please, because only thus may she be safe."

Monty frowned over it. Perhaps it made sense, after a fashion. Still, marriage to a stranger? She would be safe enough at Drummoor without marrying anyone. The letter gave Carrbridge an obligation to take care of her, and he could certainly protect her from any man with dishonourable intentions. Yet she was desperate to marry, and at once. He thought back to Merton's hints that perhaps there had been a man with dishonourable intentions, and now Miss Frost was in a difficult situation. Well, if it were so, he sincerely pitied her, but it would not alter his resolution to marry her. But only after the banns were read.

When they rejoined the ladies, Connie was at the pianoforte while Miss Frost turned the pages for her. Then Miss Frost played.

With so few visitors in the house apart from the elderly aunts and uncles, there was little call for music after dinner, and they usually progressed straight to the card tables after tea. Tonight, it pleased Monty to discover that his betrothed played rather well, and had a pleasant singing voice, too, displaying the latter in both French and Italian. And yet, that just made her all the more mysterious, for why should so well-educated a young lady end up travelling on the stage coach in a pelisse that had definitely seen better days?

As soon as the card tables began to appear, Monty headed towards Melissa, but Connie intercepted him. "Monty, I am too restless these days to inflict myself on the whist players. Will you oblige me with a quiet game of cribbage? Have Gaffney put a table over there, behind the urn, will you? I do not like to be too near the fire just now."

Monty could not, of course, refuse, and with Connie, there was never any point. If she wanted him alone, whether to question him, or ask a favour, or offer a helping of advice, she would have her way, sooner or later. He set out the cards and the cribbage board, and waited for her to settle everyone else.

"Oof," she said, collapsing heavily into her chair. "I swear each baby is heavier than the last, and this one is awkwardly placed, I feel, for I have the most dreadful aching in my back all the time."

"Not long to go now," Monty said with a sympathetic smile.

"Thank God!" she said with feeling.

"Is it really as bad as all that?" he said. "I ask because a lady came to me when I was assisting Mr Callimont in York, very distressed because she was increasing again, and why had God seen fit to bless her once more when she had eleven already? I did not quite know what to say to her. One does not like to tell a lady in such distress that it is God's will and she should be grateful. It sounds so cold and unsympathetic."

"Every child is a gift from God, naturally," Connie said, her usually smiling countenance serious for once. "There is no denying, however, that the business is... unpleasant in many aspects, and the birth itself is excessively painful. When it is over, one is so relieved that all is well that one forgets the worst of it, but... twelve! I hope that is not my lot."

"Shall you like to have a daughter this time?" Monty said.

"I shall like to have a healthy baby, and to survive the ordeal myself," Connie said crisply. "Shall we play?"

"Very well. And then you may tell me what you really wish to talk about."

Connie laughed, but, despite this opening, they played for some time before she came to the point. "I understand you and Miss Frost had... some kind of altercation this evening."

"Ah," Monty said. He made his play and moved his peg before replying. "I take it Margaret told everyone in the servants' hall of it."

"She quite properly told Harker, so that I should know of it. The mistress of the house must be aware if there is a difficulty with a guest, Monty dear. No one else knows, I assure you, but Margaret reported raised voices and tears, and also that you sent her out of the room."

"Miss Frost was distressed," he said stiffly. "I thought some privacy might be helpful."

"Indeed, but is all well between you? She seems quite herself now."

Monty hesitated, but there was no reason for secrecy with Connie. "She wishes to marry as soon as possible."

"Oh." Connie tipped her head on one side appraisingly. "And you do not?"

Monty tried not to blush, and failed miserably. "I should be very happy to... under other circumstances."

"So you do not like her?"

"Oh, no... I mean, yes, I like her very much, so it is not... not that I am *unwilling*, Connie. I should like to... I mean, the sooner the better, as far as I am concerned."

He was blushing furiously now, but Connie patted his hand understandingly. "So you find her attractive as a woman, I collect, which is a very good sign, Monty, although you will have to learn not to colour up quite so readily when you talk to your parishioners on such subjects. But I do not quite see the problem. She is keen to marry you, and you are keen to marry her, so—?"

"I know nothing about her!" he said helplessly.

"What more do you need to know? Does it matter if her father was in trade, or her mother ran off with a fishmonger, or whatever scandal may lie behind her reticence? She is an amiable, unaffected young lady, with manners which will pass muster in any company. Marry her as soon as may be, and she may live here, under my eye, until your house is in a fit state for a lady. And you know, Monty, marriage has a way of drawing people together, even if they were not close to start with. Look at my sister Hope and cousin Hugo. They married to save Allamont Hall, and before very long, they were as much in love as any two people could be. It is quite charming, and I am sure you will find married life is just the same for you and Melissa."

"Connie, you are a hopeless romantic!" Monty said, smiling fondly at her. "Are you going to make your play?"

She sighed. "Do you know, my back is aching so much, I think I might go up to bed. Tell Lord Carrbridge for me, if you please, but do not alarm him or he will fuss so. He is a dreadful worrier, my poor

Francis, and I would not have him concerned. Pray tell him only that I am a little tired, and have gone upstairs early."

"May I get you anything? Shall I send for your maid?"

She laughed. "Now *you* are fussing, and there is not the least need, I assure you. I shall be better tomorrow, I am certain. An early night always sets me to rights. Good night, Monty."

~~~~~

Melissa saw Lady Carrbridge slipping out of the room, and not long after, Monty emerged from the alcove where they had been secreted. Discussing her, she had no doubt. She could imagine the conversation. *'Melissa is quite dreadful! She cries and screams and will not be appeased. How can I get out of this dreadful mess?' 'You poor thing! And she has no manners. She had no idea how to eat the quail's eggs, did you see? Then she talked constantly to Mr March, and quite neglected Lord Jacob on her other side. And three helpings of syllabub!' 'But how can I get out of marrying her?' 'Lord Carrbridge will get rid of her, depend upon it.'*

It was understandable, of course. She felt so much of an impostor here amongst these people that they could not fail to notice it. Some of them surely did — like Lady Juliana and Lady Christopher, who asked the most pointed questions and huffed and puffed when she declined to answer. But Lord Carrbridge was unfailingly polite to her, and Lady Carrbridge was kindness itself, and had given her so many lovely gowns and not reproached her in the least when she spilt wine on one of them and ruined it, although Melissa herself could not have been more mortified, and wished the ground would open up and swallow her. She was not fit to be amongst such people!

If only she could be calm and demure, and *respectable*, but she had this terrible gnawing fear always with her, like a snake devouring her from the inside, stealing her appetite and keeping her awake at night. It never left her, for any day now might come the knock on the door or the rattle of carriage wheels on the drive, and there would be Lord Bentley and his evil brother and Mr Pontefract, and her life would be over. That creeping fear destroyed all her pleasure in being in such a wonderful house, amidst such kind people, and made her lash out at the least provocation, or none at all, even at Monty, her saviour.

Such a sweet, gentle man, so softly spoken and thoughtful, and she had been so unforgivably rude to him when he had given her such lovely jewellery. He had not come near her all evening and that frightened her more than anything else. If Monty turned his back on her, then she would be completely lost. There would be nothing to do but wait for Lord Bentley to find her. And Mr Cornelius Brockenhurst. And Mr Pontefract. She shivered.

"Are you cold, Miss Frost? May I fetch a shawl for you?"

Monty! Always so attentive, and he had been so much in her thoughts it was almost as if she had conjured him out of the air. And he had come to find her — had he forgiven her for that stupid outburst? She turned to him with a smile of relief, but his expression was serious and unyielding. He had *not* forgiven her.

Still, when she declined the shawl, he pulled up a chair and sat beside her while she played whist, joining in the general conversation that arose between hands, and it was pleasant to have him there, a reassuring presence which kept the gnawing snake at bay for a little while. Nothing dreadful could happen to her with Monty beside her, and even if Lord Bentley should burst into the drawing room now, she could cling to Monty's arm and he would protect her. Surely he would protect her! Oh, but if only they were married, for then she would be safe. The logical part of her mind knew she would be no such thing, for the marriage would not be legal without the permission of Lord Bentley, but there would be arguments and lawyers and a great deal of discussion, and before it could all be sorted out, she would have her birthday and be of age and could decide her own future. With Monty, if he still wanted her. But at all costs she had to keep him on her side until then.

But with the demands of the cards on the one hand, and the pleasure of having Monty beside her on the other, the rest of the evening flew by. When the tea trolley reappeared, and the supper dishes were laid out in the antechamber adjoining the drawing room, Monty took her through on his arm, and watched her demolish a heaped plateful of delicacies without comment.

"You must think I have never seen food before," she said at one point, as she refilled her empty plate.

"I think," he said slowly, his face serious, as it usually was, "that your guardian neglected you shamefully."

She paused, about to bite down on a cherry tartlet. Instead, she set it down and looked at him fearfully.

"You are so thin," he said. "Or you were, when you first arrived. You had not been eating properly. And no one has ever given you jewels before, or pretty gowns, and you have not had your own maid, or learnt to ride, or been much in company. You have been well educated, but otherwise your guardian, whoever he was, neglected you, and that gives me a poor opinion of him."

"Oh," she said, suddenly finding it difficult to breathe.

"Happily, you are in better hands now." And he smiled at her with such warmth that she blushed, although she could hardly say why. "I shall take better care of you, Melissa. Shall we go and see Mr Hay tomorrow to arrange for the banns to be read?"

She nodded, words deserting her. For the first time, there was no snake inside her, eating away at her vitals. When she went to her room that night, after Margaret had left she prowled around the room touching everything — the silk sheets on the bed, and the thick wool blankets, the wardrobe now half full with gowns and pelisses and fashionable bonnets, the candles and lamps, the decanters and jar of macaroons, the softly padded chairs, the elegant escritoire and the books she had brought up from the library to add to her own pitiful few. Then she knelt beside the bed and gave heartfelt thanks for all of it, and for Monty, too. Her saviour.

That night, for the first time since she had left Hampshire, she slept deeply without dreams until the chambermaid woke her in the morning.

11: Christmas

Monty's life had become one of pleasurable anticipation. A date early in January was fixed for the marriage, Connie had assigned them a suite of rooms at Drummoor until such time as the parsonage was ready, Melissa was contented and smiling, and Monty himself looked forward to married life with unexpected eagerness. He had never considered himself a passionate man, except where God was concerned, but now he found himself musing a great deal on more earthly matters and would lie awake at nights wondering just what it would be like to have a wife to turn to for his comfort and pleasure.

Before that happy time, however, he had his first service as vicar of Kirby Grosswick, and he was not to face his congregation alone. Melissa came, too, and also Carrbridge and Harriet, and when the carriage drew up outside the church, Humphrey and Reggie and their wives were waiting for them. The church was as full as it could hold, with even a few standing at the back, and oh, the joy of seeing so many shining faces gazing up at him, listening intently, nodding occasionally as if in understanding. And there at the front, in the pew now neatly labelled *'Marford'*, his own family, not looking in the least bored, and Melissa smiling up at him in the most enchanting fashion. Further back, he saw Ben Gartmore and a couple of the Drummoor gardeners.

Monty had decided in the end not to preach about sin. He had taken his text from Colossians, *'For the hope which is laid up for you in heaven, whereof ye heard before in the word of the truth of the gospel'*, and the theme of hope made for a fine, uplifting sermon. Mindful of Harriet's injunction, he kept it short, and was pleased that nobody fell asleep.

Afterwards, he shook everyone by the hand and was surprised at the earnestness with which the villagers welcomed him. *'So pleasant to have an active parson again,'* they said, and, *'Will there be a service every week?'* A carpenter offered to come and fit panelling to the parsonage walls. Another man volunteered to have a look at the roof and replace any missing tiles. A woman had a brother who was a glazier in Sagborough who would be happy to fix the broken windows. He had offers of chickens, and cats to deal with the mice, and pots for the kitchen, and vegetable seeds for his garden, and even furnishings. He accepted everything gratefully, not sure quite how much of it would come to fruition, but appreciative of the good intentions.

Then he showed his brothers and sisters over the parsonage, where they gazed in silent dismay at the devastation, and finally back to Drummoor in time for a short walk with Melissa in the gardens before dark. It was, he felt, a perfect day.

~~~~~

As Christmas drew closer, Melissa began to feel more comfortable about her situation. With each day that passed without the arrival of an irate Lord Bentley, she relaxed a little more. He had not, then, managed to follow her. Carefully recalling her journey, she realised that she could certainly have been followed to London, but from there the earl would have had to visit every coaching inn in town to discover her next destination. Perhaps, too, he had wasted time checking hotels or inns to see if she were staying in London. But even if he had found the right coaching inn, and the ticket clerk had remembered her, he would only discover that she had bought a ticket for York. Well, he would ask in vain for her in York, and would it occur to him that she might have left the coach at Sagborough? Did he know of her connection to Drummoor? Surely not, or he would have been there long since. And perhaps he did not even care that she was gone?

Truly, she must now be safe from him. She would marry Monty in January, and then there would be only three weeks until she was of age and could confess all, and surely he would forgive her? Monty was another reason for her to feel more at ease, for his attentiveness, the way he looked at her, eyes shining, the gentle little smiles — it was almost the behaviour of a lover. Or at least, how she imagined a lover would behave, for she had no experience in such matters. Even the aunts had stopped pestering her, and had begun to talk about *'When you are married...'*, and explain complicated aspects of family history that they felt a Marford bride ought to know. This was really going to happen.

By Christmas, the house was almost as full as it could hold. Melissa had moved into the marital apartment assigned to her and Monty, since her old room was required for guests, as droves of Marfords and Marches and Whittletons and Brants descended on them. Dinner moved first to the pink dining room, and then to the great hall, its massive hearth struggling to heat the room. Lady Hardy at last laid aside her mourning clothes after a full year, and declared her wish to dance again as soon as may be. She had not long to wait. There was a ball in the library, its three fireplaces ablaze, where she stood up for every dance and smiled a great deal, and, to the great interest of their friends, danced three times with Mr Merton.

The ball gave Melissa the opportunity to demonstrate her utter lack of familiarity with the cotillion, the quadrille and the waltz. Although she had sat in on lessons with Lord Bentley's children, she had been excluded from the visits of the dancing master, and consequently had only the servants' ball as her guide. Monty, unfailingly polite, helped her through several dances and then, when she professed a wish to relieve the company of her ineptitude for a while, drew her away to a dark corner beside the French poetry and kissed her gently.

She discovered that she liked being kissed very much, the resulting warmth spreading all the way to her toes. When he stopped kissing her, rather sooner than she would have liked, she sighed with pleasure and rested her head on his shoulder. He was just the right height, she discovered, just a little bit taller than her but not so tall that she developed a crick in her neck when she looked up at him. Her hand seemed to have crept its way around his neck, and was resting just above his collar, so that she could stroke the back of his head, his silky hair tangling with her fingers. So intimate, and so delightful!

He smiled at her in that way he had lately, that made her insides melt. "I cannot wait to make you my wife," he whispered.

For answer, she pulled him nearer to her, so that his lips brushed hers again, and with a little burst of low laughter, he took the hint and pulled her to him again for another kiss, much longer, that left her trembling.

On Christmas Day, he went off to Kirby Grosswick to conduct the service there, but Melissa stayed at Drummoor. Lady Carrbridge was tired and listless, and begged her to stay at home and bear her company. Melissa played cards with her, then read for a while, then walked about with her as Lady Carrbridge rubbed her aching back, but nothing answered.

"Lord, I shall be so glad when this baby is out," she said wearily. "I have never felt so out of sorts before. Dr Milligan says there is nothing wrong, but sometimes I wonder."

"I am sure there is nothing to worry about," Melissa said. "A lady I knew… she had three daughters, and was dreadfully tired each time, but the fourth child was a boy and she was filled with energy. So perhaps you will have a daughter this time, my lady."

Lady Carrbridge brightened. "That might be it — a daughter is bound to make one feel different, especially after two boys. I daresay that is all it is. You are a great comfort to me, Melissa. I am so glad you are here, and going to marry Monty, although I wish you had not to go away, you know, for although Kirby Grosswick is not far, still you will not be here. There is no one here, no one who is a real friend to me, and it is so lowering sometimes. The house may be filled with people, and that is lovely, of course, but none of them are my particular friends. Well, my cousin Mary, of course. I am very fond of Mary, although she was always a friend to Amy and Belle, rather than to me, and now that she is out of mourning… well, never mind that. As for Harriet, she flits about to her own house, or to stay with friends, or to London. Always gadding about. And Francis… well, a man has business affairs to deal with, and one cannot have a comfortable coze with a man while remaking a bonnet, however much one loves him. And I do not know at all why I am crying for I have nothing to make me sad, nothing at all."

Melissa could find no words, but she put her arms around Lady Carrbridge and rocked her gently until she was more composed.

Three days after Christmas, the snow began, falling steadily and blanketing the garden so thoroughly that everyone was confined indoors. Melissa was helping Lady Carrbridge sort out baby clothes in the nursery. Or rather, she and a nursery maid were on the floor sorting out boxes of baby clothes, while Lady Carrbridge sat in first one chair, then another, then reclined on a chaise longue, and finally walked about.

The clothes were exquisitely worked, the result of innumerable Marford ladies industriously plying their needles or exercising their lacemaking skills. Lady Carrbridge told her that every item was made by one or other of the ladies of the family.

"Aunt Jane March makes most of the lace," Lady Carrbridge said. "Aunt Theodosia and Aunt Beatrice account for most of the little gowns, although I made—" She stopped abruptly, then gasped in distress.

"My lady?" Melissa cried, scrambling to her feet.

"I think... the baby... but it is too soon."

"They come when they want to," Melissa said. Where had she heard that said? It must have been from Lady Patience. "Who shall I send for?"

"I know," said the nursery maid, rushing out of the room.

Melissa looked towards the door too, but Lady Carrbridge held out her hand to her. "Do not leave me! Please, Melissa, stay with me."

"Of course. Should you like to go to your room?"

"Yes... yes... I suppose so. But it is too soon."

They made their way slowly out of the nursery and along the landing, Lady Carrbridge holding her stomach, although she did not seem to be in great pain. Melissa had had nothing to do with birthing babies, naturally, so she was relieved when several of the senior servants appeared. But Lady Carrbridge gripped her hand tightly and would not relinquish it, so Melissa was necessarily carried along on the tide sweeping the marchioness towards her bedroom.

Once inside, Lady Carrbridge seemed a little brighter. She perched uneasily on a chaise longue, and allowed the servants to fuss around her, building up the fire, warming the bed and laying out a thick flannel nightgown for her. Two women brought in a wooden crib, and began preparing it, although Melissa guessed it would be some hours before it would be needed.

"Dr Milligan," Lady Carrbridge said. "Dr Milligan must be fetched."

"Yes, my lady," someone said, curtsying, and scuttled off.

A male voice, raised in anxiety, could be heard in the sitting room beyond, then a female voice, soothing. The male voice, louder. The door opened and Lady Hardy's face appeared round it.

"Connie, Lord Carrbridge is here, but he will not go away until he has seen you. Shall I allow him in?"

Lady Carrbridge clucked in distress. "No, no! Do get rid of him, Mary. He can do nothing useful here."

But he would not be deterred, and eventually he came in and sat beside his wife on the chaise longue, taking one hand and stroking her forehead with his free hand. "I thought it would be next month," he said helplessly.

"So did I," she said. "It will be fine, Francis. I have done this twice before, after all. Now you must go, my love. This is women's work."

"May God protect you, my sweetest love," he said, in the gentlest voice imaginable. Then he kissed her, and, with a sob, rushed out of the room.

Lady Hardy closed the door behind him. "Now, Connie, we must send for the village midwife — what is her name?"

"Mrs Hall, but I need Dr Milligan. He knows me, and I feel comfortable with him."

"But he lives at Sagborough, and the snow is so thick, no one will get through tonight," Lady Hardy said. "Let us have Mrs Hall here for tonight, and if this baby is still not here by morning, someone must try to get to Sagborough."

"Very well, very well, if I must."

The afternoon passed slowly. Lady Carrbridge was settled in bed, but her pains were mild and Melissa was given the task of reading to her. She chose *Cecilia*, partly because it was dramatic enough to be a distraction, and partly, it had to be said, because it was on top of the pile beside her bed and therefore readily to hand. She could not quite believe that she had not yet been sent away. She was unmarried and knew nothing at all about babies, and yet whenever she suggested leaving, Lady Carrbridge clung to her hand and would not hear of it.

Late in the afternoon, Mrs Hall arrived, a matronly woman who exuded calm good sense and confidence. She had, she said, delivered eight babies of her own and dozens of others around the village and on nearby farms, and her mother and grandmother had been midwives before her, so there was nothing she had not seen or heard of before.

"All you need to do, milady, is relax and let everything happen as it will. Take your time, allow the pains to come, and we'll have your baby here by morning, I promise you."

And so Lady Carrbridge relaxed and smiled, and allowed the pains to come, and Mrs Hall told her she was a very good girl and was doing wonderfully. In between the pains, Melissa read from *Cecilia,* and all was calmness and happy anticipation of the birth.

Evening gave way to night, and the pains became more intense and more frequent, and still Mrs Hall smiled and said everything was going along charmingly. "Not long now, milady."

Night faded to grey, snow-laden day, and still there was no baby. A groom was dispatched through the snow to fetch Dr Milligan, but he returned two hours later. There were snowdrifts right across the road close to Mishmere Cross, he reported, and no horse could get through. Mrs Hall's skills would have to suffice to help Lady Carrbridge's baby into the world.

This was the point at which Melissa, even ignorant as she was of babies and birthing, knew that something was wrong. The sudden anxiety on Mrs Hall's face revealed it, and Lady Carrbridge's pallor confirmed it. The poor lady no longer smiled or talked between pains, but lay back on her pillows, eyes closed. Lady Hardy, wiping her forehead gently with lavender-scented water, talked comfortably of progress and how close she must now be, but her anxious eyes betrayed her.

"Is there nothing we can do?" Melissa said to Lady Hardy.

She shook her head. "Not that I know of. Connie is in God's hands now."

~~~~~

The long day wore on. Monty stayed in the ship room with Carrbridge, who paced up and down relentlessly. Every twenty minutes, he dispatched the butler to enquire for news, but there was nothing to report. The uncles and cousins and Mr Merton came and went, but Monty stayed with his brother.

Late in the afternoon, Carrbridge turned to Monty. "For God's sake, go up and see what you can find out, for I am going mad here with waiting. There must be some news by now."

Monty climbed the stairs slowly, in some trepidation, and asked for Melissa. Her pale face and the shadows beneath her eyes shocked him.

"Is there any news? Carrbridge is distraught, as you can imagine, and all we hear is that progress is slow."

"I cannot tell you more than that," Melissa said distressfully. "It is terrible to see her suffer so, and be powerless to help. But there is nothing anyone can do, nothing!"

"Except to pray," Monty said fiercely. "I shall go to the chapel and pray for a miracle."

He went first to Carrbridge to give him the news that there was no news, and then, leaving his brother with Mr Merton and a couple of the uncles, he took a candelabra and walked through the winter-dark house to the chapel. There he lit every candle he could find and then prayed with a fervour unusual even for him. Then he sat, staring at the silver cross, its shape seeming to jump about in the candlelight, and thought about marriage and love and what it would be like to love someone as deeply as Carrbridge loved Connie, and then to lose her. He wondered how a man's Christian stoicism would survive such a loss, and how anyone could possibly offer comfort. To talk of the reunion in the afterlife could not possibly console a man with several decades of lonely life to endure first.

When the candles began to gutter, he went back to the ship room. Carrbridge was alone, one arm leaning on the mantel, head down. It was full dark, and the rest of the family must be sitting down to a subdued dinner. Monty had snatched a bite here and there, as trays of food had appeared, although he had but little appetite.

In the distance, a bell jangled. Then, a minute or two later, it jangled again. Not long afterwards, the housekeeper's head appeared round the door.

"Beg pardon, my lord, but there is a doctor arrived."

Carrbridge's face lit up. "Dr Milligan has come!"

"No, my lord. It isn't Dr Milligan. This is a Dr Hay and his sister, a nephew and niece of Mr Hay the parson. Dr Hay heard word in the village that Mrs Hall was sent for and hadn't returned, and he's asking if he might be of any assistance."

"Yes, yes! Anything he can do! Pray show him upstairs, Mrs Compton. There, now all will be well, Monty. A physician will get this baby born."

Monty wondered just what a doctor could do that an experienced midwife could not, but he said nothing, naturally, and Carrbridge must have come to the same conclusion, for he soon resumed his pacing, back and forth, back and forth.

About half an hour later, the door opened. "Dr Hay, my lord," the butler intoned.

Hay was a neat, dapper little man, well-dressed, but young, no more than thirty. Monty's face fell. What could so young a man know that Mrs Hall did not? Yet his expression was grave.

"Well?" Carrbridge said eagerly. "You have news for me?"

"I can tell you why her ladyship has not yet been delivered of her child," he said, and his tone was so sombre that Monty's insides churned with sudden fear. "The infant is lying incorrectly, crossways, rather than head down."

"So... that is why it is taking so long?" Carrbridge said tentatively. "How much longer? When do you think it will be born?"

There was a long silence. "I am so very sorry," Hay said quietly. "In such cases, there is no possibility of it."

Carrbridge went white. "And my wife?" he whispered.

Hay took a long breath. "My lord, you must prepare yourself for the worst."

Carrbridge's anguished howl echoed throughout the room.

12: Patience

"No!" Carrbridge screamed. "No! I will not believe it. Is there no chance at all?"

"There is a very small chance that the baby will turn spontaneously, leading to a happy outcome," Hay said. "It is not likely, but—"

Carrbridge groaned, a low, animal moan of pure pain.

Monty said helplessly, "And is there nothing to be done which might facilitate such an event?"

Dr Hay hesitated. "There is a technique that I have heard used in such cases, but I have never attempted it myself. It is very risky, of course, but then every option is risky at this stage. If successful, it might save both lives, but... I should not wish to raise your hopes too high, my lord."

"Will you try it?" Carrbridge said eagerly. "Please, I beg of you, try anything you can think of to save my wife's life. My poor Connie! She must live, she must! Dr Hay, do this one thing for me, and I will make you a rich man."

Hay shook his head. "I want no riches, but I will certainly do what I can, with your permission, my lord."

"Yes, yes, do whatever you have to. If you can save my wife, you will have my undying gratitude, Dr Hay."

"And you understand, I take it, that all our hopes may yet be in vain?"

Carrbridge raised his head and looked him straight in the eye, his expression bleak. "Do whatever may have some chance of success. I place my wife's life in your care, Dr Hay, but no blame will attach to you should your efforts fail at the last. We are all in God's hands."

Hay left and then the two brothers were alone again. Carrbridge, exhausted, sat on the edge of a chair, his head in his hands. Monty said nothing, having no words that could comfort his brother in his distress. All his Bible verses, his sermons, his fine words were useless in such circumstances.

A footman came in to attend to the fire, and remove an untouched tray of food. Uncle Lucius came in, patted Carrbridge on the shoulder and sat quietly beside him. Two of the cousins put their heads around the door to ask for news, then went away again. The clock on the mantel struck ten.

Somewhere far away, a baby cried. Carrbridge jumped to his feet, his face a mixture of hope and terror. For several long, unbearable minutes, nothing happened.

Running feet, and the door burst open. Melissa's face was alight with joy. "It is all right! They are both all right!"

Carrbridge burst into tears.

~~~~~

For three days, the whole house held its collective breath. Dr Hay and his sister stayed on to care for Lady Carrbridge, and Carrbridge refused to stray further from his wife's side than the sitting room outside her bedchamber. On the fourth day, Dr Hay finally smiled and declared that her ladyship was safe from the dreaded childbed fever. Champagne was opened, there were smiles and laughter,

Carrbridge emerged at last to be congratulated, and from the village, drifting faintly over the snow-covered rooftops, came the sound of church bells pealing in celebration.

A little before noon, Monty looked round the ship room, where the men had gathered, and noticed that Carrbridge had disappeared. He slipped out and asked Fitch, stationed at the foot of the main stairs, if he had seen him.

"Yes, my lord. His lordship entered the great hall about half an hour ago."

The great hall? Fitch held open the door for him, and Monty went in. With its high roof, the great hall was always chilled in winter. In the evenings, the massive hearth filled with flames kept it tolerably warm, but this morning, the air still heavy with candle smoke and goose fat and perfume, he shivered as his feet tap-tapped across the stone flags. The room was empty, the long table shining dully in the wintry light that penetrated through long, latticed windows. Monty left by the far door. Another footman jumped to attention beside the chapel stairs, then rushed to hold open the chapel door for him.

Carrbridge was there, not praying, but staring into space from a pew near the back. Monty slid onto the bench beside him.

"Do you wish to be alone?" he said quietly.

"Not at all. I... I came here to pray, to give thanks, but... I cannot seem to find the words. Will you help me? I should like to give thanks to God for his grace and mercy."

"I find the familiar words best in such cases," Monty said. "The pater noster? Shall I begin? *Our father, Which art in heaven...'*"

And Carrbridge joined in, his voice low at first, then gaining strength. When the prayer ended, he sighed and sat back on the pew. "Monty, you are a great comfort to me. I never wanted you to be a clergyman, but these past few days your faith has been an inspiration to me. I have never been resolute in my belief, as you have been. There always seemed to be more worldly matters demanding my attention, but I shall do better from now on, I am determined on that."

Monty folded his arms and leaned back too. "It has taken me the other way," he said softly. "For the first time, I wondered whether God had deserted us. That day, that endless, terrible day, I came here and prayed for a miracle, and wondered if I could possibly forgive God if he took so good, so generous a person as Connie away from us. From *you.*"

"Did you so? But then your prayers were answered, were they not? For who should appear on the doorstep but Dr Hay, a physician — exactly what was needed to save my wife and child? Was that not the miracle you prayed for?"

Monty smiled then. "Hope had deserted me by the time Dr Hay arrived, so the miracle took me by surprise rather. Even now, I cannot quite believe that the crisis is over. We came so close to losing her."

Carrbridge gripped his shoulder, his face filled with pain for a moment. "Yet we did not. Shall we go and see if she is awake? And you have not yet seen your niece."

"Two boys and now a girl," Monty said, as they made their way up the stairs. "Clever Connie! How shall you like to have a daughter?"

"It will be delightful. Two boys who will ride and fight and pretend to be Cavaliers, and a delicate flower of a girl who will embroider and sing like an angel."

Monty laughed at this optimistic familial vision. "A delicate flower like Harriet, you mean, who rides to hounds as hard as any man? She made an excellent soldier when we had our battles on the roof, as I recall."

"I do not know what went wrong with Hatty," Carrbridge said, looking bewildered. "Girls should be shy and demure and not at all forward."

"Really, Carrbridge! Where do you get these notions from? Females are certainly different, and should not trespass on the domain of men, but that does not mean they have to sit in dark corners all their lives. Connie is anything but shy, and she is perfection in your eyes, is she not? And then there is Bridget Kelly, fighting to aid her fallen women, with no one to help her but Harriet. Her forwardness is an asset to her charity, I should say."

"You think I should do something for her? Because she is our half-sister?"

"It is as you please, of course, but you had no trouble helping Ben Gartmore. The case is no different."

"A man must have some way to support himself, whereas a woman will be supported by a man, Monty."

"Miss Kelly's women are unlikely ever to find themselves in that happy position," Monty said sombrely. "In such cases, they must support themselves or go to the workhouse. A little help to establish them in some suitable occupation would make all the difference."

"Hmpf," Carrbridge said. "I shall consider the matter."

"You mean you will ask Merton's advice," Monty said, laughing. "You always ask Merton when you are unsure what to do."

"Because he always knows precisely what I should do, and how much it will cost," Carrbridge said complacently. "Here we are. I hope Connie is not asleep. I do *worry* so when she sleeps during the day like an invalid."

But when they went in, they found Connie awake and smiling contentedly at the baby sleeping peacefully in the crib beside the bed.

"Francis has said I may name her," she said to Monty as he leaned over to admire the infant. "At first, I was in difficulties, for I wanted to name her after all my stalwart helpers who stayed with me and brought me comfort in my darkest hours, but that would be four names, you know — Mary, Melissa, Miss Hay and Mrs Hall. But Mrs Hall is a Mary also, and although Miss Hay is Marina, she is often called Mary too, so that was very easy. So I have settled on Mary Melissa, you see. There! Is she not the sweetest baby, Monty?"

"She is very tiny," he said, awed, as always, by the miracle of birth, this miniature person who would all too soon grow up to be a rumbustious child and then a demure young lady and perhaps in time a doting mother herself.

Connie laughed. "So small a creature to give me so much trouble, but Miss Hay says it is often so with very small babies, that they get themselves into an awkward position. Although not often as awkward as little Mary did. But all is well that ends well, and Monty, I depend upon you to take care of Francis and feed him up and make sure he does not brood or worry about me."

"I fear you set me an impossible task, sister," Monty said, smiling fondly at her. "The feeding up I may perhaps manage, but stop him worrying about you? He will never do so."

She laughed, and Carrbridge laughed too, although a little sheepishly. When a man is an inveterate worrier, having one's wife come very close to death is not conducive to alleviating the tendency, but Monty said nothing more.

They stayed for some time, but just as they were about to leave, Connie said, "Monty, will you give *Cecilia* back to Melissa?

Mary and I read the last chapters this morning, and very affecting they were too, so pray thank her. I do so like a story where all ends happily."

She waved the book at him, and he took it, but said, "Has Melissa finished with it? If so, I will take it back to the library."

"Oh, it is her own book, not from our library," Connie said. "I do not think we have anything so enjoyable. The library shelves are all sermons or battles or some such."

Monty flipped open the cover, and there on the fly leaf was the date and an inscription, *'To dear Melissa with every good wish for a very happy birthday - Patience'.*

"So it is," he murmured thoughtfully. "I shall return it to her."

He found her in her apartment — *their* apartment, he thought, with a sudden thrill — curled up in a chair beside the fire drinking chocolate. It looked such a cosy scene, yet he felt oddly excluded. Soon, perhaps, they would drink chocolate together.

"I have brought your book back," he said, feeling awkward for having seen the inscription. "Connie sends her thanks for it." He hesitated, but his curiosity was overwhelming, and after all, Melissa would soon be his wife, and there should really be no secrets between husband and wife. "I thought it was from the library, until I read the inscription. From Patience. I have not heard you mention anyone called Patience before, I think."

Melissa looked conscious. "Just a friend. From a long time ago."

"I see," he said colourlessly. "I shall leave it here for you." He dropped the book onto a side table, and with very few more words, made his exit.

His curiosity was now positively burning, and he knew exactly where he had encountered the name of Patience recently. With swift steps he made his way to the ship room, and threw open the door. Then he stopped in surprise.

Not ten feet away, Merton and Lady Hardy were locked in a passionate embrace. They sprang apart, blushing.

"I beg your pardon," Monty said. "I will go away at once."

"No need, my lord," Merton said, laughing. "Our secret will be announced formally at dinner tonight. Lady Hardy has agreed to make me the happiest of men."

"Then I congratulate you most warmly," Monty cried, shaking his hand vigorously. "And Lady Hardy too. This is delightful news, although perhaps not the greatest secret in the world. I daresay almost everyone has observed your growing attachment over the months."

"I daresay they have," Merton said. "We have tried to be discreet, naturally, since Lady Hardy was still in mourning until recently, but it is difficult to hide so strong a preference for the company of one person in particular."

"Lord Montague, I hope you do not regard any aspect of our behaviour as improper?" Lady Hardy said.

"Not in the least. Your friendship is of many years' duration, and what could be more natural than that you should seek out each other's company? And what more natural than that friendship should deepen with time to something more? Besides, you have allowed a full year to pass since the death of Sir Osborne. No, I do not see the least impropriety."

"Then you will have no objection to marrying us?" she said anxiously. "We should so like it to be you."

Monty laughed in delight. "Oh, I should enjoy it of all things. Here, in the Drummoor chapel? How appropriate! Yes, I should be happy to do it, and if you do not delay, then it might well be my first marriage ceremony since I took holy orders.

"But we have detained you with our own affairs while you perhaps have business to undertake here, my lord?" Merton said.

"I wanted only the copy of Debrett's that was hereabouts."

"Ah. I returned it to the library. Shall I fetch it for you?"

"By no means. There is the dressing gong now, so it can wait."

That evening, everyone gathered in the great hall for dinner in a mood of determined celebration. Even Carrbridge smiled and looked relaxed. The announcement was made of Merton's betrothal to Lady Hardy, and both were declared to look suitably happy, and the bride to blush to the requisite degree.

Monty rather envied them their perfect happiness, the years of friendship which had led to this moment of truth — of abiding love, deep enough and strong enough to sustain them through a lifetime of joys and trials. And yet love was so risky. Giving your heart to another person who might die at any moment laid one open to unending grief. No, not unending, he reminded himself sharply, for death would reunite those who grieved, but in the meantime, one could only endure. And he watched Carrbridge, seemingly relaxed and contented, as affable as ever, yet the pain in his eyes was still there. Perhaps it would never leave him now, that terrible fear. Was it worth it, the pain, the fear, the possible grief? Perhaps after all he was safer marrying a woman he was not in love with.

He looked at Melissa sitting beside him, talking animatedly to Miss Hay across the table, and felt a surge of unexpected tenderness. Perhaps he was not head over heels in love with her, but he liked her very well. More than liked, if he were honest. There was something more than esteem in his response to her, something perilously close to affection, and perhaps when they were married, that little bud of partiality would blossom into something more, into love. Perhaps. And perhaps she would one day look at him with that warmth that he saw in Lady Hardy's eyes as she gazed at Mr Merton, or in Connie's eyes, looking at Carrbridge. Perhaps.

Monty's eyes fell on Dr Hay, engaged in earnest conversation with Harriet. Amidst the general rumble of voices, he caught snatches of their talk, seemingly a long discussion of his family, not just the Hays and his uncle the Mishcombe parson, but another branch of the family which was related to the Duke of Camberley and through him to the Earl of Humbleforth, whose sister-in-law had been wife to the seventh Marquess of Carrbridge. And that was how it was done in all the families of the *ton* — one laid out one's connections until one found, inevitably, that one was connected in some way to everybody else.

Except when one married a bedraggled stranger who turned up on one's doorstep. Monty's eye fell again on Melissa, now contentedly eating her second helping of syllabub. He knew nothing at all about her, except for the few scraps of information she had seen fit to reveal, which might not even be true. Her parents, of whom she knew nothing, were dead. Her guardian was dead. Her name was Melissa Frost. She was not already married. And now he knew she had once had a friend called Patience. It was not a great deal.

She noticed him watching her, and laid down her spoon. "Do I displease you, my lord?" But her tone was bantering, not cowed.

"Not in the slightest," he said, smiling.

"Ah. You looked so severe that I thought I must have transgressed in some way."

"I beg your pardon, my mind was wandering. Should you like some more syllabub? There is another dish of it further down the table."

"Oh, no. Or rather, yes, I should like it very much, but if I eat any more I might explode, so it is best if I do not."

He laughed at that. "We cannot have you exploding, Miss Frost. That would never do, at least not before the wedding. I should be most disappointed if my bride were to explode before the happy day. Or afterwards, now that I think about it. In fact, I am tolerably certain that I should not like you to explode at all."

She giggled, and tucked one hand in his in the most comfortable way imaginable, so that his heart performed a little somersault of pleasure. "You are very silly sometimes, Monty. I thought you were terribly stuffy at first, but now I see that you are not stuffy at all. We shall get along famously, shall we not?"

"I hope so," he said, finding it oddly difficult to speak with his throat so tight. Then, as much to reassure himself as her, he said again, "I do hope so."

After the ladies had gone, the men rearranged themselves around Carrbridge, to talk about little Lady Mary and chaff him about the difficulties of daughters. Monty had nothing to contribute to the discussion and after a while he slipped quietly away. It was a good opportunity to find the library empty, and check Debrett's without being observed.

But he was again out of luck, for as soon as he entered the library, he saw a candelabra lit about half way down the room, and someone leaning over a table, engrossed in a book. His head came up as Monty entered, and with his own candle in his hand casting its light on him, there was no escape. But as he drew near, he saw that it was only Merton.

"My lord," Merton said. "I thought to forestall you by retrieving Debrett's for you. Here — is this the page you wanted?"

It was. The history of the Earls of Bentley was laid out from the knighthood under Henry VIII to the creations of barony and viscountcy and earldom, right to the present earl, the fifth, and his three wives, Anne, Emilia and Patience. Patience. There it was, just as he had remembered.

"Lady Hardy told me about the inscription on Miss Frost's book," Merton said. "I wondered if that was what impelled you to refer to Debrett's."

"That is two connections now to the Earl of Bentley," Monty said frowning. "Two names that occur in Melissa's life, and also in Bentley's. Thomas and Patience. Yet both are common enough names. There is a Patience in my own family, and two cousins by the name of Thomas. What do you make of it, Merton?"

"The obvious solution, the one that must arise to anyone after some thought, is that the earl conceived a natural daughter by a Miss Frost. Subsequently, he took the child into his own household, passing her off as his ward. His third wife — Patience — clearly had some affection for the child, to give her a book in that manner, and Miss Frost has perhaps received the same education as the legitimate daughters, but was still treated as a poor relation. Probably she was destined for a life as a governess eventually, had her father not bumped into *your* father one drunken night, and gambled her away. It would make his actions a little more understandable — the shameful little secret, living under his own roof? No wonder he tried to get rid of her. I daresay your father mistakenly believed that she was a legitimate daughter, for he would hardly have agreed to marry her to his son otherwise."

"Poor Miss Frost, not wanted by anyone," Monty said. "But she said her guardian was dead?"

"So he might be. This edition of Debrett's is a few years old now. It may be that the fifth earl is dead, and the sixth earl... let me see..." He scanned the page. "Randolph. If he has the title now, he may well want to get rid of his father's little by-blow." Merton looked up at Monty thoughtfully. "Does this change anything, my lord? If Miss Frost is illegitimate, I mean. Do you think Lord Carrbridge would disapprove? He is very conscious of the family's honour."

"As he should be," Monty said. "But he is a marquess, and I am merely a country parson. Miss Frost will, I am sure, make me an admirable wife, and we will hardly be moving in society. This is all supposition, of course, although I agree with your reasoning. It does seem likely that Miss Frost is a natural daughter. If so, it explains her reluctance to divulge any details about herself, and she has not lied at all."

"So far as we know," Merton said.

"True. But there is nothing here to make me regret my decision to marry her."

13: A Wedding

Dr Hay and his sister had become fixtures in the house, by one of those unspoken agreements that no one questions at the time but everyone wonders about afterwards. At first, they were indispensable to Connie, keeping watch over her night and day, and providing reassurance to the rest of the household. Then, the continuing snow kept them there. But even when the necessity for medical attention had been reduced to a daily chat over a cup of tea, and the roads were passable again, they lingered on and showed no inclination to return to Mr Hay's house.

Monty could well understand it. Mr Hay and his sisters always had the parsonage as full as it could hold over Christmas, and the place was a riot of hissed family quarrels and rampaging children. Undoubtedly Dr and Miss Hay were very glad to escape the tumult and enjoy the relative tranquillity of Drummoor, which was also full but large enough to accommodate scores of guests without the least discomfort. They were often to be found in the library, quietly reading, or making notes, Dr Hay in a strongly upright hand, and Miss Hay in neat, precise lettering.

Harriet got on tremendously well with them, although it had to be said that Harriet got on pretty well with everyone, when she was around. She tended to hop here and there a lot, but when she was present she was very good company, if she chose to be. Now, it seemed, she chose to be good company to the Hays, and, to judge from the laughter emanating from her when she was with them, she was good company for them too.

The Hays were a curious couple, with a strong family likeness which manifested to odd effect in them. They both had hair of an auburn tint, which looked striking on Miss Hay, but was merely a nondescript red on her brother. Her delicate, small-boned prettiness on him looked like frailty. Both of them were so slender that one feared a strong wind would blow them over. On her, this made men rush to protect her, whereas they thought her brother a weakling. He was, however, very clever, and when the covers were removed and the port was passed around, he could discourse sensibly and with a great deal of cogency on almost any subject. Monty suspected Miss Hay of the same capability, but if she had such a skill, she wisely kept it to herself.

"Well, Hay," Carrbridge said one evening after dinner, as the gentlemen lingered over their port, "I promised you the earth if you would but save my wife, and you have delivered on your part of the bargain. It remains for me to keep mine. What would you ask of me, and if it be reasonable and within my power, you may have it."

"My lord, I ask nothing of you," Hay said at once. "I entered upon my profession with the aim of saving life, so I expect no undue reward for doing so. Under normal circumstances, I would present you with the bill for my professional services, but it seems to me that I have eaten enough of your beef and drunk enough of your excellent claret to more than offset that amount. There is no further debt to be discharged."

"No professional debt, perhaps," Carrbridge said with a smile. "Nevertheless, I would express my gratitude to you in some way. Do you want to practise your skills in London? Then let me buy you premises, and tell everyone I know about your abilities."

"I have no wish to minister only to the very wealthy," Hay said quietly. "The poor, the hard-working and suffering poor, who cannot pay for a doctor, or even an apothecary, and must depend upon the village herbalist for treatment — I should always wish to help them as well."

"Then let them be helped," Carrbridge said. "How would you do it? Travel from place to place, treating all who need you? Or a hospital, where your patients may come to you?"

"Sagborough has no hospital," Merton put in.

"I..." Hay stopped. "My lord, you would do that?"

"Of course, if that is what you wish."

"The Carrbridge Hospital," Merton said, and there was a murmur of approval around the table.

"No, no," Carrbridge said. "The Hay Hospital. Credit must be given where it is due, to the man with skilful hands, not the man who happens to have inherited a great deal of money. How wonderful it must be to be *useful*, Dr Hay, to be able to use your talents to do some good in the world. I may have a noble lineage, but I am a very ordinary fellow at heart and sometimes I feel very ineffectual."

"But you have a seat in the House of Lords, my lord," Hay said in astonishment. "You have the best position in the world to do some good. You could take a role in government, you could introduce bills to protect those unable to protect themselves, you could mitigate the effects of poorly worded bills. You have great power, my lord."

"Good lord, I suppose I do! I could make speeches when something comes up that I disagree with, instead of merely grumbling about it. I have the right, after all."

"The right and the duty," Hay said. "Just think how much good you could do."

"Careful, m'boy," Uncle Ambrose said, patting Carrbridge on the arm. "Fellow will turn you into a Whig if you are not on your guard."

Hay smiled. "There are worse things to be, Lord Ambrose."

"Not many," he muttered.

~~~~~

Melissa was thrown into a whirlwind of preparations for her wedding. Every day, she spent hours in the library attic choosing rugs and chairs and sideboards and paintings to fill the house at Kirby Grosswick. The villagers had rallied round, and already several of the main rooms were ready to be furnished, more servants had been engaged and they had the use of the marquess's third best carriage, for they could not afford their own. Monty had been to the village several times, riding through the snow-covered fields, for the roads were still impassable, to conduct services or to oversee the repair work, and he reported that there would be several rooms ready for use not long after the wedding.

"I shall be able to sleep there occasionally," he said. "But you will want to stay here until all is in perfect order."

They were in their apartment, engaged in putting books on shelves in the sitting room, her four books, and his scores of collections of sermons and theological works.

"Why should you think so?" she said. "I am not used to grand living, so having only a few rooms open will not trouble me at all. So long as there is a parlour and dining room, and enough bedrooms for ourselves and a guest, that will be enough. It will be exciting to watch all the work going on around us."

"A guest? Are you planning to entertain so soon?" He stopped, book in hand, to gaze at her in bewilderment.

"I thought Miss Hay might like to stay," she said. "I like her. She is not so grand as all your relatives, and she wishes to do something for the villagers. She has a great deal of medical knowledge that she would like to put to use."

"Oh. Well, why not?" Monty said. "If Connie can spare her."

"I think it is more a question of whether her brother can spare her," Melissa said with a laugh.

Monty looked puzzled. "Why should her brother not spare her?"

"Because she helps him with his medical work. That is why she came with him, when he arrived that dreadful night. She knows as much as he does about anatomy and medicines and illness."

"Surely not! For he has trained at university and at several hospitals, and must have attended many patients."

"And she goes with him. She reads every book and journal and treatise that he does, and he relates to her the information he learns in lectures. She is every bit as capable a physician as he is. It would be very helpful to have her examine some of the poorer villagers at Kirby Grosswick, who cannot afford even the apothecary's fees. Unofficially, of course."

She could see Monty struggling with this idea. "I am not convinced," he said at length, "that a woman is suited to such work. A woman may have practical skills, in midwifery, for instance, but for diagnostic work and for the proper management of illness, why, that is more suited to the abilities of men, I should say. It is not seemly for a woman to step outside her own sphere."

"It may or may not be seemly," Melissa said, "but Lady Carrbridge would have died without Marina. She it was who suggested a way in which the baby's position might be altered, and she it was who put the attempt into practice. She has such small, delicate hands, and she is very deft, and so she succeeded, where Dr Hay, perhaps, might not have done. Think how dreadful it would have been if Lady Carrbridge had died, and the child too. Yet now they are both well, and there is only happiness in this house, instead of grief. Is that not a conclusion worth having, even if it required a woman to step outside her own sphere?"

He thought about it. That was something she liked about Monty, he never dismissed an idea immediately, he always thought through the ramifications first.

"It is a dangerous way of thinking," he said, and his face was serious. "To argue that the end result is good, and therefore the steps necessary to achieve it must be good — that is false logic. If a family is starving, and a man steals food for them, why, they are no longer starving and that is a good thing, therefore the theft must be good, too. Is that what you would assert?"

"No, because stealing removes something from a person with a legitimate claim to it, so there is a loss to balance the good. But if Marina helps one of her brother's patients — where is the harm? No one is injured by the action."

"Only society itself, which is unsettled by the event. Life goes on a great deal more smoothly if everyone knows their proper place, and keeps to it. But let us say no more of this. It pleases me that you chose to tell me of this matter, for there should be no secrets between husband and wife, but it would do no good to broadcast it more widely."

She bowed her head under this husbandly edict, rather uneasy at his reference to secrets. No doubt he still wanted to know all her history, but she had no intention of telling him — not yet! When her birthday came and she was of age, then she would confess all and let him respond however he saw fit, but oh, not yet! He must not know yet.

"This one," he said, with a heavy volume in his hand. "This must go beside my bed, for I refer to it every morning. Which is my bedroom?"

"This one," she said, opening the door to the empty room, waiting for Monty to stamp his own character on it. "Your dressing room is through that door, and that door—" She broke off, blushing.

"Your room?" Monty said, gently.

She nodded, almost unable to speak. But she must! She had to try, in order to keep things right. "Monty…"

He was not listening, for he was staring at the door, mesmerised. "I daresay I shall spend more time in there than in here." And he turned his head, and smiled down at her in a way that made stomach flutter.

Oh, if only! How lovely it would be! But she must try to deter him. "Monty… would you mind if… if… you stay in this room… just at first?"

The disappointment on his face tore at her like a knife wound. Poor Monty! But he answered her with the utmost gentleness. "You are still upset about Connie. That is understandable. And your life has been very unsettled — so many changes, and… and all happening so swiftly. It is a great deal to come to terms with. I will not press you, although… no, you must do what is best for you, Melissa."

"Thank you," she said, with heartfelt sincerity. It was one less thing to worry about in the coming weeks.

The final days until the marriage flew past. The village road was still so deep in snow that, in the end, it was deemed too bad to take the horses out, and several grooms were dispatched to the parsonage with a hand-pulled sledge to bring Mr Hay to Drummoor. There in the chapel Melissa became Lady Montague Marford, and wondered greatly at her elevation in rank, from nobody in particular to a titled personage, and even though it was only a courtesy title, nevertheless as she walked out of the chapel everyone, from the kitchen maids to the marquess himself, bowed or curtsied, and addressed her as *'my lady'*.

The wedding breakfast featured a vast array of delicacies, and twelve different flavours of syllabub, which made Melissa laugh, although she felt obliged to try every one. That evening, Lord Carrbridge took her in to dinner as the guest of honour, and later, when the carpets were rolled up for some impromptu dancing, he led her onto the floor to take her place at the head of the set. Then she danced with Monty, and then with Lord Reggie, and Lord Humphrey, and everyone was wonderfully kind to her. Even the aunts were smiling. She felt like the worst kind of impostor, and wondered what they would say when they discovered that she was not yet of age and the marriage was invalid.

Later, much later, Monty took her arm and they made their way upstairs to their apartment, where he kissed her gently and bade her good night in that soft voice of his without a hint of reproach, and disappeared into his own room. And when her maid had readied her for bed and left her, Melissa buried her face in the pillow and cried herself to sleep.

14: Hopes And Fears

Monty felt curiously changed by marriage. Becoming a clergyman should have been more of an earthquake in his life, but he had wanted that, had dreamt of it, for years, and he accepted it as his God-given right, something he was destined to be. But he had never seen himself as a married man, and it was a strange experience. Sharing morning chocolate in their little sitting room, still in their robes, or hearing his brothers speak about Lady Monty, or receiving letters of congratulation addressed to *'Lord and Lady Montague Marford'* — all of it was oddly different. He would get used to it in time, but for the moment it was unsettling.

Merton came to see him the morning after the marriage. "My lord, I am having a little difficulty with the notice of your marriage to be sent to the Gazette."

"You want to know something of the lady's father, I daresay," Monty said with a sigh.

"It is usual," Merton said apologetically. "*'…daughter of Mr So-and-so of the county of Something.'* Or even, *'Miss Melissa Frost, lately of Wherever.'* What should you prefer me to say, my lord?"

"Since we know nothing of her home or her family, or even whether she has a father, legally, it is best to say nothing. Just put, *'…lately married to Miss Melissa Frost.'*"

"Might I enquire of Lady Montague what her wishes are in this respect?" Merton said.

"If she wished us to know anything of this nature, she would have disclosed it," Monty said. "Therefore let us not trouble her needlessly about such matters."

"Very good, my lord."

That Saturday, Monty rode over to Kirby Grosswick with his valet and groom to spend his first nights at his new home. He expected to find a parlour fit to be used. What he did not expect was to find his sister and a dozen other ladies in residence there, with fabrics and ribbons and thread spread over every surface, and several small children playing with wooden toys on the rug before the fire.

"Hatty? I am very pleased to see you, and pray feel free to use my home as your own, but whatever are you doing here?"

She laughed. "Oh, Monty! You are such a good brother, not to explode with outrage, for I am taking advantage of you shamelessly. Is Lady Monty with you? Oh, thank goodness, for I knew you would not mind but Melissa is more of an unknown."

Monty could not but agree with her on that point.

"This is Bridget, Monty," Harriet went on. "You have heard all about Bridget Kelly, of course."

"Of course. How do you do, Miss Kelly."

"And these are Bridget's girls. They have been obliged to leave the house in Sagborough rather suddenly, and Carrbridge has been so stuffy and refused to do anything at all for Bridget, just because she is female. He is perfectly happy to help all father's little offshoots, but only if they are male, which is *so* annoying. I plan to make Westbury House over to the girls just as soon as I can get the tenants out, for it will be so much better for the children to be out in the country, would you not agree? And no censorious neighbours to worry about. But that will take time, so we were a little stuck for somewhere to live just for the moment, until I remembered the house you leased for the female servants, which is perfect, quite perfect. But then there was not enough coal at Oakdown House and so we came over here so that they can work, you see, just until I can get some coal delivered. Please say you do not mind, Monty dear."

"I do not mind, so long as *'obliged to leave rather suddenly'* is not a euphemism for *'burnt the house to the ground'* or *'hiding from the constables'*, or anything of that nature."

Harriet chuckled. "Nothing of the sort, but the neighbours discovered that Bridget's girls are not, as they had supposed, respectable widows of soldiers killed in the Peninsula, and took umbrage. They seemed to think that having a child out of wedlock is an infectious disease, and all their daughters would be struck down by it immediately."

"Oh dear," Monty said.

Miss Kelly rolled her eyes. "We lived in that house for three years, my lord, without the least difficulty, living very quietly, but then Lady Harriet came along and—"

Monty laughed. "Harriet is not terribly good at living quietly. Well, you may have Oakdown House for the moment, at least so long as the Drummoor maids do not mind, and you may use my coals and, no doubt, eat my mutton, too. Do you have everything else you need? Beds and so forth?"

"Oh yes, the house is decently furnished, unlike yours, and Bridget was able to pack up everything from Sagborough, so they have blankets *and* mutton, and you need not fear that you have to feed anyone. And it will only be for a little while... a few months, perhaps, until Westbury House is empty."

"I believe grandfather expected *you* to live at Westbury House when he gave you the use of it," Monty said, smiling.

"And so I did, for a while," Harriet said. "But it is so dreadfully *dull* living out in the country on one's own. One cannot always fill the house with friends, and you know me, Monty, I like to flit here and there. So Bridget may have it, and we must hope I live for a great many years, because it reverts to Carrbridge when I die. Monty, it is very late in the day to be arriving. I was just about to go back to Drummoor myself. Are you staying here tonight?"

"And tomorrow night also. That way I shall be able to conduct two services tomorrow, and I shall expect Miss Kelly and her ladies to attend one of them."

"Three days married, and already you are leaving Lady Monty all alone at night," Harriet said with a sigh. "There is no romance in your soul, Monty."

"As a clergyman, my first duty is to God and my parishioners, not my own wishes," he said gently, but his heart was filled with sadness. Lady Monty was always alone at night, and so was he, and only one of them was happy about it.

That evening he dined alone, and retired to the truckle bed in what would one day be his dressing room. On Sunday, he conducted Matins and a sung Eucharist, preached a sermon on the subject of love, for he felt his congregation would expect it of him, and returned alone to the parsonage.

He had not been there long when the newly engaged housekeeper, Mrs Prince, admitted Ben Gartmore to the parlour. Monty laid down the book of sermons he had been attempting to read.

"Ben? This is a surprise. Do come in."

"Beg pardon for disturbing you, my lord, but... none of the others would say nothing, and I thought you ought to know."

"That sounds ominous. Will you sit, Ben?" When he hesitated, Monty added, "We are brothers, after all."

Ben smiled, and perched uncomfortably on the edge of a chair. "It's just that... the ladies that have moved into Oakdown House..."

"Ah," Monty said, understanding.

"Exactly, my lord! After church, there were... some comments. Some of the villagers are not at all happy about it. They think..." He went crimson. "They're worried that the house might be—"

"A brothel?" Monty said.

Ben nodded. "I mean, several of us said it's not like that, they're just chambermaids and such like that got taken advantage of. Well, not all of them. Kitty was with a circus, would you believe? A tightrope walker. But most were in service, and there are plenty of tales of what goes on with the footmen and grooms, or the sons of the house, so it's not as if it's anything unusual, but you know what people are like."

"I know," Monty said. "I never heard of it at Drummoor, though."

"Mrs Compton's very strict with the maids, keeps them well away from the footmen. And from Lord Gilbert. Oh, maybe I shouldn't have said that?"

Monty smiled sadly. "Gil is a disgrace, but I do not believe he would amuse himself with a housemaid. Still, it is better not to give him the opportunity, so I cannot fault Mrs Compton for her caution. Thank you for telling me this, Ben. I shall have a word with the verger and sexton, so that they may at least correct any misinformation about Miss Kelly's young women. And perhaps next week, I shall preach on the subject of Christian charity and compassion."

After Ben had gone, Monty dined alone again, spent a couple of hours staring into the fire and then went early to bed, only to lie awake for hours thinking of a lady with green eyes and a mass of dark hair that he had never yet seen tumbling loose about her shoulders. Melissa. Lady Monty. His wife.

~~~~~

Melissa's days were busy. As a new bride, there were wedding callers almost every day, struggling through the snow to offer their congratulations and ask awkward questions about her family and look down their noses at her when she chose not to answer. Some of them were very stiff and she understood that. She would be stiff about it too, in their place. Who was she, after all? Nobody. A girl of unknown parentage, with no rank, no fortune, no position in society.

Until now. Now she called a marquess brother-in-law, and she was humbled by the way Lord Carrbridge always appeared in the drawing room when there were callers, and gently steered away difficult questions by talking about Monty's living, or the progress on the parsonage. Lord Humphrey and Lord Reggie and their wives came often, too, riding over the fields on alternate days so that one or other pair were always there. The aunts and uncles were still rather unbending, but from Monty's brothers and their wives she received nothing but kindness.

It surprised Melissa to discover that she missed Monty when he was away at Kirby Grosswick. She had barely noticed his absence when he had gone north to see Lord Gus married, but at the time she had not long arrived at Drummoor and everything was new and strange and difficult, and she was quietly terrified. Now, she had been there for almost two months, and it had begun to feel like home. She was no longer frozen with fear, and the bad dreams had almost vanished. It seemed unlikely that Lord Bentley would appear in wrathful pursuit.

As for the quiet man she had married, he had begun to grow on her rather. He never shouted at her or rebuked her, and although he had grumbled sometimes, in the end he had always surrendered and given her exactly what she wanted. And here she was, safely married. Well, not quite safely, not yet, but in a little under three weeks she would be of age, and then she might be safe. Surely then she would be safe.

But she felt guilty, too. Poor Monty! He had looked at her with such warmth, such *anticipation*, and she had turned him away. Yet not a word of reproach had he spoken. He went off to his own room every night as she went to hers, and he made not the least protest. Good, kind Monty! Always so understanding, so tolerant, so forgiving.

Had he ever lost his temper? She had asked Lady Carrbridge that question once, and she had laughed and said, "I have only heard of him rising to anger once. You know Ben Gartmore, I believe? And you know his circumstances, that he is a natural son of the eighth marquess, so, of course, when Lord Carrbridge found out about him, he expressed a wish to help Ben, in short, to set him up in a profession of his choosing. Monty remonstrated with him quite forcefully, I am told, since he had always been refused his wish to take orders and here was the illegitimate son getting something that the legitimate son could not have. He was very cross about it, apparently, and one can quite see his point."

"He got his wish in the end," Melissa had said, wondering what a very cross Monty might look like.

"Oh yes!" Lady Carrbridge had chuckled and added, "He made a thorough nuisance of himself, spending all his money on anyone who asked for it. In the end, it was easier to let him have his way. At least he is being useful now. And he will not give away all his money when he has you to consider, my dear. Marriage always settles a man."

Melissa wondered about that, for Monty seemed very settled already to her. On the contrary, his wife was very much an unsettling factor, arriving out of nowhere and claiming a husband, and then pushing him to marry quickly, and concealing matters of import from him. And she wondered, too, in her darker moments, alone in her bed at night, how he would react when he knew everything, and whether he would be *very cross* with her, or whether his forgiving nature would be dominant that day.

~~~~~

Monty returned to Drummoor both eager to see his wife again, and at the same time nervous about it. At least at Kirby Grosswick she had not been constantly in front of him, sharing their apartment, and the breakfast table, and the whole long evening. Connie, in her delightful way, had outfitted the new bride in some ravishing gowns well suited to her new status, but Melissa's décolletage, the slender throat and that mass of artfully arranged hair distracted him beyond endurance. He dared not touch her, and certainly not kiss her, and yet how much he longed to. He was half mad with longing. He spent the hours after dinner pretending to read a book, and avoiding Melissa as much as possible. It was just as well that Connie was still confined, or otherwise she would certainly have noticed and asked awkward questions.

His refuge was the library, where he could usually find the solitude he needed for his peace of mind. One morning, not long after breakfast, he went there in search of a particular book of sermons for inspiration. He found, instead, Lady Hardy weeping quietly in a corner.

"Lady Hardy? Are you unwell? May I get you anything to relieve your distress?"

"Oh... oh, no, I thank you. You are most kind, but... I am quite well."

"Shall I send for your maid?"

"No, no! I shall be better directly. I beg your pardon, this is most unlike me."

"It is indeed," he said, "which makes me the more concerned. Have you... forgive me if this is impertinent, but have you quarrelled with Mr Merton?"

"Oh, no! Nothing of the kind, I assure you, it is just that—" A long pause. "Forgive me, I must not burden you with my troubles."

"I am a man of God," he said, gently. "If it will help you to talk, I am very happy to listen."

"Thank you!" she said. "And you are a married man, now, so you may advise me, may you not?"

Monty's heart sank, but he answered sincerely, "I will offer my advice, if I can."

She wiped her eyes, and turned to him with such hope in her face that he was shaken. This was his life now, to be accepted as the recipient of every trouble, a confidant and adviser, and however ill-qualified he felt himself to be, he could, perhaps, impart some comfort to a distressed lady. So he sat, and composed himself, and prepared to listen.

"My story goes back some years, to when I was sixteen," Lady Hardy began. "I was an innocent but..." She paused, took a deep breath. "I beg your pardon, but is there any brandy here?"

He fetched her a glass, and one for himself, for he suspected he might need it. She took a gulp of the liquid, then set the glass down.

"You did not know my cousin, Mr William Allamont. Connie's father. He died long before Lord Carrbridge met his wife, but I grew up in his shadow. He was an evil man, Lord Montague, evil. He did things... forgive me, but I must be specific. He did something to me that no man should do, except to his wife."

"Good God!" Monty exclaimed, unable to suppress his revulsion. "That is... I have not the words!"

"Indeed," she said, with a wry grimace. "So most normal men would say. It only happened once, I made sure of that, but it left me with... the deepest fear of... of men. Of... the intimacy between a man and a woman."

"That is not to be wondered at. And yet you married."

"Indeed, for my situation at home with my step-mother was such that anything was preferable, even marriage. And I had the most astonishing good fortune, for it so happened that my husband was a man who felt a similar revulsion of intimacy."

"Ah," Monty said, understanding. That accounted for the lack of children of the marriage.

"But then something miraculous happened, for I fell in love with Daniel Merton, and he with me. And with my husband dead, and my year of mourning over, our betrothal was the natural and happy conclusion. But..."

"But you are terrified," Monty said gently.

"I am. You understand, do you not? And Daniel knows all my story, so he would understand, if I asked him to... to wait. To give me time. Do you think? Am I wrong to ask it of him? Must I submit? For I am so afraid!"

"No man of honour would force you to submit," Monty said slowly. "Mr Merton would certainly understand, and if he loves you he would willingly give you all the time you need to accept his love. But..."

Her face fell. "But? You think it wrong of me to ask such a thing of him?"

"Who can say what is right or wrong, within a marriage? It is for the husband and wife each to make their peace with the other and their commitments and wishes and fears. It is not wrong, but it is, perhaps, cruel."

"Cruel?"

"Lady Hardy, let me be very frank with you. For a man, such matters are not confined to the bedchamber only. He cannot set them aside at will. He spends the whole evening with his wife, admiring her smooth skin, the softness of her form, the gentle tones of her voice and the brightness of her eye. His thoughts are inevitably drawn to that hour when they will be alone together and all these delights will be his. He cannot help this, for it is his nature. So it is, anyway, for almost all men. The need for a woman is as real, as urgent, as the need for food in a starving man, and just as painful. And imagine then how it feels to be turned away at the bedroom door, to be rejected — only a saint could not feel hurt and resentful."

She nodded, saying nothing. He could see it was not the answer she had hoped for.

"A man needs his wife," Monty said quietly. "He needs the comfort of her arms, and if that need is not met, it will eat away at him until he becomes a different man."

"Then I must submit," she said in a low voice.

"Do not think of it as submitting," Monty said. "Rather, you offer your husband a great joy, the gift of your love, and trust him to deal gently with you."

"That I understand," she said. "But his great joy is nothing but pain and fear to me. I do not know how women force themselves to it time after time."

Monty smiled. "Would it surprise you to know that women — some women, anyway — enjoy such occasions every bit as much as men do? You look astonished, but it is so, I assure you. My father had a mistress who took it upon herself to initiate each of his sons into the gentle arts of the bedchamber. I was seventeen when my turn came, and I can assure you that she enjoyed herself a vast deal, and just as much as I did. Perhaps not all women are so, or perhaps their husbands have not had the benefit of such expert tuition, but most women do not dislike the act of love at all, and as for pain… there is no pain after the first time."

"No pain?"

"No. I imagine that humankind would have died out long since if that were so. Put your trust in your husband, Lady Hardy, and in God's infinite wisdom, and all will be well."

And she smiled for the first time. "Thank you! So many clergymen are nothing but censorious, or would tell me only that it is my duty — which I already know. But you understand matters temporal as well as spiritual, and have shown me nothing but compassion. You are a good man, Lord Montague."

But Monty was left hollow and empty, and wishing that he had less understanding of matters temporal, at least where they concerned his own hopes and fears.

15: Currant Cake

The cold, snowy weather had now given way to milder days, which set the Drummoor gutters gurgling with meltwater. The wagons of furniture for the parsonage were sent off while the roads were in that brief interlude between deep snow and deep mud.

Melissa was wild to move there too. Drummoor was very pleasant, there was no denying, but she must not get used to scores of servants, and two full courses on the table every night. The longer she delayed the move, the harder it would be. And there was always that niggle of worry that Lord Bentley might still be looking for her. If he traced her to Drummoor, then he would be told that she had married and moved away, and then he might give up and not follow her to Kirby Grosswick. Whereas if she were still living there, she could not avoid receiving him.

"If we wait, the roads will be nothing but bog for months," she said to Monty over their morning chocolate. "There are three bedrooms ready, and a room we can use for dining in as well as a parlour, and the kitchen is in good order. I do not want to wait here for months and months."

"There is still a great deal of work going on," Monty said, frowning. "It is not fit for a lady. The parlour is the only room with a carpet."

"So far, but it will not take long to make the other rooms presentable."

"But the carpenters are still replacing the wood panels," he objected. "Truly, Melissa, there is no purpose to you living in a half-derelict house. It will not be comfortable for you. Pray let me be the best judge of what is appropriate for my wife."

She slammed down her chocolate cup. "Really, Monty, do not treat me like a child! I may judge for myself what is appropriate, and I assure you I am not at all accustomed to luxury. If you had seen my attic bedroom at Ben— at my home, you would appreciate that two rooms and a bedroom is more than adequate for my needs. I do not want to stay here indefinitely, an unwanted guest in your brother's house, when I might be enjoying my own establishment. You are cruel to deny me the pleasure of my own home, Monty."

His lips thinned, and his breathing grew ragged, as if he struggled with some violent emotion, and for a moment she held her breath, wondering if she was now to be confronted with *very cross* Monty. But he composed himself, and when he spoke, it was with his usual calmness.

"Let it be as you wish, my dear. What kind of husband would I be to deny you such pleasure?"

And then she felt like a worm.

~~~~~

The move was made, and Melissa had to agree that the house was half-derelict. Someone had repaired the roof, and all the chimneys had been swept, but most rooms were stripped down to bricks, with the woodwork gone, even the floorboards in some rooms. But she had a warm parlour to sit in, and a dining room to eat in, and she had a cook and a housekeeper and two house-parlour maids, and a groom who acted as a footman, and she had Margaret as her lady's maid. In addition to Monty's valet, and Ben Gartmore and another man who was bringing the garden back from its previous wilderness, they were quite a large household. And just next door lived Bridget Kelly and her girls, who were in and out all day long, filling the house with girlish laughter and warmth. As the repair work went on, the constant banging and whistling and sawing reminded her that eventually the house would be just as she had imagined it.

In her mind's eye, the house was very like Bentley Hall, as it had been in the happy years after the late earl's third marriage, when the halls had echoed to childish laughter and Melissa herself had almost been caught up in it. Patience had been something like a mother to her, and Alice, Charlotte and Delia something like sisters, and the earl had been away a great deal and the two boys were at school. But gradually things had changed. Money was suddenly in short supply, and Randolph and Cornelius had grown up to be unpleasant young men. Patience changed, too, and was often to be found weeping in corners, or was ill for long, dreary spells. Melissa had retreated to her former invisibility, but she had never forgotten the good years, and now she walked through the empty, echoing rooms of the parsonage and saw them filled with light and colour and music and joyful faces.

Their first dinner at the parsonage was not a success. Since the cook had had no notice of their coming, there was no meat in the house, and not much else either, but Monty made no complaint, and they played cribbage together very companionably after dinner, and went early to bed.

But the next day was a disaster. The morning chocolate was late, and barely palatable, although Monty drank it all, with a grimace. But then breakfast was nothing but stale bread and cheese, and Melissa spent the next two hours going through the stores with Mrs Green and trying to persuade her to do better.

"It's not what I'm used to, milady, and that's a fact. Always had my own kitchen maid before this, and how I'm supposed to manage without neither kitchen maid nor scullery maid is beyond me. What with a full dinner for his lordship every day, and meals for the servants' hall as well, I don't see how I have the time to make cakes and all these fancy breads you asked for, milady."

"I shall see if I can get someone from the village," Melissa said helplessly.

"I've tried already, and no one wants the work, seemingly. You'll have to get someone from Sagborough."

"Very well, Mrs Green. I am sorry you have been put to so much trouble. Do you have currants? I can make a cake for our supper."

"Well, now, that's a handsome offer, milady. Let me show you where I keep the bowls."

And she wondered how on earth they would have managed on two hundred pounds a year and only a couple of maids of all work. But she liked baking, and had often helped out in the kitchen at Bentley Hall, so before long she had an apron on, a mixing spoon in her hand and was humming as she stirred. She put the currant cake in the oven to bake, and was just flouring a board ready to roll out pastry for a pie when Susan, one of the house-parlour maids came in, very flustered.

"Oh, milady, you're looked for all over, for Mrs Sopwith is here."

"Who is Mrs Sopwith?"

"Oh, milady, she lives at the big house with the holly just down in the village."

"Hmm. Better tidy myself up. Mrs Green, we shall need tea… and cake! Oh, goodness, cake! If mine is not ready, Susan must run round to Oakdown House — I am certain they will have cake we may borrow. Oh Lord, look at me! I am covered in flour! I shall wash in the scullery, and that will have to do."

Melissa rushed into the parlour rather breathlessly. Monty was looking harassed. "Ah, my wife," he said. "Lady Montague, these are our neighbours, Mrs Sopwith and Miss Sopwith. Mrs Sopwith, may I present to you the Lady Montague Marford."

Mrs Sopwith was a severe-faced matron of some sixty years, dressed from head to toe in black bombazine, with a voluminous black lace cap edging her bonnet. She brought with her an unmarried daughter, who was the very image of her mother, all thin limbs and sharp angles, except that she wore unflatteringly pale muslin. Miss Sopwith's nose was red, and she held a handkerchief to it constantly.

Melissa curtsied, Mrs Sopwith looked her up and down, and Miss Sopwith sniffed, although whether from disapproval or from her cold was uncertain.

"May I congratulate you on your marriage, Lady Montague," Mrs Sopwith said, with a twist of her face that might have been intended as a smile. "I hope you mean to entertain, for the area is sadly lacking in families of quality with whom one may dine. We ourselves cannot afford to open our doors to all and sundry, can we, Sofia? I am but a penniless widow, quite retired in the world, but we are happy to accept invitations, are we not, Sofia? And my dear Lady Montague, I should be most pleased to correct any small deficiencies I may observe, for you have not my experience in the world. Why, I have dined at Carlton House once, and twice at Buckingham House, have I not, Sofia? So you see that I may instruct you in the styles in vogue amongst the highest in the land. There is no need to thank me, for I am happy to offer my advice wherever I see that it may be needed."

"How kind," Melissa said faintly, not knowing quite how to respond to this outpouring.

"So my friends all say," Mrs Sopwith said smugly. "Did not Lady Halpeth say so only the other week? *'How kind you are, Mrs Sopwith,'* she said, *'to be offering the benefits of your wisdom so generously.'* Did she not say so, Sofia? And my very good friend, the Viscountess Markham, is forever telling me that I am altogether too kind."

"May I offer you some refreshments?" Melissa put in hastily. "Some tea, perhaps?"

Miss Sopwith brightened noticeably, and her mother managed a genuine smile. "Why how kind! A glass of Madeira would be most acceptable, just a very small one, of course, so early in the day. And ratafia for my daughter. She cannot take wine. And if you have any pastries? No? A seed cake, perhaps, or a cherry cake, and a plain sponge for Sofia, for too much fruit is bad for her digestion. No sponge? Well, whatever you can manage."

Mrs Sopwith worked her way steadily through three large glasses of Madeira, and several slices of currant cake, still warm from the oven. By the third glass of wine, she was smiling widely, calling Melissa *'my very dear girl'*, while Monty was *'my dear vicar'*. She had forgotten Miss Sopwith's digestion, and was urging her to try the currant cake, advice which she accepted with alacrity. She had sipped her ratafia without enthusiasm until Monty had surreptitiously left a glass of Madeira at her elbow.

There was only one sticky moment, where Mrs Sopwith tipped her head coquettishly on one side and said, "And do tell me all about yourself, my dear Lady Montague. You were Miss Frost before your marriage, I understand? And where are you from?"

It was such a simple question, but Melissa answered without hesitation. "Near Falmouth."

"Ah. Then, my dear girl, you must know Dr Harting and dear Lady Elizabeth?"

"No, I have not had that pleasure," she said composedly. "I did not move in society. More Madeira, Mrs Sopwith?"

"Oh…but no, we had better be on our way. Sofia has some errands to run for me in the village and she must be back in time to bring me my tonic before dinner. I am a martyr to my nerves, Lady Montague, you cannot imagine how difficult life is when one's nerves are all to pieces. And this is just a very quick call to make your acquaintance, and make you aware of our willingness to accept invitations whenever you should commence to entertain. And if you should require introductions to any of the noble families in the district, you may always apply to me. I know everybody of true *quality*, is it not so, Sofia? Do sit up straight, girl, do not slouch in that disagreeable manner."

The Sopwiths left shortly afterwards, and Melissa collapsed onto her chair with relief. "I hope we do not have to put up with *them* too often. A quick call? They have been here an hour, at least. Poor Miss Sopwith! She said not a word, the whole time she was here."

Monty's face was as rigid as stone. "Melissa, is that flour in your hair?"

"Oh… probably. I was making a pie for our dinner."

"But why? Is Mrs Green indisposed?"

She flushed. "No, but… she is finding it difficult. She is used to a larger household, and there is no kitchen maid. I do not mind, Monty. I like to be useful, and if I can help out in the kitchen—"

"We employ enough servants that you do not need to do so," he snapped, eyes cold. "I do not want you helping out in the kitchens or anywhere else from now on. Your place is here, in the parlour, to receive any callers, or if there are none, to employ yourself with suitable tasks for your rank. Try to remember that you are a lady now."

"Was I not a lady before?" she cried, trying very hard not to cry.

"I have no idea," he said, his tone icy. "Were you?" He stood up. "Falmouth," he said, in disgust, and stalked out of the room.

~~~~~

Monty stomped off to his bedroom, his anger too great to spend any further time with his wife. In the fullness of time, he would have a book room which would be his personal retreat, a room that was his alone and into which no other might enter without his express permission, but until that day his bedroom, or rather the small dressing room attached to it, was his sole refuge. Apart from the small truckle bed and a wardrobe, there was a writing desk and chair, and here he sat, head in hands, contemplating his lamentable loss of composure.

Had he been unreasonable? A little, perhaps, for Melissa was very young and had never had charge of a household before, or so he assumed. And here he halted, remembering once again that he knew nothing at all of her history. His brother's words still rang in his mind, *'But she could be an opera dancer, for all you know. Or some man's rejected mistress.'* And so she could be. Or, most likely, the by-blow of the fifth Earl of Bentley. It had never mattered much to him what she had been, only what she might be — a wife who would look after him and attend to his comfort, and there, it had to be said, she fell down lamentably. But it was his own fault, he thought gloomily. He had rushed into this marriage and now he would have many years to reflect on the wisdom of it.

But he had not much time for reflection that day, for he soon had another visitor. This time it was Peter Herbert, the verger.

Monty saw him in the dining room, so that he need not disturb Melissa's parlour with business talk.

"Mr Herbert, how are you?"

"I'm worried, that's what I am, your lordship."

"Then sit down and tell me all about it."

But Peter would not sit, instead twisting his hat awkwardly in his hands, and chewing his lip. Monty waited.

"It's these… women!" Peter burst out eventually. "There's a lot of talk in the village, your lordship, a *lot* of talk, and the ladies don't like it. They don't like it at all."

"You mean Miss Kelly's young ladies at Oakdown House, I collect?"

"Aye, your lordship. Sinners, that's what they are, and they shouldn't be mixing with decent folk and going to church, as bold as brass. Be better if they moved somewhere else, your lordship, and it's not just me sayin' so neither. Everyone thinks the same. There's women afraid to step out on the streets in case they meet any of them, and worried their men will be drawn in."

Monty tried to curb his annoyance. "Really, Mr Herbert, the ladies are perfectly harmless. They made a mistake and now wish to be allowed only to raise their children well and earn their bread. What is the harm in that?"

"They're sinners, your lordship. They should keep out of sight, and I'd expect you, as our parson, to take the lead on matters of morality. We don't want them in church."

"Heavens, Mr Herbert, who better to go to church than sinners? Are we not all sinners?"

"Aye, but—"

"What did Our Lord say about sinners?" The verger shuffled his feet awkwardly, and Monty went on relentlessly, " *'He that is without sin among you, let him first cast a stone'* and when Peter asked him, *'Lord, how oft shall my brother sin against me and I forgive him?'* and Jesus answered—"

"Aye, seventy times seven," Peter muttered.

"Exactly. I hope we might all exhibit Christian charity towards these poor unfortunate women, Mr Herbert, and I trust you will express that view to everyone you meet. My next sermon will be on the subject of compassion."

Peter grunted, and went away, but Monty was not sure he was convinced. It was one thing to put a farthing in the poor box now and then, but heaven forfend that these God-fearing folk should be required to mingle with the poor and unfortunate.

Dinner was adequate, although Monty thought the beef tough and dry. Ben Gartmore had brought some fish, however, with pheasant and pigeon hanging in an outhouse ready for Sunday, and Melissa's apple pie was delicious.

After the servants had withdrawn, when Melissa rose to go to the parlour, Monty said, "Sit a moment longer, Lady Montague. We must talk."

She paled, and plopped back to her seat, saying nervously, "That sounds ominous."

"Do not be alarmed," he said quietly. "There is no censure implied, and indeed I was wrong to upbraid you earlier for the deficiencies of the household. These early days are bound to be difficult, for both of us, and I hope you will forgive me my... intemperance earlier."

She nodded her acquiescence.

He went on, "Melissa, the situation is not easy for either of us, but it is made a great deal more difficult by your continued refusal to confide in me. I am your husband, can you not trust me?"

She made no response, merely lowering her head, avoiding his eyes, but he saw the tension in her posture.

"I do not ask you to tell me everything, but surely you can tell me where you lived before? It is not Falmouth, of that I am sure, and it will not do for you to say so to everyone. I am a clergyman and it is very bad to have my wife telling such lies." He paused, but still she said nothing. He went on more gently, "There should be no secrets between husband and wife, but if you must have them, will you not at least tell me why? Why must you keep your previous life hidden?"

Her head shot up. "I cannot tell anyone! You speak of trust, but *you* do not trust *me!* Oh, leave me alone! You are so... so *righteous*, Monty!"

And something in Monty snapped. He jumped to his feet, shaking with anger. "I am a clergyman, I am *supposed* to be righteous!" he hissed at her. "And you are a clergyman's wife and you ought to be righteous too, or had you forgotten that? Did you not stand before God and promise to honour and obey me, but you do not even *trust* me. All I get from you is arguments and wilfulness and *lies*, and I am sick of it, Melissa, sick to the heart of all this, and so I tell you. Even if you do not much like me, it is your duty as a wife to behave properly, to me and to everyone else, do you understand?"

"I understand you!" she cried. "You do not care two farthings for my feelings at all, that is what I understand. You are just selfish and horrid, and I *hate* you, Monty, I hate you! I wish I had never married you!"

And with that, she stormed out of the room, and he heard her footsteps thumping on the uncarpeted stairs as she retreated to her bedroom.

16: Rain

Monty had the greatest difficulty sleeping that night. His thoughts were tormented by Melissa's angry face, and for once it was not the memory of her warm kisses that kept him awake, but the violence of her response, and his own lack of control. She had provoked him beyond endurance, there was no doubt about it, but he should not have responded in like manner. It was unforgivable in him. He was not a child any more, he was four and twenty years old and a man of God. Beyond all that, he was a gentleman, and should never speak so to a lady, and whatever Melissa had once been, she was a lady now. Her marriage had made her so.

Yet still she would not be open with him. Why was she so distressed whenever he mentioned her past? Why could she not confide in him? If Lady Hardy could trust him with her most intimate thoughts, how was it that his wife could not? Such distrust upset him more than he could say.

He had never had great expectations of his marriage, but he had hoped that Melissa would enhance his comfort and attend to his wishes, even if she never learnt to love him. He had wanted them to be on easy terms with each other, if nothing else. And deep inside, he was aware of a yearning for something more from her, a liking, perhaps, or some glimmering of affection. He wanted her to smile when she saw him, or to reach out a hand to him, or to show him the small attentions due to a husband from a loving wife. He so much wanted her to be a loving wife.

Monty understood the implications of that line of thought. When he considered the matter dispassionately, he could no longer pretend to himself that he was indifferent to her. When she was in a gentle, contented mood, she was everything he wanted in a wife, and they had spent hours and days together without the slightest friction. Those times were happy ones, and he delighted in her company then. But these spikes of rage appeared without warning and shattered his peace, leaving him desperate to restore her good humour.

Perhaps that was within his power to achieve. Trying to impose his will on her always failed, for she only became distressed, and eventually all would end in argument and disharmony. Besides, there was some truth in her words. She had called him *'righteous'*, and he remembered that Humphrey had called him a *'sanctimonious prig'*. Was that really how he appeared? Very well then, he must take a different approach. If he refrained from criticism, if he were gentle and loving with her, then it may be that she would become so in her turn. And at all costs he must not mention her past life, for that set off her outbursts more than anything else. He determined that he would begin anew with his wife.

There was no cosy sitting room beside their bedrooms in the parsonage, so they took their morning chocolate separately, in their rooms. Monty went across to the church to discuss some matters with the sexton, and therefore had no opportunity to see Melissa before breakfast. She was red-eyed, as if she had been crying, and she looked so downcast that his heart ached for her. As soon as they were alone, before he could even begin to form the words of his own apology, she jumped up and ran round the table to Monty's chair and threw herself at his feet.

"Oh Monty, I am such a bad wife to you, and a harridan, always shouting at you! You must be wishing you had never married me. I am so sorry — can you ever forgive me?"

"There is nothing for me to forgive," he said, smiling in relief at this outpouring. "Indeed, it is entirely the other way round. It is I who must crave forgiveness for my appalling outburst of temper. I have been like a bear, and I am not normally so cross, I assure you. I hope we may forget yesterday altogether, and say no more about it."

"You are so kind, and I do not deserve you in the slightest. But there is something I *must* say to you. Yesterday, you asked me to trust you, and I *do*, truly I do. I would trust my life to you, Monty. So I will tell you this much — that I have very good reasons for being secretive, but not for much longer. Everything there is to know about me, I will tell you, withholding nothing, but... not yet. I must ask you to give me a little more time — not long, just another ten days or so, and then I promise you shall know everything."

"Melissa," he said, lifting her hand to his lips with a thrill of delight at the touch. "Think no more of it. Tell me whatever you want, whenever you want — or never, if that is your wish. None of it is of the least importance, for what you once were is immaterial. You are my wife now, and a lady, and a Marford, and a perfectly capable person, well able to decide your own way in the world. I do not need to guide you, nor shall I, and if you want to make currant cake and apple pie, I shall be very happy with that."

"Truly?" she said, her face brightening.

"Truly. The apple pie was delicious."

She shook with laughter, and then lifted his hand so that it rested against her cheek. "Oh Monty, I have been so horrid to you."

"And I to you," he said in a low voice, for he was finding it hard to speak suddenly.

She looked up at him with a warmth that set his heart spinning and looping with joy. Was this love, this crazy weakness he felt, this strange mixture of incredible exhilaration and shakiness, like a fever? Was this what it felt like to be head over heels in love with someone?

"We shall go on better now," she said, and then, to his delight, laid her head on his lap, his hand still pressed to her cheek. He would have stayed so all day quite contentedly, had not Mrs Prince come in just then with another plate of bread. Laughing, Melissa jumped to her feet and took her place at the table again, with a charming blush suffusing her cheeks, and Mrs Prince smiled knowingly.

It was enough, and he was happy again — more than happy! She trusted him, she cared for him, just a little... surely she did, or she would not have felt such remorse after their quarrel, at least the equal of his own.

And he was beginning to know a little more of her background, even though she had as yet told him nothing openly. He could guess the significance of the date ten days in the future when she would confide in him, and he also felt tolerably sure of the name of her home, which began 'Ben—'. Bentley... the home of the Earl of Bentley, her guardian or perhaps her father, the man who had given her the education of a lady, yet kept her in rags. The home she was running away from.

And that, the heart of the matter, was the one piece of information he did not yet have. He recalled, though, that one speculative idea had now fallen by the wayside — Melissa had not welcomed him to her bed, and therefore she was not trying to pass off an already-conceived child as his. But it made her reasons for marrying him even more obscure. It was all very puzzling.

~~~~~

After their huge quarrel, Melissa had been gripped by terrible fear. Even though she had shouted back at him just as wildly, when she had reached her room it was to collapse on to a chair from sheer weakness. She had been shaking from head to toe, terrified that he would somehow send her away, reject her, annul the marriage… could he do that? She was not quite sure, but she thought he could.

The very thought terrified her, and she had paced her room, crying, and eventually crawled into bed, still crying, curled up into a ball trying to imagine a future that did not have Monty in it, and failing. She could not lose him now! It was unthinkable, unendurable. She could not live without him.

And slowly, very slowly, it dawned on her that the fear that had haunted her for many weeks of being returned to Lord Bentley and the unspeakable Mr Pontefract had given way to very different fears, concerned with a much handsomer man, with dark eyes and full lips, who had taught her how to kiss.

She loved him, that was the truth of it, and how he must hate her for her shrewish behaviour. But she would do better! She would grovel at his feet and beg his forgiveness and tell him as much of herself as she dared — for she could not tell him the truth, not yet, it would be fatal — and hope that would be enough. She had taken the first opportunity to do so, and he had responded so kindly. Dear, generous Monty, to be so understanding!

After this, Melissa found that he seemed more relaxed, and there were no more outbreaks of his *very cross* incarnation, which had struck such fear into her heart. He was calm and smiled at her and complimented her on her good management when she succeeded in presenting him with a half-edible dinner each night.

Monty, who was used to Drummoor standards! He was so good, so wonderfully good, and surely she did not deserve him, of that she was sure.

"That was delicious, my dear," he said, after she had daringly ordered two courses for their Sunday dinner, and although the dishes were spread about rather, to fill the table, still there were enough removes and roasts to justify the description. "You have brought Mrs Green well up to scratch, and the blackberry and apple tarts were wonderful."

Melissa blushed, and could only murmur, "Thank you. She is much happier now that she has a kitchen maid."

"Did you find someone from the village?"

"In a way. Rose from Oakdown House used to be a kitchen maid, before… um, once, so she was happy to do it. I am afraid we now have seven indoor servants, and three outdoor. That is too many, is it not?"

"We are living a little beyond our present means," he said, but his smile did not waver. "I am not sure that we shall be able to afford our own carriage this year. However, I have some money saved to tide us over these early days, and after a few months we shall review the situation. Four of our present establishment are from Drummoor, so we may send them back at any time we choose."

"I do not see that we need so many," she said. "Mrs Green we must have, and one house-parlourmaid, and a groom for your horse, and your valet, of course. But I do not need a lady's maid, nor a housekeeper, and I can help in the kitchen, and with dusting and laying fires and so forth. We could get a woman from the village once a week for the heavy work, and the laundry could be sent out. I do not quite know how we came to have so many servants."

"You do not like to sit at your leisure while the servants take care of everything?" he said gently.

She only hesitated a moment, wondering how much she should say, before remembering that Monty was her husband and the least judgemental man she had ever met. "I am not used to it... to being the mistress of such an establishment. There were scarce more servants at Ben— at my home, but I was... well, not quite one of them, but I was not family either. And I got on better with them than with—" She stopped, wishing she had not said so much.

"I understand," he said in his quiet way, and she thought probably he did. "The thing to remember with servants is that they are there to do your bidding. One should never abuse them or insult them, for they cannot answer back and they live in fear of being turned off without a reference, but they are yours to command. If ever you need guidance about dealing with them, you now have four sisters-in-law who would be delighted to advise you."

"Thank you, Monty," she said, but it was lowering to think of Lady Carrbridge, Lady Reggie and Lady Humphrey, all so respectable, and perfectly suited to their new positions, whereas Melissa felt like an impostor. Even the unseen Lady Gus was reputed to be sweetly angelic, and probably never shouted at her husband but was always demure and composed, and undoubtedly knew how to manage ten servants without once getting flour in her hair.

Still, it was better to talk of her work rather than his, for she did not like to mention the day's services or the noticeably reduced congregation, due to Bridget Kelly and her friends. They all came to both services, although they kept to themselves and made no attempt to mingle with the other villagers. Even so, there was a great deal of muttering about it, and several prominent villagers, among them Mrs and Miss Sopwith, had stayed at home. But Monty said nothing of it, and seemed not in the least discomposed by it, talking with equal ease to everyone after the services.

It was fortunate that the complexities of domestic management kept Melissa at home, because the snow had given way to relentless rain. Monty had to splash down to the village once or twice to visit parishioners, and reported everywhere drenched and the road churned to deep mud.

"The stream beside the road is running very fierce at the moment, and some of the cottagers' gardens are under water, but I daresay there is not much growing at the moment anyway. At least it will reduce the number of our callers, with the roads so bad. I hope you will not think of venturing out in such foul weather, Lady Montague."

"Oh no, I have not the least idea of it," she said hastily, rather glad that she would not have to visit the Sopwiths.

She had no trouble filling her days. When she was not in the kitchen helping Mrs Green, she was in one of the upper rooms with Mrs Prince, with Ben Gartmore and Luke the gardener for the heavy lifting, sorting through the vast array of furniture brought from Drummoor, and deciding on what to put in each room, when all the renovations were complete.

From the high windows, she could look down on the whole village, as each day the stream grew fiercer and wider and began to engulf the low-lying pasture and vegetable gardens. And still the rain poured down.

"Those cottages will be under water if this keeps up," she said.

"You'd think so, wouldn't you?" Ben said. "But at the ale house they say they've never been flooded. The gardens, yes, that happens often, but the cottages are all built on earth mounds. The water's got to be high before it would get into them."

But Melissa watched the rain falling and the stream rising, and wondered.

17: Rescue

Monty woke to the odd feeling that something was wrong. Pulling back the bed curtains, he discovered it was still dark outside. When he went to the windows, he could see nothing but the rain still falling, although perhaps less heavy than it had been. Opening the front-facing window and leaning out got him rather wet, but afforded a view of lower down the valley where torches wavered about. Distantly, he heard shouts, and a baby crying.

He dressed quickly, wrapped himself in a old cloak of thick wool, and ventured out to see what was happening. The problem was not difficult to find. Not far below the church and parsonage, the rain-swollen stream had grown to monstrous proportions, and a lake now filled most of the land between the road and the wooded hills to the south. As his eyes adjusted to the darkness, he saw the roofs of several cottages poking above the water.

A large crowd had gathered along the road with lanterns and torches and ropes, shouting across the swollen waters.

"Is everyone safe?" Monty asked the first group he came to, which included Ben Gartmore.

"Aye, seem to be. They had enough warning to get out in time, and they've got across the bridge to the mill road, but it's under water in both directions and rising. The bridge itself will be drowned any moment. I don't know what more they can do. It's too dangerous to swim or try to get a boat to them."

The sky was already lightening, but although dawn brought a welcome respite from the rain, it also revealed less hope for those stranded. It could now be seen that some seventy souls stood on the last remaining hillock, entirely surrounded by water, which continued to rise. The daylight showed that many were old or frail or very young, who could never brave the stormy waters around them.

The crowd watching the disaster unfolding was increasing. Amongst them were Bridget Kelly and several of her women.

"Can they not be rescued?" Bridget said. "Is there no boat or raft?"

"Nothing that could survive those waters," Monty said. "Look how fast the flow is. And swimming is too dangerous."

"We can't even get a rope to them," Ben said sadly. "We've been trying for hours, but it's just too far to throw. I thought of trying the dogs, because they swim pretty well, but I couldn't persuade them into the water. But someone will have to swim it, I reckon."

"Even if anyone were strong enough to swim across with a rope, and not get swept away," Monty said, "there are many over there who could never make the swim back, rope or no rope."

"Then is there no hope, my lord? Must we just give up?"

"What we need is a bridge," Monty said thoughtfully.

"All the bridges are under water now," Ben said.

"Then we shall just have to make one. Axes... what we need are axes. And plenty of rope."

"My lord?" Ben said hopefully.

"That oak tree there would make a fine bridge, if we could get it to fall at just the right angle. It would reach right across the water to the dry land. But we shall have to be quick — the water is still rising fast. *Axes! I need axes here! And a woodcutter.*"

There was a scurry of activity, as men ran to fetch axes. Two men were found who had some expertise in felling, and knew where to make the cuts to have the tree fall in the right direction. Before long, the valley echoed to the sound of chopping wood, and many willing hands took their turn. Monty watched in desperate anxiety. Progress seemed so slow, and the hillock gradually shrank as the angry waters continued to rise. Over the grunted efforts of the choppers and the roar of the water, the cries of terrified children rose.

"Will we be in time?"

Monty turned to see Melissa's anxious face peering up at him from the voluminous folds of her cloak.

"God willing," he said, and never had he felt more truth in the familiar phrase.

"I shall go and help Mrs Green make soup, and ensure the fires are built up," she said. "Send everyone to the parsonage to dry off, rescuers and rescued alike." And she strode away, leaving Monty proud of her thoughtfulness.

The tree swayed, then lurched, and with a great creaking and cracking, it fell, and the direction was perfect. There were shouts and a few screams as the stranded villagers waded into the water to avoid being hit, but a cheer of relief went up as the tree settled in a great flurry of broken branches.

"Ropes!" Monty yelled, almost before the tree had stopped moving. "Where are the ropes? There must be something to hold on to. Bring me a rope, and I will take it across." He unfastened the hampering cloak and cast it aside.

"No, my lord, let me go!" cried several voices, as someone dropped a coil of rope at the tree's foot.

"No arguments—" Monty began, but he was too late.

A small figure darted out from the crowd, picked up one end of the rope and leapt onto the fallen tree trunk.

"Kitty!" Ben yelled, but she was gone, running full pelt along the tree trunk as sure-footedly as if it were a road. In the time it had taken for the crowd to gasp in alarm, she was across and into the tangle of branches at the far end. She tied the rope to a thick bough, and then disappeared into the thicket of torn branches. Moments later, she emerged carrying a baby and ran just as agilely back to the roots, where waiting arms reached to grab the infant. Back and forth she went, and by the time the rope was secured at both ends as a hand rail and two or three men had begun to inch their way over the makeshift bridge, she had brought half a dozen small children across in her arms.

"Good Lord, she is fast!" Monty said. "She must be the circus performer, I think?"

"Aye, a tightrope walker," Ben said, with a sudden grin. "She's certainly something, isn't she?"

"Indeed she is," Monty said.

By this time, some of the more agile amongst the stranded had begun to climb into the tree, and there were shouts of distress and cries of "Help! Help!" from the shrinking hill. Those remaining were beginning to panic as the water encroached ever nearer.

"No pushing!" Monty yelled, and then, when that did not answer, climbed onto the fallen tree trunk and himself began to walk across. The trunk was wet, and the rope rail flopped about in an unsettling way. As more people tried to clamber onto the tree, it suddenly lurched downwards. Monty was thrown to his knees, the water raging not two feet below him. Screams and shouts suggested he was not the only one caught out. He clung to the rope, and gingerly manoeuvred himself to his feet again.

"Everyone stand still!" he yelled, and this time his words had some effect. "Grab hold of a branch, if you can, and do not panic! And no pushing!"

Carefully, step by cautious step, he made his way across the bridge. One of the rescuers had fallen into the water, with Kitty desperately holding onto his arm. With Monty's help, the man was lifted back onto the bridge.

"Go to the parsonage and warm up," Monty said to him.

Shivering violently, the man crawled away.

"Cold as ice in there," Kitty said. "Stop them all trying to cross at once, if you can, milord. I need to get some more rope."

And with that she was gone, back to the dry side of the valley.

Monty reached the far side to find a mass of terrified faces looking at him through the fallen branches. Those lower down were already up to their waists in water.

"Women and children first," he said sternly, "then the old ones. The able must help the less able. And no more than two or three on the trunk at once, in case it moves again. You there," he said, pointing to a young man who was blocking the way for two women behind him, "come up here and help the women up. The rest of you, hold tight to a solid branch, and try to support anyone having trouble. Here, give me your hand, madam. Now hold the rope and do not let go, understand? Walk slowly. You next, then the old gentleman down there who looks as if he will fall at any moment. Go slowly, very slowly. Take your time, and go straight to the parsonage. Yes, pass the child to Kitty, and she will take him.

Your turn will come, sir, but there is a woman just behind you who must go first. Give her a hand up will you?"

In this way, one by one, with encouragement and sternness mixed, Monty got them through the tangle of branches and up onto the tree trunk and to safety. His was the voice of authority, both aristocratic lord and church preacher, and they could no more have disobeyed him than flown to the moon. With the help of Kitty, who tied some of the more terrified to the rope rail to stop them falling into the water, even the oldest and youngest reached safety without loss of life.

The parsonage was full. Every room on the ground floor that had floorboards and a fireplace had a blazing fire in it, and sodden villagers huddled around the flames, bowls of steaming soup in their hands. Monty caught sight of Melissa bustling about with a tray of buns fresh from the oven. He grabbed one as she went past.

"Are you all right?" she said.

"Perfectly. A little damp, that is all."

Then, with a quick smile, she said, "I did not know I married a hero. What next, dragon slaying?" So saying, she disappeared into his future book room with her tray.

Monty ate his bun, changed into dry clothes, and made his way downstairs again. This time he found Melissa in the kitchen, overseeing the dispensing of soup.

"Would you like some?" she said, with a smile that warmed him inside, but he shook his head.

"Are you coping? This is not overwhelming the household?" he said, taking in Mrs Green standing at the range, grumbling steadily as she stirred a pot.

"No, indeed, for Mrs Shaw and her daughters are making the next pot of soup, you see, and Mr Pargeter and his brothers are in charge of the coal." Monty saw several village women busily chopping vegetables, while a troop of young men passed through with scuttles of coal. "We are using a vast deal of coal, I hope you do not mind," she said anxiously. "Also, I have put Mrs Carter and Mrs Wainwright to bed in the spare room, because they were so cold, and they have been up all night. And I should like to put Mr Simpson to bed, too, but it must be a room with a fire. Would you mind if I use your dressing room? I can get more beds set up later, but just for now—"

"Of course," he said at once. "These people have had a dreadful experience, and we must do everything we can to look after them. Has the doctor been sent for?"

"The doctor will not get through from Sagborough today, for the stream is right across the road down in the village, but Mr Hissop is here."

"Mr Hissop?"

"The apothecary. He is very good, and his daughter is almost as knowledgeable as he is."

"Ah. Excellent."

~~~~~

All day people came and went from the parsonage. The labourers were in and out, watching the water continue to rise and engulf their houses, and then returning to warmth and safety. A few people from lower down the village waded through the shallow water covering the road to bring blankets and food, or just offers of help. So much mud was tramped into the house that Melissa wondered if the rugs would ever be clean again. Still, everyone was safe, and what else mattered? She cheerfully doled out hot soup and bread for hours, and then ordered a whole side of beef to be roasted for the visitors' dinner. When her path crossed Monty's, she could not help smiling at him — her hero! So brave, to clamber out

185

on that fallen tree, when he could have been tipped into the water at any moment, and swept away. But that was just like him, only thinking of others and not himself.

After the beef had been consumed to the last morsel, and everyone was warm and dry, Monty led those willing across to the church, where he lit every candle and held an impromptu service of thanksgiving. Never had Melissa heard hymns sung with such gusto, or prayers recited with such feeling. They had all had a lucky escape, and if Monty was the hero of the hour, the heroine was Kitty. The men shook her hand, the women cried over her, and Bridget Kelly's fallen women were absorbed into the village as if there had never been the least question of their respectability.

By dusk, it was clear that the cottage folk would not be able to return to their houses for some days yet. A few had been claimed by friends in the village, but most remained, having no friends except the other poor folk.

"They must stay here," Melissa said anxiously to Monty. "We cannot throw them out."

"No, of course not. I take it we have enough supplies to feed them for a few days more?"

"Oh yes! And there is plenty of room for everyone. We have so many empty rooms here, and blankets enough. I will have all the mattresses brought down, but Monty, Mr Smith is still in your bed, and I do not like to move him for he is so old and frail, and he is very comfortable there, and his daughters are looking after him. But you can share my room — just for tonight, and tomorrow we can arrange something better. You will not mind that, will you?"

Mutely he shook his head, but there was an expression on his face that she could not read, although it made her uncomfortable.

They had no proper dinner that night, for Melissa hardly liked to ask the harassed Mrs Green to cook anything more, but they had supper alone in their dining room, and then read for an hour in the parlour, the only two rooms downstairs not taken over by cottagers. Hardly a word was spoken, and Melissa was aware of her own tension. The coming night would be difficult. Would Monty take the opportunity to claim his rights as a husband?

And a part of her, perhaps the major part, very much wanted him to. How she longed for him to kiss her again, to hold her tightly and whisper in her ear and look at her in that way that made her dizzy and weak. And in just five days, she would be of age and could marry him again, properly, and it would be perfectly all right for him to do so. But until then... and what if, when she told him the terrible truth, he rejected her? She could end up as one of Bridget Kelly's fallen women. No, it was better to keep him at arm's length until they were truly married.

So they went upstairs in silence, and Melissa allowed Margaret to ready her for bed in her room, while Donovan did the same for Monty in one of the empty rooms. Then he came into her room, eyes downcast, and stood uncertainly beside the door. Poor Monty! So decisive, so assured at other times, yet now he looked lost and fearful.

"Where will you sleep?" she said gently. "The chair by the fire might be comfortable, or we could make up a bed for you on the chaise longue."

He licked his lips, lifting his head to look at her, and she saw the agony in his eyes. "I cannot do this," he whispered. "To be so close to you and yet unable to touch you... no, I cannot."

She stared at him helplessly.

"You torment me, Melissa," he said bleakly. "I will keep to your wishes, but do not ask me to share your room."

"Oh Monty," she said, tears rising to her eyes. "I am so sorry. If I had realised... perhaps some other arrangement could have been devised. I did not know it was so difficult for you." She rested one hand on his chest, shocked to feel the rapid beat of his heart beneath it.

"How could you?" he said. "I hardly knew it myself... until now. It is not your fault that you are so lovely, so enticing. I could bear it better if your hair were less soft..." He reached a hand to stroke a loose curl. "... if your skin were less smooth..." One finger traced its way down her cheek, making her shiver in delight. "...if your lips were less rosy..." His thumb rubbed against her mouth, and she uttered a soft mewing sound. Then, his voice so low the words were almost inaudible, "...if I loved you less well."

"Oh Monty. My dearest Monty." Almost of its own volition, her hand found its way behind his head, so that she could pull him towards her. His lips touched hers, hot and sweet, and he gave a little groan. Then they were in each other's arms, held fast in a passionate embrace that caused every rational thought to flee. There was only her and Monty and the great blazing fire that was consuming them both.

When, an eternity later, they broke apart, he picked her up and carried her to the bed.

18: Guests

The sun woke Melissa the next morning, for they had forgotten to close the bed curtains. The first thing she saw was Monty's smiling face, his eyes shining. Guilt washed over her for an instant, but she set it aside sharply. What was done was done, and there was no going back. Now she must hope that Monty loved her well enough to forgive her deceit.

That day, they drank their morning chocolate in bed together, like a proper married couple, and between Monty's happiness and her own, and a spate of chocolaty kisses, Melissa wished with all her heart that they might stay thus all day and never leave their cosy nest.

But there were voices all over the house, and somewhere a baby crying, and a couple arguing in the distance, his angry rumble contrasting with her shrill invective. Monty went off somewhere to dress, and Melissa rang for Margaret. After three rings, she put on her wrap and ventured out of the bedroom to find her. Two men on the landing, shirts hanging out of their trousers, stared at her in surprise.

"Beg pardon, mistress," one said, and he bowed, but his eyes dropped only a little, so that he was staring at her exposed shoulders, only half hidden by her unbound hair.

"Milady," hissed the other, nudging his fellow in the ribs. "'Tis Lady Montague, see?"

"Beg pardon, *milady*," said the other, but he grinned in an abominably rude manner.

"Go away," Melissa squeaked, feeling horribly vulnerable. "You should not be in this part of the house."

They bowed again, and walked away, but they had not taken three steps when the rude one whispered something to his friend, and they both burst out laughing.

Margaret came running up at that point, and Melissa retreated back into her room, wishing she could lock the door, but the key had been lost. She was safe with Margaret, but she was quite unsettled by the whole incident, and all her pleasure in the day was gone.

Not an hour later, Melissa and Monty were just sitting down to breakfast and she had barely begun her tale of the two discourteous men, when a carriage rolled up to the door, mired to the axles in mud.

"Good gracious! Surely no one thinks to call today," Melissa said crossly, but Monty merely laughed.

"It is only Reggie and Lady Reggie, come to see if we have been washed away."

And so it was, their faces anxious as they were shown into the dining room.

"Good Lord, Monty, have you taken leave of your senses?" Lord Reginald said. "There are men on your front step smoking, if you please, as if they own the place."

"And a woman sitting in the front window feeding her baby," Lady Reginald added.

"They have no homes to go to, until the flood water recedes," Monty said in his mild way. "I can hardly turn them out of doors, not when they have elderly and sick and young children in their midst. It would be inhumane at this time of year."

"Shall I send for tea?" Melissa said, stepping in quickly to avoid an argument.

"Thank you but we will not stay," Lord Reginald said. "The roads are so bad and there is more rain coming, according to our coachman, so we must not delay. We heard last night of the flood, and came at once to assure ourselves of your safety. We might have known you would be playing the good Samaritan, Monty."

"What else should I be doing?" he said, with his gentle smile.

"That is all very well, but it is most inconvenient for Lady Monty, to be living amongst such people. I am sure they are very good sorts at heart, but they will take advantage of your generosity and it is not as if you might confine them to a spare wing where they would be no trouble. They are everywhere. Why, we had to step over three children crawling about in your entrance hall. If you must fill your house with peasants, at least let us take Lady Monty back to Great Mellingham with us, where she might be comfortable."

"Yes, do come, Lady Montague," said Lady Reginald. "I should not have a moment's peace were you to stay on here amongst such... such *rough* people."

Melissa hardly knew what to say. She had no wish at all to leave Monty, yet she had to agree that it was awkward to be surrounded by working men, and in her own home, too.

"That is a very kind offer," Monty said slowly.

"You think I should go?" she said, downcast.

"It would be for the best," he said. "Just for a few days, until all these people have somewhere else to go to."

"But my place is here, with you," she said. "It is my responsibility to look after you."

"And mine is to ensure your safety," he said softly. "It is not fitting that you should be here, and it would please me to know that you were well protected and not exposed to offensive behaviour."

"Then it shall be as you wish," she said in a low voice.

"Excellent," Lord Reginald said. "We shall await you in the carriage."

But when the door has closed behind them, Melissa burst into tears of despair. To be torn away from Monty now, when they were so happy! It was unbearable.

"I do not want to leave you!" she sobbed.

"Nor do I want you to go," he said, holding her tight. "I wish you could stay with me, but Reggie is right — it is not fitting for you to be here. It will only be for a short time — a few days, perhaps, and then we will be together again, my darling. And at least you will be safe, and I need not worry about you."

And he kissed her, and hugged her, and kissed her again, and then he sent for Margaret and told her to pack a box, and within the hour Melissa was in Lord Reginald's carriage, rolling slowly away from the parsonage. Monty stood on the drive waving farewell, but she could hardly see him for the tears streaming down her face.

~~~~~

Great Mellingham was a fine house, built in the style fashionable more than a hundred years ago, with two splendid wings flanking the central portion, and the whole having a pleasing symmetry. It had not Drummoor's imposing grandeur, but it was indubitably more elegant. But if the exterior dated to a previous century, the same could not be said of the furnishings, which were all brand new. The house smelled strongly of fresh paint and plaster and newly cut wood, and every door had its shiny new lock and a matching key.

Melissa was assigned a large bedroom in the Chinese style, with an adjoining dressing room almost as large. Footmen lifted her box up the stairs, under the watchful eye of a stern-faced butler, and two maids scuttled about under Margaret's direction unpacking. When Melissa had changed her gown, and put on her best indoor shoes, leaving her boots to be extricated from the quantity of mud which had affixed itself thereto, the butler led her in stately procession to the morning room, where Lord and Lady Reginald awaited her. Tea was sent for, and other unspecified refreshments, which Melissa rather hoped would be cake, for her breakfast had been interrupted rather.

Lord and Lady Reginald were a pleasant couple, polite to a fault, who made decorous conversation for at least half an hour before the squeaking wheels of the tea trolley could be heard. There was no cake, only some rather stale Bath buns, which Melissa ate hungrily. Lord Reginald excused himself, and Lady Reginald picked up some sewing.

"I forgot to bring my work bag," Melissa said soulfully.

"There are some journals from London if you would like something to read."

"Oh, you are very kind! May I? Thank you!"

Melissa picked up a journal at random, and began to flick through the pages. There were plates of the very latest styles from Paris and London, and she wondered just how much they cost, and whether she could ever afford to buy anything so elaborate. Then she realised that one of the evening dresses depicted was very like one that Lady Carrbridge had given her. How she was raised up in the world, to be mingling with such fashionable people!

"Do you like such styles?" Lady Reginald said with a smile. "I confess, I find them a little ostentatious for my taste. Lady

Carrbridge carries off such modes charmingly, but I am a simple person with simple tastes."

Melissa looked at Lady Reginald's high-necked morning gown of kerseymere, with a wealth of decorative stitchery around the bodice, sleeves and hem, and thought that only a very wealthy lady would think such attire simple. She could see little difference between it and the gowns in the journal, apart from a little extra trimming.

"It is the same with me," Melissa said, "although I confess it has been most enjoyable allowing Lady Carrbridge to outfit me. It is difficult to know how I shall manage when I must make my own gowns, for how should anyone contrive anything so elegant? These hats might be managed, however. The construction would be easy to copy, I fancy."

Lady Reginald stared at her. "How clever you are, to make your own gowns! And hats, too. I can trim a bonnet, but only if a milliner has made it for me first, and as for a gown — I might make an adjustment here and there, but no more than that."

Laying the journal aside, Melissa picked up a book instead, and finding it to be a novel from the circulating library, she settled down contentedly to read.

Not long afterwards, horses were heard approaching, and then a female voice in the hall, and, moments later, a face appeared in the doorway — Lady Humphrey.

"Lady Monty! How dreadful the news is from Kirby Grosswick," Lady Humphrey said, entering the room with the train of her riding habit carelessly looped over one arm. "I have just come from there and all is in chaos, and Lord Monty in the thick of it, as always. If there is trouble, there will Lord Monty be. Such a sweet man. But how are you? Oh, may I have one of these buns, Robinia? I am so hungry all the time. I am sure I shall be as large as an elephant before this baby is born."

The butler materialised in the doorway. "The Lady Humphrey Marford, my lady."

"Yes, yes, yes, thank you, Marston. There is no need to announce Lady Humphrey when she is already in the room." The butler bowed and, without haste, withdrew, closing the door behind him with an audible snap.

"Marston is still giving you trouble?" Lady Humphrey said.

Lady Reginald sighed. "He is so *grand*. He was head footman for the Duke of Camberley before, and he thinks he has come down sadly in the world," she said to Melissa. "He quite disapproves of me, I know it. The butler we had at home was lovely, like everyone's favourite uncle, but Marston—!"

"I have resolved the problem by not having a butler," Lady Humphrey said. "It is most disagreeable when the servants sneer at one, and I am so disreputable, Lady Monty — oh, but may I call you Melissa? I am so disreputable that even the scullery maid sneers at me."

"Disreputable?" Melissa said, faintly.

"Oh, indeed. I am quite beyond the pale. My father made all his money from trade, you see, and I am liable to shoot people if I take a dislike to them. Now Robinia here is frighteningly proper, and always behaves as she should, but I do not."

"Ah, but I am so dreadfully *provincial*," Lady Reginald said.

"So you are," Lady Humphrey said. "I had forgotten that. No wonder your butler looks down on you." Both ladies laughed. "Robinia, these are yesterday's buns, I swear it."

"I *asked* for a cherry cake," Lady Reginald said, plaintively. "Or something with coconut. But Mrs Launceston does whatever she wants."

Melissa's eyes were round. "I thought I was the only one having trouble with the servants."

The two ladies roared with laughter. "My dear, *everyone* has trouble with the servants."

Melissa laughed too, and suddenly her spirits lightened. Despite her misery at leaving Monty, this was a good day, for she had acquired two new friends.

~~~~~

Despite the grumbling about the servants, Great Mellingham was a pleasant place to be, the days spent in quiet employment with Robinia and, very often Hortensia too, and a good dinner every night. Reggie and Robinia both professed themselves to be delighted to have a guest, having had the house full at Christmas and feeling very flat when everyone had left. They said this so often, and with such sincerity, that Melissa could not doubt them. All that was wanting, they said, was a fourth for whist.

Two days after their arrival, the opportunity arose to remedy this defect. A carriage broke an axle almost outside the gates of the property, and its occupant, a well-dressed woman of above fifty, requested aid and was invited inside while their own coachman conferred with hers to assess the damage.

She introduced herself as Mrs Horace Chesterfield, from Hertfordshire, a widow of some years' standing, although she still wore black. She was a handsome woman with a fine figure, although her looks were marred by a scar across one cheek.

"Where are you bound, Mrs Chesterfield?" Robinia said. "For this is a very quiet road, and we do not get much traffic from Hertfordshire."

"Oh, that is Richard's fault — my coachman," she said with a merry laugh. "He will take these shortcuts, and they always go wrong! I am on my way to York for a spell, but he decided to turn off the main road and — well, here we are, broken down and very far from help. If he were not so careful a driver in other ways, I should have turned him off years ago."

The report from the two coachmen was not optimistic. The axle was completely smashed, and the carriage could not be moved until the wheelwright could be got from Mellingham village. Even then, it might be days before the axle could be repaired.

"Oh dear!" said Mrs Chesterfield. "What then are we to do? Is there a respectable inn anywhere nearby?"

"Is your business in York urgent?" Robinia said.

"Not in the least. It was merely a whim of mine, for I am so restless since my dear Horace died."

"Why, then you must stay with us."

"Oh, indeed, I could not impose—"

But Robinia insisted and Mrs Chesterfield graciously agreed, and so it was decided.

That evening was a pleasant one. Mrs Chesterfield was good company at dinner, although Melissa thought she devoted rather too much of her attention to Reggie. It was not that she flirted, exactly, for how could a respectable widow of such years be said to flirt? But she listened intently to every word he said, and responded in the most respectful manner, in contrast to her more casual tone with the ladies. However, she played whist competently, so the four played several rubbers and only retired to bed when the clock struck midnight.

Melissa was restless that night. Even though Hortensia brought news from Monty every day, she still missed him, and however comfortable Great Mellingham was, she wanted to be back in her own home with her husband. She lay wakefully in bed for some time, then, with a sigh, threw back the covers. She had another book from the circulating library to read, and she had left the characters within it at a dramatic moment. She would read for a while until sleep overcame her.

There was still a little light left in the embers of the fire. She was still fumbling around for a spill to light her candle when she heard a noise, just a quick scuffling sound, gone at once. Mice, she thought, reaching again for the spills jar. A soft click stayed her hand. She froze, ears straining, for mice did not, in her experience, make clicking noises. Then, to her horror, she saw a sliver of light from the crack under the dressing room door. Someone had entered her dressing room from the landing.

She crept towards the door, weak and trembling with fear. Who could it be? And why would anyone enter her dressing room? Did they mean her harm? The light wavered, moved this way and that, as the interloper walked around the room. Melissa stretched out her hand to the door, found the knob, felt around some more and her fingers fell on the cold metal of the key. Slowly, keeping one eye on the wavering line of light below the door, she grasped, turned and prayed it would make no noise. Silently the key revolved. The lock engaged with an audible clunk, and Melissa held her breath. The light continued to bob about. She breathed a sigh of relief. Quickly, she moved to the bedroom door and locked that, too. She was safe!

The light under the door stopped moving, and then came some slight sounds that Melissa could not identify. Metallic, she thought. What on earth was going on? But this did not seem like the behaviour of one who planned to murder Melissa in her bed. A burglar, perhaps. And if so, she could not sit in her room listening while some housemaid stole the silver.

She crept to the bedroom door and gently unlocked it, then stole out onto the landing. The dressing room door was ajar, the faint glow from the burglar's candle scarcely showing. Very, very cautiously, inch by careful inch, Melissa pushed the door open. Someone could be seen scrabbling around by the fireplace, but she could not make out who it was.

But she did not need to, for she knew what she was going to do. Her hand felt around the door. No key on the outside, so it must be on the inside — there it was! Slowly she withdrew it, and when she was sure she had it firm in her hand, she slammed the door shut and locked it.

Then, with cries of, "Help! Help! Burglars!" she ran off to wake the household.

It took some time to rouse enough men to tackle the burglar, who had grown in Melissa's eyes to the size of a giant. She would be disappointed if the door were opened to reveal only a wisp of a kitchen maid. But when Reggie and his troop of footmen and grooms, unlocked the door and streamed inside, the room was empty. Soot covered the rug in front of the fire, and a window had been opened, suggesting that the culprit had fled. Melissa was terribly disappointed. Why had she not thought of the windows? Although how she could have secured them, she knew not, and the room was on the first floor.

But when Reggie peered down from the window, he laughed. "Our burglar did not get far, I see."

And there, perched precariously in the branches of a tree and looking terrified, was Mrs Chesterfield.

19: Theft And Deception

Two gardeners brought ladders and the burglar was retrieved from her tree, clutching a sooty metal box. She glowered at them all, not in the least cowed, and only put up a fight when Reggie asked her to hand over the box.

"It is mine!" she said defiantly. "I have done nothing wrong in reclaiming my own property."

"That remains to be seen," Reggie said sternly. "Lampton, Walker, relieve Mrs Chesterfield of the box."

There followed an unseemly tussle, but two large footmen were more than a match for one rather stout middle-aged lady, and Reggie soon had the box in his possession, and Mrs Chesterfield was led away with what dignity she could muster to be locked into an empty portion of the wine cellar, with the two footmen left to watch over her in case she escaped.

Then they all returned to bed, to snatch what hours of sleep were left to them.

The metal box, which had been hidden behind loose bricks in the chimney, was found to contain rolls of money, some coins and several bags of small but valuable jewels, as well as titles to several properties.

"That is curious," Reggie said thoughtfully, as they examined the contents the following morning. "Murchester Hall... I remember hearing of that. It seems to me that it was one of Carrbridge's properties at one time. Merton will know, if anyone does. The others do not sound familiar, though."

"But so much money!" Robinia said. "And these diamonds must be worth a great deal."

"Is it possible that Mrs Chesterfield truly owns the box, as she claims?" Melissa said. "Perhaps she lived here once, and left it behind."

"Then why not ask for it, like an honest woman?" Reggie said. "No need to creep about at night if it is her property. It is more likely stolen, perhaps by highwaymen, and was left here so that the thieves would not be caught with stolen property on their persons. The house has been empty for some years, remember. It would not have been difficult to break in and find a safe hiding place."

"It would not be difficult to break in, perhaps," Melissa said. "Finding a chimney that happened to have loose bricks in it would be a lucky chance, I should think."

"That is true," Reggie said. "Well, we shall do nothing further except to keep Mrs Chesterfield locked up. I sent word to Drummoor at first light, so I am hopeful that Carrbridge and Merton will come and advise us."

Not long after noon, Lord Carrbridge and Mr Merton arrived, accompanied by two grooms, and Lord Carrbridge's valet, in case they should be required to stay the night. The marquess was irate, pacing about, arms waving, most aggrieved that anyone should be sneaking about in the middle of the night retrieving boxes from chimneys.

"This is quite unacceptable!" he cried. "Why, Lady Monty was only in the next room, and suffered the greatest fear and alarm, and

I will not have it! This person — this Mrs Chesterfield, if that is indeed her name, and personally I doubt it — should not be allowed to terrorise honest people in this way."

"We are all agreed upon that, Carrbridge," Reggie said. "But Lady Monty was more than equal to the occasion, and had the presence of mind to lock the lady up so that she might be caught. Otherwise, she might have got clean away, you know, and the box of valuables with her."

"And what of her coachman?" Mr Merton said.

Reggie looked chagrined. "Gone, and the groom and maid with him. We think they had another carriage, one without a broken axle, parked in a field nearby, ready for their escape. The coachman and the others must have run for it when Mrs Chesterfield was caught, and they saw that the game was up."

"What were they like?" Mr Merton said. "The coachman — was he an older man?"

"No, rather young. Twenty five, perhaps, and the groom even younger. The maid, about the same."

"Interesting," Mr Merton said. "May we see the box of valuables?"

When it was all spread out before him, he examined every item with great care, and then he asked to see the chimney where the box had been secreted. When he returned to the drawing room, he was smiling.

"Do you wish to interview Mrs Chesterfield?" Reggie said. "She will not tell you much, but you might find out a little more about her, with judicious questioning."

"I should certainly like to see her at some stage," Mr Merton said. "However, I do not need to ask her any questions, for I know exactly who she is, and what she is about."

They all exclaimed in amazement, but he smiled, and pointed to the contents of the box. "The titles here are all properties which rightly belong to Lord Carrbridge. Murchester Hall, for instance, was held by Lady Millicent Marford for her lifetime."

"Great-aunt Millicent?" Lord Carrbridge said. "But she has been dead for years. Her house should have reverted to the estate long ago."

"Indeed. Lannimont Lodge… I have only seen one mention of that, in a letter to the eighth marquess, but no other sign of it. Yet here it is. And Barnfield I assumed was lost at the faro table or some such. It is obvious, therefore, who is behind this attempted theft, and who Mrs Chesterfield is."

"You speak of Sharp, I presume," Lard Carrbridge said.

"Certainly," Mr Merton said. "Who else but your agent would have access to the titles of your properties? And remember that Great Mellingham was empty for some years, with renovations overseen by Sharp. He had every opportunity to loosen bricks in the chimney, in order to hide money and documents. He has been concealing such caches in many different places. Now that he finds himself pursued by the law, he is trying to retrieve some of his hidden funds. He was foiled at Drummoor by Lady Humphrey, and now he has been thwarted by Lady Montague's quick thinking."

"Yes, Lady Monty was both quick-witted and courageous, and we are all greatly indebted to her," Lord Carrbridge said with a bow which put Melissa to the blush. "But I do not understand. Who is this Mrs Chesterfield, and what does she have to do with Sharp?"

"Why, she is his wife," Mr Merton said.

There was a long silence, and Melissa tried to call to mind the nondescript little woman, rather tired-looking and worn out, that she had encountered once or twice at Drummoor, and reconcile that image with the robust Mrs Chesterfield.

"I do not understand you," Lord Carrbridge said plaintively. "I have seen his wife, and not only is she nothing like Mrs Chesterfield, but I cannot imagine her doing anything of this nature."

"The wife I speak of is his other wife, who was known as Mrs Ballard, from Drifford mill town in Northumberland." Mr Merton said. "As soon as I see her, I shall be able to confirm it."

"Ah," Lord Carrbridge said. "But she was supposed to be confined to an asylum."

"So we were told by Ballard, but since we believe he is Sharp, it seems unwise to take his word for anything," Mr Merton said. "Bear in mind that Sharp has lost his position as your agent, my lord, he has lost his foothold in Drifford and he has lost a great deal of the income that supported his lavish lifestyle. He must be getting desperate, so he sends his wife to recover a secret store of money. But not only does his plan fail, but she is captured. It is a pity he was not here himself. I had hopes of the coachman, but Sharp is too slippery to be caught that way. Still, we will get him before long, I am sure of it. And if I am right that this is Mrs Ballard, then the Duke of Dunmorton will be very pleased to hear of it. She tried to poison his grandson, so we may send her to Northumberland to be tried for attempted murder, and perhaps she, at least, will hang for her crimes."

After the trials of the night, the evening was a pleasant one. Lord Carrbridge and Mr Merton decided to stay overnight, and since it was one of the regular occasions when Lord and Lady Humphrey came to dinner, they sat down seven to table, and then played a cheerful game of loo afterwards. If Monty had been there, then the evening would have been quite perfect.

Melissa had not previously had much occasion to talk to Mr Merton, who was rather a dour, quiet man with a forbidding countenance. In such confined society, however, she had her opportunity and he proved to be an easy conversationalist, making sensible suggestions for the management of the flood victims, and recommending several craftsmen to work on the interior of the parsonage. When she asked him how Lady Hardy was, his thin face lit up with a broad smile and he grew animated, revealing their plans for an early wedding and the small changes he was making to his house for the comfort of the future Mrs Merton. His affection for his betrothed was quite charming.

She was curious about how he came to be secretary to Lord Carrbridge.

"Ah, that was Lady Carrbridge's influence," he said. "I was known to her when I worked for Lady Hardy's husband, Sir Osborne Hardy, and his death coincided with Lord Carrbridge's realisation that his finances were amiss. I was invited to investigate, and then taken on permanently."

"I do not know what we would have done without him," Lord Carrbridge said. "My agent has been swindling me for years, and I had not the least idea until Merton looked into it."

"And had you no secretary before, my lord?" Melissa said.

"Once, many years ago. He was the chaplain, but he became my secretary briefly. Poor Mr Penicuik! A dreadful business!"

Melissa paused, the card she was about to play suspended in mid-air. "Oh dear! Whatever happened?"

"We never speak of it," Lord Carrbridge said with a shudder. "It was all too horrible to contemplate."

Lady Humphrey sighed. "And that is all anyone will say of the matter. It is most mysterious. I have made enquiries everywhere, and have discovered only that a butter churn and a pig were involved. Beyond that, no one will say a word, except *'Poor Mr Penicuik!'* as if the man were dead."

"He is not dead, although he might as well be," Lord Humphrey said, mournfully.

The party played in silence for some time, out of respect for poor Mr Penicuik, until Lord Carrbridge, his mind still on his former chaplain and secretary, began to talk of his plans to acquire a new chaplain.

"It was so pleasant when Monty was able to take services in the Drummoor chapel," he said. "Lady Carrbridge found it a great convenience not to have to go down into the village on a Sunday, and one does not like to take the horses out in bad weather just for that little distance. I daresay Monty will know someone we might engage as chaplain, and since Lady Carrbridge delights in filling the house with as many aunts and uncles and cousins and mere acquaintances as it can hold, we shall hardly notice the extra expense of one more at table. What do you say, Merton?"

"You can bear the expense very well now, my lord."

"Indeed, for my income is twice what it was, and my expenses much reduced, is it not so? Everything is perfectly comfortable, with nothing of that nature to worry me," he said with satisfaction. "Even with the cost of the hospital, I shall have sufficient to enable me to disburse small sums to other worthy souls."

"If you have money to spare, perhaps you could do something to help Bridget Kelly?" Melissa said diffidently. "She is family, after all. In a way."

"But female," Carrbridge said gently. "The charge Father laid on me was to help his sons, not his daughters."

"A thoughtful man helps both, although perhaps in different ways," Mr Merton said. "You will teach the Earl of Deveron to be a marquess in his turn, and establish Lord William in a career. And for little Lady Mary, you will give her a season or two in London and a good dowry. As for your father's less official children, you gave Ben

Gartmore and Charlie Wilkes the chance of careers, so why not help Miss Kelly, too?"

Lord Carrbridge looked pensive. "Humphrey, Reggie, what do you think?"

"I would do it in a heartbeat," Humphrey said. "She is an independent sort of woman, it seems, and needs only a helping hand to get started. She will not be a drain on the estate."

"It is unorthodox," Reggie said, "and one would not wish to be seen to be condoning immorality, but Miss Kelly herself is respectable enough. Why not?"

"You have not asked for my opinion," Hortensia said, "but I shall give it anyway. Bridget is to be applauded for giving respectable employment to these unfortunate women. I have already promised my help."

"Then I need not intervene?" Carrbridge said. "Perhaps it is a project best suited to ladies?"

"If I may suggest, my lord," Merton said, "there is one favour that only you may dispense. Lady Harriet plans to accommodate these women at Westbury House, which is hers for her lifetime but thereafter reverts to the estate. It would be an act of great charity to make the house over entirely to Lady Harriet, without conditions."

"An excellent idea," Hortensia said. "That would give Miss Kelly and her women far greater security than they have at present."

"Then let it be so," Carrbridge said. "I told Monty how it would be. Merton always knows what is best to be done."

~~~~~

The following morning a large quantity of mail was delivered to the house.

"Letters are getting through at last after all this bad weather," Robinia said in satisfaction, sifting through a great pile of them. "Oh, Melissa, there is one for you."

"For me? How? Who knows I am here? It is not Monty's hand, that much I can see. Oh… it is from a Mr Haddington."

"The cloth merchant in Sagborough?"

"He offers me three free lengths of any fabrics I choose, as a wedding gift. Should I accept, do you think?"

"Why, certainly! I go to Gorton's as a rule, but Haddington's is highly thought of. Lady Forth goes there, after all. Let us go today! I have not been anywhere for an age, and I shall call on Lady Forth while you choose your wedding fabrics, and I can also return all those books to the circulating library, so that you may have new ones to read. What an excellent scheme!"

Melissa thought so too, and the weather agreed, for the sun shone on them as the carriage rattled down the drive of Great Mellingham. The road was bad all the way to Sagborough, but they arrived without mishap and Robinia left Melissa and her maid at Haddington's warehouse. It was not a prepossessing building, looking no different from a thousand other warehouses up and down the country, but the number of carriages waiting outside was reassuring, and within they found a warm and inviting emporium. Bales of calico and velvet and silk and muslin and bombazine were stacked to the ceiling, the walls were lined with drawers no doubt filled with kid gloves and buttons and ribbons, while glass-fronted cases displayed a dazzling array of fans, snuff boxes, bandeaux, combs and other trinkets.

There were seats near the door, and here Melissa and Margaret waited until an elderly woman bustled over to attend to them. Melissa showed the letter.

"Oh, Lady Montague Marford — oh, how honoured! How gratifying! If your ladyship would be so obliging as to wait just one moment, I shall fetch Mr Haddington at once."

Melissa watched her thread her way through the pillars of cloth towards a dapper little man in a rather splendid embroidered coat, so dazzlingly beautiful that she rather regretted that such styles were no longer fashionable. Mr Haddington wore his hair lightly powdered, and little frills of lace at his throat and wrists in the old style, which made him look like a quaintly old-fashioned uncle. When informed of her arrival, he immediately left the two ladies he had been attending to, and rushed to Melissa's side.

"So… hmm… condescending of your ladyship," he said with such a low bow that it was a wonder he did not fall over. "Pray allow me to… hmm… show you everything of interest amongst our newest stock, and perhaps… hmm… there will be something to entice your ladyship's discerning eye. Now here are the very latest…hmm… silks, just arrived from London last month. Is not this… hmm… very fine work? And here…"

Melissa passed a very pleasant half hour walking about with Mr Haddington, examining this or that material. Seeing the prices attached to each bale, she was astonished at his generosity in giving away three lengths, until she remembered that he hoped to secure her custom for many years to come, and perhaps also hoped that she would spend more today in gloves and silk stockings that his gift would cost. She had made her choice at an early stage, but there was something so agreeable in such deference after years of being treated with neglect, that she was not minded to hurry the experience.

Eventually, when they seemed to have exhausted every possibility, Mr Haddington said, "And now, if your ladyship would like to see the most special items, which I keep in the rear store room?"

Even more choices! Melissa could not resist, so she and Margaret followed Mr Haddington through the warehouse to a door hidden behind a curtain. Beyond was a smaller room, furnished in much the same way, but colder, there being no fire. Melissa shivered a little, but listened willingly enough as Mr Haddington began his descriptions of the figured silks and muslins so fine they were almost transparent.

"These are what the grandest London ladies wear," he whispered.

"They are too delicate, I fear," she said. "I should be afraid to put a needle to them."

"I can recommend one or two excellent seamstresses, if your ladyship—"

"That is enough," came a male voice that Melissa recognised, a voice that sent her innards roiling with terror.

"No!" she whispered.

But it was true. From behind a stack of bales appeared Lord Bentley, and behind him Cornelius Brockenhurst.

"No, no, no! Go away, go *away!* What are you doing here?"

"Collecting my property," Lord Bentley said with a sneer. "Did you think you could just walk away from your obligations, Melissa?"

"My lord?" Mr Haddington said, in puzzled tones. "I do not understand. You assured me her ladyship would be delighted with your little scheme. An amusing way to tender your wedding gift, you told me."

"And you being such a trusting fool believed it," Lord Bentley said. "Rope, Neil."

"No, please!" whimpered Mr Haddington.

"Wait a minute," Melissa said. "You cannot do this. I am leaving here this moment."

"Men!" said Lord Bentley, and at once four more faces materialised, all large, muscular types, with the bent noses and scars that betokened a life spent not running away from confrontation. What could two women and a rather delicate middle-aged man do against so many? And if Melissa had had any thought of running away, Cornelius settled the matter by producing a pair of very business-like pistols with a wide grin.

"If you all do exactly as you are told and behave yourselves," he drawled, "then no one dies today."

Melissa went cold, but all thought of resistance fled. Whatever they wanted, they were not planning to hurt anyone, it seemed, so she could only go along with it for now, and hope for the best.

Mr Haddington and Margaret were bound and gagged and tied to chairs in no time, and with a wave of one pistol, Cornelius directed Melissa towards the door at the back of the room. She threw one glance at Margaret, whose eyes were huge with terror above the gag, then turned and walked, head high, to meet her fate.

20: The White Hart Inn

There was a carriage waiting outside in the yard, but Melissa was surrounded and the men bundled her into it with no opportunity to look about her for help. Lord Bentley, Cornelius and one of the bruisers got in beside her, the steps were drawn up, the door slammed and within moments they were moving. The blinds were drawn up, but there was enough light to see the triumphant sneers on their faces.

"Where are you taking me?" she said coldly.

"You will see," said Lord Bentley.

"What do you hope to achieve by abducting me in this foolish manner? You were lucky that I responded to that letter from Mr Haddington."

"You walked into the trap very readily, it is true, but we could have found another way just as easily. Once we discovered your whereabouts, it was not difficult. As to the purpose, we shall achieve what we set out to do three months ago, which is to marry you to Pontefract, and be done with you."

"If you wish to be rid of me, I wonder you put yourselves to so much trouble, since I was already gone from Bentley Hall." She could feel tears prickling, but she was determined not to give way to them. Lifting her chin, she said, "Anyway, I cannot marry Mr Pontefract, since I am already married."

All three men laughed, and that chilled her more than anything else.

Lord Bentley leaned forward until his nose practically touched hers. "Just because you stand before the parson and put a notice in the paper don't make you married, my dear. You need my permission for that, or had you forgotten?"

Melissa had no answer to that. She sat in the darkened carriage as it rumbled slowly over cobbles and jolted into deep ruts, with no idea where she was being taken or how she could possibly escape her captors or Mr Pontefract. Nor was there any hope of rescue. Robinia would soon discover what had happened, and Margaret and Mr Haddington would be released from their captivity, and then Monty would hear— Monty! Her heart quailed. How could he possibly find one insignificant travelling carriage amongst the thousands on the roads? She was alone, and no one, not even Monty, could help her now. She would never see her darling Monty again. Closing her eyes, she could not prevent the tears from falling.

~~~~~

There was no knowing how long they had been travelling, but eventually they came to cobbles again, and all the odd noises and scents of the town. The carriage slowed, turned, stopped. Running feet and voices. Doors slammed in the distance. Melissa could smell something meaty — a stew or soup, perhaps, and beneath it a hint of rotten vegetables and the stronger odour of the stables.

After a while, someone rapped on the carriage door.

"Remember that there are two pistols pointing at your back, and Cornelius is an excellent shot," Lord Bentley murmured.

Melissa wondered whether perhaps it might be better to be dead than to be married to Mr Pontefract, but then she reminded herself sternly that so long as she were alive there was a possibility of escape, and finding her way back to Monty, so when she stepped down from the carriage, she made no attempt to run or shout for help.

She was surprised to find herself in the yard of a bustling coaching inn. *The White Hart*, according to the sign over the door. Several private carriages were drawn up in the large yard, and the London to York mail coach was about to depart in a great confusion of bags and passengers and boxes and ostlers running hither and thither. But she was quickly surrounded and hustled into the inn, up some narrow stairs and into a private parlour.

Two men were already there, Mr Pontefract and a man who, by his attire, was a clergyman. Her heart sank. So they were determined to do this at once. But she was still optimistic, for she could not be forced to marry against her will. Or so she told herself, but looking at the implacable faces of Lord Bentley and his brother, who had followed her into the room, she began to wonder.

"You may begin," Lord Bentley said to the clergyman.

Immediately he opened his prayer book and began to recite. "Dearly beloved, we are gathered here together—"

"You may skip the preamble. Get to the point."

"Yes, indeed," said Melissa. "Do get to the part about impediments, so that I may explain all the ways in which this marriage is unlawful."

"It *is* lawful," Lord Bentley snarled. "Look!" He drew papers from a pocket. "Special licence. My consent to the marriage. We have a clergyman. The proper fees have been paid."

"But *I* do not consent," Melissa said.

"Irrelevant. Continue, parson, and get to the *point*."

The parson licked his lips, and spoke in a rapid stream of words. "Norman Henry, wilt thou have this woman to thy wedded wife, to live together after God's ordinance in the—"

"Oh, this is ridiculous," Melissa said.

"—holy estate of Matrimony? Wilt thou love her, comfort her, honour, and keep her, in sickness and in health; and, forsaking all other, keep thee only unto her, so long as ye both shall live?"

"I will," said Mr Pontefract, leering at Melissa. Dear God, that leer had given her so many nightmares, and now here it was again, in the flesh.

"Melissa, wilt thou have this man to thy wedded husband, to live together after God's ordinance—"

"Certainly not," Melissa said.

"—in the holy estate of Matrimony? Wilt thou obey him, and serve him, love, honour, and keep him, in sickness and in health; and, forsaking all other, keep thee only unto him, so long as ye both shall live?"

"No, I will *not!* I will *not!*"

"She will," Lord Bentley said.

"Who giveth this woman to be married to this man?"

"I do, and for God's sake get on with it, man."

"This is madness! I—"

"Repeat after me. *'I, Norman—"*

"She is never going to say all those words. Just get to the *point.*"

"You cannot do this! I am already—"

In a great rattle of words, the parson said, "Those whom God hath joined together let no man put asunder. I pronounce that they be man and wife together, In the Name of the Father, and of the Son, and of the Holy Ghost. Amen."

"Amen," said all the men, loudly.

"Right, Pontefract," Lord Bentley said. "We have done our part, now it is up to you. Let us get her upstairs."

"With the greatest of pleasure." And the leer assumed even greater proportions.

Melissa screamed. It seemed, at that point, the only recourse still open to her. Surely there was one person in the inn who would not ignore a lady screaming for help? But it appeared there was not, for she was rushed out of the parlour, half carried and half dragged, still screaming until someone jammed a hand over her mouth, up two more flights of stairs and almost thrown into a bedchamber, so that she landed on her hands and knees. Mr Pontefract entered the room just behind her, and the door was slammed shut. There came the ominous sound of a key turning in the lock. Outside the room, male voices, laughter, then receding footsteps.

She scrambled to her feet. A quick look around the room suggested no possibility of help. The furnishings consisted of a bed, a chair, a wash stand and some pegs on the wall. The narrow window was uncompromisingly barred. But there was a fireplace, and a set of fire irons, and a quick grab put her in possession of the poker.

Mr Pontefract was struggling for breath after the rush up the stairs, wheezing slightly as he mopped his brow with a handkerchief.

"No need... for that..." he muttered, collapsing abruptly to sit on the edge of the bed, his corpulent weight causing a great creaking and shifting beneath him. "Good God, but I could do with a brandy."

"This is an outrage," Melissa said. "You do realise that this so-called marriage is entirely illegal, I suppose?"

"Not what... Bentley says," he wheezed. "All... perfectly... above board."

"It is *not!*" she cried. "I do not agree to any of this, and besides, I am already married."

"Not valid," he said. "Bentley said so." He got up and banged on the door. "Brandy! Bring me some brandy, dammit!" Then he returned to the bed, sitting down again with a heavy sigh. "Hardly matters. Married to me now. Just have to con... consume... do the business. All right and tight, once that is done."

It occurred to Melissa that Mr Pontefract's grasp of the law was tenuous at best. Her own was not exactly robust, but this was not a time to display the least hesitation. "You are wrong, sir. My marriage to Lord Montague Marford is perfectly legal, and even if it were not, that shambles of a marriage downstairs would not convince a single judge in the country. Both parties must be willing, and I am not, and never have been."

"No matter," he said. "We were betrothed, which is legally binding, so we were as good as married anyway. So Bentley says. Now we are properly so, and I just have to... to... consume the marriage."

A knock on the door announced the arrival of the brandy. Mr Pontefract rose, scrabbled in a waistcoat pocket and produced the key. Unlocking the door, he took possession of a tray with a bottle and two glasses, then slammed the door shut and locked it again. The key was returned to its pocket. This small occurrence lifted Melissa's spirits immeasurably. At least the key was inside the room! There were possibilities in that, if only she could retrieve it.

Mr Pontefract poured himself a large measure of brandy, downed it in one gulp, and poured another. Then, with a sigh of satisfaction, he arranged himself on the bed with his legs stretched out in front of him, and the brandy bottle conveniently to hand on the chair nearby.

With another of his stomach-curdling leers, he said, "Protest all you like, my dear, but you may as well accept the inevitable. I like a girl with a bit of spirit, myself, so feel free to put up a fight. It makes the eventual surrender all the sweeter."

Melissa kept hold of the poker, wondering whether it would even be possible to take a sufficiently decisive swing at her supposed husband, or whether, despite his bulk, he might be agile and strong enough to overpower her. But before she turned to violence, she still had some arrows of logic in her quiver.

"You are very sure of yourself, sir. But suppose you are wrong. Suppose this farce of a marriage is, as I have suggested to you, invalid. If you violate me, you commit a very serious crime."

"Not if I genuinely believe that you are my lawfully wedded wife," he said smugly.

"If you *are* my husband, then you may do as you please," she said softly. "And if you are not, then you may be hanged for what you propose to do."

The brandy glass paused on its way to his lips. Then he laughed, drank his brandy and set down his glass. Resting his hands on his ample stomach, he said, "Certainly I am your husband."

"You are very sure of yourself," she said. "I should not be so confident, in your place."

"Bentley said—"

"Lord Bentley will not be hanged for this night's work. *You* are the one whose life is at stake if he has misjudged the case. Have you talked to a lawyer? I should want to take legal advice, myself."

And now at last she saw the doubt in his eyes. He swallowed the last drops of brandy in the glass and refilled it. "Hanged?"

"Hanged. That is the penalty for violating a woman, Mr Pontefract." She spoke with the utmost conviction, although she had no more idea than he did of the law. "If we were married... but we are not, since I did not consent. You heard me, did you not? When the parson asked if I were willing, I said I was not. My intent was very clear. No one could mistake it. And so... no marriage. Violation. Hanging."

He was silent now, drinking, trying to think it through but failing to reach any rational conclusion.

"Best not to risk it, do you not agree? Take legal advice tomorrow."

For a long time, he said not a word, drinking, refilling his glass, drinking again, then abandoning the glass and drinking directly from the bottle.

Then, "Damnation!" he said. "Hellfire and damnation! They swore to me— Damnation!"

~~~~~

It was several hours before Melissa could be sure that Mr Pontefract was sufficiently soundly asleep for her to risk retrieving the key. He drank steadily for some time, glowering at her, and she did not dare to move or to set the poker down, in case he became drunk enough to lunge at her.

This gave her ample opportunity to wonder why on earth her guardian would go to so much trouble over her. Even if Cornelius owed Mr Pontefract money, surely she had no value to offset the debt? Mr Pontefract had never met her before that night when she had been summoned to join the family for dinner, so he could not be harbouring a secret passion for her. He was a man of some wealth, so he could find a wife in a more conventional way if he had the desire for one. Yet all three of them had come tearing north from Hampshire, had hired thugs to ensure her compliance, had bribed a clergyman, had obtained a special licence and were prepared to use the most despicable means to accomplish their foul plot. Yet why? She could make no sense of it.

And when her racing brain finally gave up the puzzle, there was Monty to fill her thoughts. He was so sweet and loving and everything the brutish Mr Pontefract was not. Dear Monty! Her heart ached for him. If only he were there to rescue her! She beguiled the long, lonely hours by imagining him riding through the night on his sturdy steed to save her. Except that he could not, for how could he ever find her? He had no idea where she had been taken — she did not even know herself! Somewhere to the south, and on the main London to York coach route, but how would anyone know where to begin looking? It was hopeless, and therefore she could not depend on aid reaching her. She would have to be her own rescuer.

Eventually Mr Pontefract fell asleep, or lost consciousness, she could not tell which, the almost empty brandy bottle slipping from his fingers to the bed. Even then, she waited until he was snoring loudly. When she plucked up the courage to lay down her poker and venture nearer, her first attempt to retrieve the key succeeded only in half rousing him, so that he rolled over onto his side, facing away from her. Now she would need to crawl on the bed to recover the key, and she dared not, for if he woke, she would be completely in his power and he might not remember in his drowsy state the unwisdom of violating her.

Again she waited. Outside the door, there was no sound, and she was hopeful that no guard had been set on watch. Below the window, the inn yard was quiet, but every hour or so it came alive with the clatter of coach wheels and horses' hooves and the shouts of ostlers and passengers and guards. But regular coach departures were a good sign. If she could ever escape from her little prison, she would have a means to return to Sagborough.

After an interminable wait, Mr Pontefract again rolled over, this time facing Melissa, and the pocket of his waistcoat gaped invitingly open. It was the work of a moment to retrieve the key. Then she stood beside the door, trying to find the courage to open it and face the unknown that lay beyond. But it could not be worse that what lay, snoring in stentorian manner, within. The lock gave a great clunk as it disengaged, but she did not wait to see if Mr Pontefract woke, opening the door and slipping out in seconds. Then she locked it behind her, but left the key in place. It was a risk, she knew, but she could not quite bring herself to take it with her. It hardly seemed fair to the innkeeper to force him to break down his own door.

There was no one on the landing. As quiet as a mouse, she crept down the many flights of stairs, feeling her way where the lamps had guttered out, and after many false turns found her way out to the yard. It was quiet just then, but she heard voices in the stables and from the kitchen, the occasional clatter of a pan or a pot chain. There was still a hint of stew in the air, making her stomach rumble. When had she last eaten? Breakfast, most likely, and that must be yesterday now. But she dared not draw attention to herself by going into the tap room, so she found a dark corner with an upturned bucket, no doubt where the scullery maid sat when she was supposed to be working, and waited quietly.

Before too long, horns could be heard in the distance, and the yard came to life. Ostlers rushed out with horses, doors were thrown open from the inn, and several people wandered out into the yard. In a few minutes more, a coach rumbled under the arch and came to a halt, the horses steaming and blowing and stamping, amidst a great confusion of inn workers and passengers and postilions and boxes and horses. The coach was bound for London, so it was of no use to Melissa, but in the gaggle of passengers disembarking and making their way to the tap room, she was able to follow along and hand over her coins for coffee and bread and meat like everyone else.

This raised her spirits greatly, and in the crowds milling about here and there, she ventured under the arch and looked up and down the main street. Tadcaster, she had heard the coach guard announce as they arrived, but she had no memory of the place from her previous journey by coach. Nor were there any other inns within sight where she might go to find a coach northwards. The White Hart seemed to be the only one with any traffic, and surely soon there would be a York-bound coach?

It seemed she was out of luck. These quiet hours of the night saw little traffic, and after a while she was forced to go into the inn in search of warmth. The tap room was almost empty, just two men stretched out on settles, fast asleep, and a family with three young children waiting patiently. Melissa found a seat near the fire and settled down to wait. But it was hard to sit patiently, when every footstep on the stairs, every voice from the bed chambers aloft might mean discovery. She tried to sit still, and tried not to cry, but a few tears escaped anyway. She closed her eyes, and rested her head against the back of the chair.

Half asleep, Melissa sprang to alertness only when the noise of the coach passing under the arch became deafening. She jumped to her feet and rushed outside, where the first light of dawn was already casting grey fingers over the yard. At last! The board showed that the vehicle was bound for York, although it was the mail coach and not likely to wait.

She raced across to the driver.

"Can you take me to Sagborough? Please? I can pay."

"Are you on the waybill? Then no. Buy a ticket, get tomorrow's coach."

"I can pay," she said again, producing a gold sovereign from her reticule. Oh, the pleasure of having money to wave under the noses of these people!

The coachman turned to look at her. He was quite a young man, and she imagined that he might have a wife and children back home in London, and the inducement would be tempting.

"There are rules…" he began.

She produced another coin. He hesitated. A third and then a fourth lay in her palm. He waited. One more, then.

"Sagborough? Get inside." And he scooped the coins from her hand, gesturing towards the open door of the coach.

She was so engrossed in her transaction that she failed to notice the door of the inn open. It was only when Lord Bentley's voice could be heard even above the hubbub of the yard that she recognised her danger.

"Melissa? Melissa! Get back here this instant!"

21: Confrontations

She froze. He had a cloth in his hand, as if interrupted in the middle of his breakfast, and his face was dark with anger.

"Come here at once!" he yelled. "You are the most troublesome child."

Her hand was already on the door of the mail coach. So close to freedom! But what could she possibly do? No one would help her. Already people were stepping away from her, looking uncertainly from her to the earl, judging the situation, seeing, perhaps, nothing but a family dispute, a man accompanying his niece or ward, who was giving him trouble. He would box her ears and haul her back inside where, no doubt, they would both laugh about it later. Just a joke, that was all it was. For who would guess the truth? No, she could not depend on anyone coming to her aid. It would take a miracle to save her now.

There was no miracle, just a lone voice from the crowd.

"What is your claim on this girl?" The man from the family in the taproom. They were waiting to board the mail coach, she now saw.

"Claim on her?" The earl's face was enough to curdle milk. He threw down the cloth and strode across the yard. "She is my ward, that is my claim on her, and she is trying to run away from me."

"I'd say she has reason," the man said stoutly. "I watched her in the taproom, and the poor child was terrified and in tears. You must have mistreated her badly. I say we find a magistrate and let him judge the situation."

Melissa could scarcely believe her luck. In the watching crowd she saw heads nodding, and some people glared at Lord Bentley.

"He is trying to marry me off to a horrid man," Melissa cried, seeing her opportunity. "He is trying to force me!"

The earl only laughed. "Nonsense, my dear," he said, with a softer tone. "What strange ideas you do take! Come inside and eat your breakfast, and let me explain again all the benefits of the match." Then, to the man from the taproom, he said in confiding tones, one man to another, "These young girls! They always think they know best, and make the deuce of a fuss, but really they need a great deal of guidance from wiser heads, would you not agree? Oh, forgive me, I have not introduced myself. The Earl of Bentley."

And that was the end of it. No challenge could prevail against a peer of the realm. No one could save her now. She was so sunk in despair that she scarcely noticed the expensive travelling coach that swept into the yard just then. It was only when a familiar voice hailed her that she turned.

"Melissa! Melissa! At last!"

And there, racing across the yard, weaving expertly between horses and heaps of bags and packages, was a true miracle — Monty, his face alight with joy, arms outstretched.

"Oh, Monty!" she cried, hurling herself into his waiting arms and bursting into tears. Here at least was one person who would not be the least cowed by the earl.

"There, now," he murmured into her bonnet. "Hush, hush. Did they hurt you?"

"Not at all."

"Nor shall they. You are safe now, my love."

And with his arms wrapped tight around her, she felt utterly safe and protected.

"Well, now, how touching," drawled the earl. "Pray unhand my ward, sir."

"Lord Bentley, I presume?" Monty said calmly, turning to face him, although without loosening his embrace of Melissa in the slightest. "She is no longer your ward, since she is my wife."

Lord Bentley laughed, a harsh sound that sent shivers down Melissa's spine. When she dared to look at him, the earl was smiling in a twisted sort of way. "She is *not* your wife. My ward is not yet of age, and therefore needed my permission to marry you, which I did not give. Therefore her marriage to you is invalid. She has, however, this night contracted a legal marriage to another. You are too late, sir."

"Your grasp of the law is faulty," Monty said, his quiet tones yet ringing with authority. "Your permission is only an essential prerequisite if the marriage is conducted by licence. If the banns are called and no objection is lodged, then the marriage is valid."

Melissa gave a gasp of astonishment. All this time, she had been mistaken — Monty was truly her husband. For the first time, she saw doubt pass across Lord Bentley's face, but he masked it quickly.

"Nonsense! How could anyone object to banns read in a different county entirely? That is nonsense."

"Shall we go to York and ask the Archbishop?" Monty said. "I am certain he can give us a definitive ruling. And as to the so-called marriage conducted this night, I am very sure my wife did not give her consent and that *is* a prerequisite of any legal marriage."

By this time, Melissa saw that the Marquess of Carrbridge, Lord Reggie, Lord Humphrey and Mr Merton had all descended from the marquess's travelling carriage, as well as several grooms. Behind Lord Bentley, however, his henchmen had arrayed themselves, with Cornelius and Mr Pontefract now pushing through to stand beside the earl. But Monty was very calm, his arm firmly around her waist, and she clung to him as if to a floating spar in a flood.

"What is going on?" Mr Pontefract said, his face red. Then, seeing Monty, he cried, "Unhand my wife, sir, at once!"

To Melissa's amazement, Monty actually laughed. "And who are you, pray?"

"Norman Pontefract, of Winchester, and that, sir, is Mrs Pontefract. And *this*, in case you are too ignorant to know, is Lord Bentley. The *Earl* of Bentley, you know. Kindly respect his lordship's wishes in this matter."

"By all means, let us introduce ourselves," Monty said affably. "I am Lord Montague Marford, and you are acquainted with Lady Montague, I believe. This gentleman is my brother, the Marquess of Carrbridge."

"Ah." Mr Pontefract looked from Monty to Melissa to the marquess and then to the earl. "Bentley, I do not think—"

"Have no fear, Pontefract, we shall have the little whore back in your bed before long."

"Bentley—"

"Really, Lord Bentley," Monty said, "that is no way to speak about your sister."

There was an abrupt silence. Melissa looked at Monty in astonishment. *That* story would never fly! The earl knew perfectly well— Yet he did not speak. He only exchanged a quick glance with

Cornelius and made no effort to deny it. Surely it could not be possible?

Mr Pontefract threw up his hands in surrender. "I care not who she is, but this is too tricky by half for me. You are not worth it, my dear, fortune or no. You may have her, and welcome, Lord Montague. She is a little termagant, and will make your life a misery, I daresay."

"But she is *my* little termagant," Monty said complacently.

Pontefract stumped back to the inn, and Lord Bentley seemed flummoxed. His mouth opened and closed once or twice, but no sound emerged.

"Well, I shall bid you all a good—" Monty began in amiable tones.

It was Cornelius who let out a shriek of pure anger. "Are you just going to stand there, Randolph, and let it all slip away? Well, if you have not the guts to take action, I do." He produced a pistol from one pocket. Several people in the watching crowd screamed, and jumped backwards in alarm. "If Pontefract is not to have your money, you little witch, then you will not either."

And he pointed the pistol directly at Melissa.

Monty spun her abruptly round to put himself between her and the gun. There was a violent bang, Monty gave a squeak of surprise, and then slid silently to the ground.

~~~~~

Monty could not quite work out what had happened. He was lying down in a public place, which was something a gentleman ought never to do, and somewhere nearby there seemed to be a mill going on, for he could hear shouts and scuffling and shrieks and the unmistakable sounds of fists colliding with bony structures. And then there was this searing pain that made it hard to think.

"Monty? Oh, Monty! Is he alive? He is alive, I think."

Melissa. He tried to say her name, but it came out as a groan.

"His feet, Merton. Now... lift."

The world shifted, pain exploded everywhere and Monty screamed. Then, darkness.

When he came to himself again, he was in a carriage which was, it seemed to him, being jounced about with the sole intent of aggravating the pain in his side. No, not his side, his arm, he thought. His eyes stayed closed but he could hear voices.

"Is he going to die?" Melissa, sounding terrified.

"Nobody dies from piffling bullet holes like that. Went straight through." The confident voice of Humphrey.

"But I do not understand..." Carrbridge, in plaintive tones.

Another excessive jolt brought a groan to Monty's lips.

"Monty? Oh, Monty! You are going to be perfectly all right. We are just taking you to a surgeon."

He opened his eyes a fraction, and there she was, his lovely Melissa. "'Lissa," he murmured happily. "Per... fectly a' right." And he was, he decided. Everything was all right as long as Melissa was there. "Don' go 'way 'gain."

"I shall not, I promise."

Then there was the surgeon's house to be got into, and the fellow poking him about in the most abominable way, and then bandaging him up tightly. After a dose of laudanum, however, he felt much more the thing.

"There, you'll do, my lord," said the surgeon. "How far do you mean to travel today?"

"Just beyond Sagborough," Carrbridge said.

"Ah. Good roads most of the way, then. Get him straight to bed when he gets home, and have your own man look at him every day, and he will do well enough. I'll have your carriage brought round." And he disappeared to attend to it.

"Well," Monty said, looking around at the sombre faces of Melissa, his brothers, and Merton afterwards. "A fine set of fellows, these Brockenhursts. I suppose they will get away with it."

"I suppose they will," Carrbridge said gloomily. "For Lady Monty's sake, we do not want to announce to the world that she spent the night at a coaching inn with a fellow like Pomegranate or Pomfret or whatever his name was."

"Pontefract, like the town," Melissa said.

"Did he... injure you?" Carrbridge said gravely.

"He did not. I told him that he would be hanged if he touched me, and he was in sufficient doubt not to risk it. When he fell asleep I was able to escape."

"How clever you are!" Monty said, reaching out his hand. She took it, and knelt beside him.

"Oh, Monty, but is it really true? We are properly married even though I am not of age?"

"As a man of God, I never lie," he said solemnly. "Yes, we are properly married. I took care we married by the banns, and not by licence to be sure of it."

"But you lied about the other thing — you said I was his sister, and that cannot be true."

"And yet it is. Here, I have — ow! You will have to fish in this pocket for me, my love. You will find a letter in there from Gus. It was appallingly delayed by the weather, but it reached me yesterday. Read it out, for I have not yet told the others about it."

She unfolded the paper, which was filled with a strongly masculine hand. *'My dear brother, Dunmorton remembers the whole business of the wager of the daughter, but it was not anyone called Frost, for he knows no one of that name. It was the Earl of Bentley who wagered his daughter. She was his eldest daughter, and the only child of his second wife, a Miss Emilia Davenport, who was half French. When the child was six months old, the mother ran away with a French tutor, and took the child with her. Bentley thought they were both dead, and refused to have them mentioned in his hearing. After some years, the mother died and Bentley discovered the child was living only ten miles away with her nurse's family. He greatly disliked her, for she reminded him too much of his late wife, and Dunmorton thinks he would have been glad to be rid of her. Hence the wager. Monty, is it possible this Melissa Frost is in fact this daughter?'*

"No," she said softly. "It cannot be... The late Lord Bentley was my father?"

"It must be so," Monty said. "Merton, pray explain it. My brain is a trifle muddled just now."

"Of course, my lord. Lady Montague, the late Lord Bentley wagered his daughter, the late Lord Carrbridge confirmed it in writing and that confirmation contains your name and came to you. The inescapable conclusion is that you are Lord Bentley's daughter. Since you have the same birth date as that recorded in Debrett's for the Lady Emily Brockenhurst, clearly Melissa Frost and Lady Emily are one and the same person. Why you have been called Melissa Frost all these years is unknown, but you are indeed the earl's legitimate daughter."

Her expression was suddenly fearful. "If I married in the wrong name... does that invalidate the marriage?"

Monty gave a little smile. "No, because it is the name you were commonly known by. We are legally married in every way, Melissa. You cannot escape me now."

"Thank heavens!"

The surgeon came in just then to announce that the coach was in readiness, and willing hands supported Monty into it. Melissa took her place beside him, but her face was ashen. It was a shock, of course. She had been brought up thinking herself nobody at all, an unwelcome charge on her guardian, and Monty knew it would be hard for her to get used to the idea of being the daughter of an earl, and sister to the present earl.

As the coach lurched into motion, Merton coughed delicately. "My lord, it would be helpful to have this new information confirmed as soon as possible. One would not want there to be any doubt about the matter."

"What do you propose, Merton?" Carrbridge said.

"We could talk to Lord Bentley now, discreetly. With his brother liable to be hauled away by the constables, he might be amenable to being open with your lordship, if Monty agrees not to pursue any charges against Mr Cornelius Brockenhurst. And we could find out about this fortune that was mentioned."

"Yes, I did not understand that at all," Carrbridge said in aggrieved tones. "Lady Monty came to us in rags, almost, and now there is talk of a fortune."

"There had to be some reason why Lord Bentley would go to such lengths to recover his ward," Merton said. "And Lady Montague will be of age in just a few days and would probably have control of her own money. Unless she should happen to be married."

"Well, let us go back to the inn, then, and see if these people are still there," Carrbridge said.

"I do not want to see them again," Melissa said distressfully. "I *never* want to see them again."

"And you need not," Carrbridge said soothingly. "You may stay here in the carriage with Humphrey and Reggie to protect you, and John Coachman and the grooms. Mr Merton and Monty and I will see Lord Bentley, if he is even there. It may be that he has left already and the point is moot."

Monty had no great desire to delay their departure from Tadcaster, but he supposed it made sense. Bentley would be in a position to confirm that Melissa was indeed his sister, something which might otherwise be very difficult to prove. So they returned to the yard of the White Hart Inn, which was now engaged in its regular occupation, and one would be hard-pressed to recognise it as the scene of such drama not two hours earlier.

The innkeeper was very pleased to see them. "For the constables is here, your lordship, and very wishful to talk to the young gentleman that was shot and not taking kindly to you whisking him away, like."

"They had sooner he expired on the cobbles, I daresay," Carrbridge said. "Good heavens, when a man is shot and wounded, one can hardly deny him the attentions of a surgeon in case the constables might wish to talk to him."

"Exactly what I said myself, your lordship," the innkeeper said. "This way if you please."

"The constables may have five minutes to talk to Lord Montague," Carrbridge said. "He is still fragile, indeed, we are extremely lucky he is alive."

The constables were engaged in a futile attempt to interview Cornelius Brockenhurst, who, owing to the circumstance of being locked into the inn's wine cellar, was availing himself rather freely of the refreshments therein. He was reclining on the floor, a bottle in each hand, singing a bawdy song at the top of his lungs, while his brother remonstrated with him.

The constables retreated thankfully to the more civilised surroundings of a private parlour, and Monty was glad to sit down, for he was feeling rather wobbly. His tale was soon told, and the innkeeper pushed a brandy into his hand and told him to "Drink up, my lord, and you'll be right as a trivet in no time."

Monty doubted it, but the idea of drinking up seemed a good one to him. He drank and let the others tell their versions of events, interrupted no more than twenty times by Lord Bentley, who had followed them with a glowering expression.

"There, now you have got all the information we have to give you, so you may take yourselves away, my good fellows," Carrbridge said to the constables. "We wish to talk privily with Lord Bentley."

"But—"

"Out."

And they went tamely, perhaps not liking to argue with a marquess. Monty was glad of it, and hoped there would be some refreshing silence for a while, for his head was beginning to hurt. But silence was not to be had.

"Now, Bentley, do sit down and let us talk," Carrbridge said. "Merton, explain to Lord Bentley."

Merton coughed slightly. "My lord, it would be helpful to everyone if this matter could be resolved as expeditiously and quietly as possible. You undoubtedly hope that your brother may be spared any... unpleasant consequences, and Lord Montague wishes to spare his wife any social awkwardness that may arise from this night's work. I am sure all those concerned will readily agree to remain silent on the details of what has occurred, knowing that any attempt to discredit Lady Montague would inevitably lead to ruin for Mr Cornelius Brockenhurst. You understand, my lord, I am sure." Bentley nodded curtly. "To that end, Lord Montague is prepared to withdraw any complaint against your brother, if you would be willing to provide the evidence for Lady Montague's birth rank, and supply details of her fortune."

Bentley's eyes grew speculative, but Carrbridge said firmly, "Bentley, we are both peers, so let us recall both the privileges and the obligations of our rank, and try to merit the nobility that God has seen fit to bestow upon us. Really, you had much better earn my gratitude than my enmity. All I ask for is a little sensible cooperation."

"Very well, very well, although I do not know what evidence I can give you."

"A signed statement that Melissa Frost is also Lady Emily Brockenhurst would be sufficient," Merton said.

"I suppose I might do that."

"Why *is* she called Frost, by the way?"

"I have not the least idea. As to the fortune, the size of it, or the identity of the trustees, or any other matter, I know nothing, except that a man met me every year in London asking me to confirm that Melissa was still living in my care, and thereafter five hundred pounds was transferred to my bank. If she married, that sum would go to her husband, and the whole amount when she reached the age of one and twenty. Everything else about it is a mystery to me, except that it kept us afloat for years. Not sure how we will go on now."

"Your brother is a personable young man, I imagine, when he is not shooting people," Carrbridge said. "Have him look about for an heiress. Lady Carrbridge has some skill in that line, and if we can settle matters satisfactorily between us, I am sure she can help."

Bentley nodded slowly. "That is… generous, Carrbridge. I say, your brother is a very queer colour."

Monty was hot, and his head was spinning. No, the whole room was spinning, which was very odd. He could hear voices talking, but it was a distant rumble, like a waterfall. Or was that his own blood rushing in his ears? He wished they would… he wished… Why was his face resting against the carpet? He could not make it out at all, so he closed his eyes and let sleep overwhelm him.

22: Letters

When Monty woke, he was lying full length in the carriage, covered with a rug. It had been Great-aunt Zinnia's carriage, of course, he had forgotten that. The old lady had abhorred inns, and had arranged her travelling coach so that she need never stay in one, instead sleeping in her coach and driving through the night. It was very convenient now to have a travelling carriage whose interior converted so readily to a bed. The blinds were drawn up, although a little daylight crept around the edges. The steady motion and lack of bumps suggested they were on the main road. His arm throbbed a little and he was weak and dizzy, but the carriage was warm and comfortable.

He wondered where the others were, but it was not a particularly pressing problem, for if he turned his head by the tiniest amount he could see Melissa curled up beside him, fast asleep. If Melissa were with him, then there could not be anything amiss. He shifted slightly so that he could gaze at her whole face, calm in repose. If there were more light, he suspected he would see the evidence of her tears on that calm face. What a dreadful night she had endured! Had she had any sleep at all? Probably not. Nor had he, come to that, and then he had been shot and lost a great deal of blood and given laudanum and brandy... no wonder he had fallen asleep.

After a while, the carriage jolted more than usual, and Melissa's eyes fluttered half open, and then, abruptly, fully open.

"Monty? How do you feel? Oh, what a stupid question! I mean, are you in pain? Or dizzy? Or... or anything untoward?"

He smiled at her. "Apart from a bullet hole in my arm, nothing in the least untoward. Oh, Melissa!" He ran a finger down her cheek — so soft, so deliciously soft! "I thought you were lost to me, that I would never see you again, my dear one."

"That was my fear also," she said. "To have so much happiness in my life, and then to have it snatched away! If Mr Pontefract had— But let us not speak of that, for nothing happened and you came to rescue me, dear, sweet Monty. I know not how you managed to arrive at just that inn at just that moment, but I thank God for it."

"You had rather thank Mr Haddington," he said. "He was outraged to be used in such a manner, and for a lady to be abducted from under his very nose. By the time Lady Reggie had driven back to Great Mellingham with the dreadful news, and Humphrey and I had been fetched, and we all returned to Sagborough to pick up the trail, Mr Haddington had done all our work for us. He was able to furnish us with an excellent description of your abductors and their vehicle, and to inform us that it was last seen heading south on the London road. After that, it was a matter of enquiring at every inn along the way. We were fortunate that they never turned off the main road, and that the earl gave his own name everywhere. How foolish of him. If ever I have occasion to abduct a lady, I shall be sure to manage the affair more deviously."

She smiled, and stroked his face. "Clearly you are feeling better if you can manage to joke about it."

"How could I not be better when my Melissa is with me?" he said simply.

"Oh, Monty!"

She moved closer and then, to his infinite joy, brought her lips to his. Such sweetness in her kiss! If only he could stay like this for ever, warm, comfortable, one lock of her hair tickling his neck, the carriage rocking them gently as happiness fizzed inside him like champagne. A sudden jolt threw her sideways, and then they were both laughing, and kissing again, and laughing even more. But then she became serious.

"Monty, I cannot tell you how sorry I am for making your life so miserable. I was so terrified that Mr Pontefract would find me, or that you would send me back to him, that I think I was half mad with fear. I should have told you everything at once."

"That is all in the past," he said. "You need never fear that dreadful man again, or your brothers. You are mine to protect now, and to love, and to cherish always."

"As you are mine," she whispered. "I am going to make you so happy, my darling. I do love you so, Monty! I never imagined it was possible to love someone so much. When I thought I would never see you again… I have no words for what I felt. Such utter despair! I was afraid that nothing would ever be right again. My life has not had many happy times, my love, but these few short weeks with you have been so blissful, I cannot tell you—"

And then the tears came, and he wrapped his good arm around her, and pulled her close, kissing her forehead and then, when she lifted her face, her lips again. And despite the aching in his arm and the jolting of the carriage, he felt life could furnish no greater felicity. He was the luckiest man alive.

~~~~~

The carriage took them directly to Drummoor, and Lord Carrbridge refused to countenance any alternative.

"Lady Carrbridge will be beside herself with anxiety, and will never forgive me if I do not take you to her at once," he said firmly, and not all Melissa's protests could shift him on the matter.

In truth, she was not sorry for it. Her home at Kirby Grosswick was still full of displaced labourers, not to mention innumerable men with saws and hammers and paintbrushes and buckets of plaster. It was not a comfortable place. And when she saw Lady Carrbridge's white face waiting to greet them, and found herself led to the rooms she had shared with Monty before, fires burning merrily and servants busily arranging everything in the most comfortable manner, she was glad of it. Besides, Dr Hay was still in the house, and so Monty would have the best care as he recovered.

It was rather strange, Melissa found, to sit down to dinner in the green dining room, just as if nothing had happened at all. Only Monty's sling suggested the momentous events of the last two days. The conversation was mostly about the forthcoming wedding between Lady Hardy and Mr Merton, and the progress of little Lady Mary, and all the other domestic trivia of the house. But when the second course had been removed and they had arrived at the dessert, Lord Carrbridge rose to make the announcement that the former Miss Melissa Frost had been discovered, in fact, to be the Lady Emily Brockenhurst, eldest daughter of the fifth Earl of Bentley, and that a fresh notice of her marriage would be sent to the Gazette so that the whole world would know the truth of the matter.

"Is that really necessary?" she whispered to Monty when Lord Carrbridge sat down. "Must the whole world know of it?"

"It is best," he said. "The original notice was incorrect, you see. Besides, it is shameful that your father denied you the position due to your rank for all those years. The world is entitled to know of it and judge him accordingly. And also, one does not want there to be any doubt in the matter. Carrbridge has a signed statement from your brother attesting to the truth, and that will ensure that the entries in Debrett's may be made correctly. Everything must be done in proper form."

"My brother…" she said wonderingly. "I have three brothers and three sisters, and never realised it before. How odd!"

"I do not think your two eldest brothers are a particular asset to you," Monty said, with a wry smile. "One tried to force you into marriage, and the other tried to shoot you. I hope your younger brother and sisters are more civilised."

"They are lovely!" she cried. "I helped to raise them, and became their unofficial governess and loved them dearly. I wish I might see them again."

"And so you shall," he said, smiling.

"But I do not even know where they are."

"That can be discovered. We shall find them, have no fear. Another helping of syllabub?"

When the ladies withdrew, they all gathered around Melissa and she was left in no doubt of their sympathy.

"I am very sorry to say it of Lord Bentley and Mr Brockenhurst, for they are your brothers, after all," Lady Carrbridge said, "but I cannot like them. They have behaved abominably towards you, and kept you as an unpaid servant, and withheld your fortune from you, and I do not intend to acknowledge any acquaintance with them if they are in town. I shall never forget your appearance when you arrived here."

"Oh, indeed, her clothes so old and worn," said Lady Juliana.

"And she was so *thin*," said Lady Carrbridge. "That is despicable, to keep one's own sister without adequate food, for look how you have filled out since you first arrived, dear Melissa.

Why, you have a charming form now. I do believe we shall need to let out your gowns a little before too long."

And that set the aunts twittering and hinting about other possible causes for the tightness of her gowns, and although Melissa blushed, she knew that it was entirely the result of her fondness for syllabub. Still, perhaps before too long there might be another reason for a little extra stoutness?

~~~~~

The following morning at breakfast, Mr Merton entered with a great stack of letters.

"Everything was held up by the snows," he said. "Most of these came yesterday, and I have only just now sorted them out. Lady Carrbridge... my lord... my lord... my lady... oh, and one for Lady Montague."

"For me?" Her stomach clenched in sudden alarm. "Who writes to me?" She turned it over and over in her hands, all her fears rushing back to swamp her.

"You will not know unless you open it," Monty said gently.

With shaking hands she broke the seal. "Oh! It is from Lady Bentley... Patience, Lady Bentley, that is. The fifth earl's third wife."

"Your step-mama, then," Monty said.

"Oh yes! So she is... I had not realised. Oh, Monty, she must have written to me before... *'My previous letters...'* she says. I hardly know what it says. What does she say, Monty? Has something happened to one of the children? I cannot make it out."

He took the paper from her trembling hands. "Shall I read it to you? *'My dearest Melissa, It was the greatest surprise to see the notice of your marriage in the newspaper, for I had not the least notion that you were acquainted with that family. But perhaps Randolph finally did his duty by you and arranged it all. However it came about, I wish you the greatest joy, my dear, and it pleases me so much to know that you will at last be valued as you should be. We are all well, and William's arm has mended beautifully and he is already riding again, although more circumspectly! As I mentioned in my previous letters, we have no hope that Randolph will do anything at all for the girls, but my godmother has a niece to bring out next season and has offered to take Alice to London with her, and will even pay for her gowns. It is the greatest kindness, and she is so pretty and good-natured that she is bound to marry advantageously, although we do not tell her so, for there is nothing so fatal as the weight of one's family's expectations, as I know myself only too well. Alice herself is in transports to think that she will see you in town, but I do not think it likely you will move in the same circles. You are very much risen in the world, my dear Melissa! Might I hope that you will be able to write to me now? I daresay Randolph would not frank your letters, and you wished to spare us having to pay, but perhaps the marquess might be so obliging as to frank them? It would delight me so much to hear from you. Your loving friend, Patience.'"*

The room had fallen silent, everyone listening in astonishment. Melissa was too choked with misery to say a word, dashing away tears with the back of one hand.

"You never received her letters, did you?" Monty said softly. She shook her head. "You did not even know her direction. And this Lady Bentley is the present Lord Bentley's stepmama, and Alice is his sister, yet they seemingly live in poverty."

"That man is a disgrace," Lord Carrbridge said loudly, laying down his own sheaf of papers. "I will frank every letter you write, Lady Monty, and when you write to Lady Bentley, you will oblige me by finding out what I may do for her. Schooling for the boy, perhaps. As for the daughter—"

"I shall take care of Lady Alice," Lady Carrbridge said, tears sparkling in her eyes. "It is within my power to give her a season such as all girls dream of, and if she is amenable, she may look as high as she pleases for a husband. And we shall make sure everyone knows that her own brother would not do it."

"As to that, perhaps it would be best not to rub Bentley's nose in it," Lord Carrbridge said mildly. "We are trying to put the recent difficulties between the two families behind us, after all."

"Well, that will diminish the fun a little, to be sure," said his wife. "Nevertheless, I shall enjoy showing off Lady Alice. In fact, let us have her to stay here, now that the weather is a little better. Where does she live?"

Monty looked at the letter. "Birmingham."

"Birmingham. Good gracious. I never knew anyone from Birmingham before. But by all means let her come. And her mother and her brother, if they are so minded."

"There are two other sisters, as well," Melissa said, laughing. "You should perhaps know the exact numbers before you issue a general invitation."

"The more the merrier," Lady Carrbridge said at once. "We have been very quiet since Christmas and it is weeks yet before we go to town, so let us have some company. There are a few others I could invite. I shall go and make a list at once."

"There now," said Lord Carrbridge, as his wife bustled out of the room. "That has done her a world of good. She has been so quiet since Mary was born, not at all herself. A little company will be— Oh, of all the vexatious things!" He waved the letter in his hand in annoyance.

"What is it?" Monty said. "Shall I fetch Merton back? He is very good at dealing with vexatious correspondence."

245

Lord Carrbridge threw down the letter he had been reading. "Gil is being sent home. Of all the foolish—! That boy will be the death of me, I swear it."

"What has he done this time?" Monty said, but he was smiling as he spoke. "Is his leg healed?"

"Not properly, for the little idiot will not stay quiet and rest. His colonel says that he has been getting into fights and has aggravated his injury, not to mention making himself unpopular with his fellow officers. And there is somebody's wife involved, as well."

"There is always somebody's wife involved, where Gil is concerned," Monty said, laughing.

"True, but this time they are sending him home to spend some time in the soothing bosom of his family, according to his colonel. We may expect him within the week, and then we shall no doubt have him up to his high jinks here instead of there. Mrs Compton will need to keep the house maids out of his way. Good Lord, whatever did I do to deserve a brother like Gil?"

"He will settle down," Monty said. "We all went through a foolish phase and got into a great deal of trouble, and we all grew up eventually. I am sure that Gil will too, one of these days. And he has never played around with the house maids. His tastes always ran to married women, who cannot see beyond that angelic face of his. He is not one to corrupt innocents. You worry about him too much, Carrbridge."

Lord Carrbridge stared at him, then turned to Melissa. "Lady Monty, I congratulate you. You have wrought a great miracle with Monty, and turned him into a normal human being. He was quite a saint before, and very wearing it was to be with him, let me tell you. But now he hardly ever quotes the Bible at us, and is far less inclined to burst into prayer. It is a great relief to us all."

Monty laughed. "I was a sanctimonious prig. Humphrey said so, and he was quite right. But now I am far too happy to be sanctimonious. You may all do as you please without the least censure from me, except on Sundays, when I shall don my vestments and terrorise my congregation with visions of eternal damnation for those who fail to show the proper respect to Lady Monty."

"Ah, yes — love," Lord Carrbridge said, smiling fondly. "It makes contented slaves of us all, in the end."

~~~~~

On the following Saturday, Monty left for Kirby Grosswick. His arm was well enough healed to contemplate resuming his duties as vicar, and he was curious to see what state the village was in and whether the flood waters had receded sufficiently to enable the labourers to return to their cottages. He had no desire to leave Melissa, but he could not shirk his obligations. But to his delight, she asked if she might go with him.

"I do not want to spend even one night without you," she said, hugging him tightly, and this was so much in accordance with his own wishes that he agreed to it at once.

He sent word ahead to ensure that he would at least have good dinners to look forward to, however great the disruption to every other part of his establishment. But he found no such disruption. The labourers had gone, some back to their homes, some to friends and a couple of families to the stables, where they had turned the unused side of the hayloft into a comfortable temporary home, repaying the debt by helping in the kitchens and gardens. The house was clean, and two more rooms had been finished. Monty now had a book room, and Melissa a drawing room, so they spent the afternoon in the pleasant task of arranging furniture to their liking.

The church was as full as it could hold for both services, Monty was pleased to see, and after each service there was no restraint between the residents of long-standing and Bridget Kelly and her women. In fact, several men could be seen in close attendance, among them Ben Gartmore, chatting to Kitty with an easy to read expression on his face.

"I daresay you will be wanting a permanent position here," Monty said to him with a smile, as they made their way back to the parsonage after the second service.

Ben looked conscious. "I'd like that, if you'd be willing to have me and if his lordship the marquess don't mind. There's plenty for me to do in the garden, and you'll need a gamekeeper to manage your coverts. They've been a bit neglected, by the look of them. And… those old cottages behind the stables just need a bit of doing up."

He looked so hopeful that Monty could not help laughing. "Then choose one and do it up, Ben. Far be it for me to stand in the way of true love."

"Thank you, my lord," Ben said, with the wide grin that reminded Monty forcibly of Gil. Ben was so much a Marford, it was almost a shame he could not have the name.

One surprise was that Callum, the former vicar's manservant, had begun attending services again. He joined in the responses loudly and displayed a fine baritone voice during the hymns. He even smiled at Monty as he filed out of church.

"He looks a lot better," he whispered to Melissa.

"I think he was driven half mad by being cooped up with Mr Whittaker all those years. Mrs Green says he is helping in the kitchen, and she does not mind him mumbling to himself all the time. I am glad we never sent him to the work house."

"That would have been too cruel for words," Monty said. "What is our dinner tonight, my love?"

"Goose for you and syllabub for me," she said, laughing.

"Splendid," he said.

And so it was. Afterwards, Melissa decorously withdrew upstairs to the drawing room. Monty sat over his port for perhaps five minutes before rising to join her. But first, he went to his bedroom to retrieve a neatly wrapped package.

"I have a small gift for you," he said, as he entered the drawing room. "I promised you some proper jewellery once we were married, and here it is."

Her astonishment and pleasure were all he had hoped for. The emeralds caught the candlelight and created a thousand dazzling points of light.

"Oh, Monty, you are so good to me! These are beautiful."

"Then they are well suited to their owner," he said complacently, taking them from her and fastening the jewels around her neck. "There! And there are ear drops and a bracelet too. Happy birthday, my darling one."

"My birthday! I had almost forgotten," she said.

"But I had not. You are of age now, and your fortune is your own."

"Except that I do not know where it is or how to claim it!"

"A minor detail. We will make enquiries when we are in town."

"I daresay it will turn out to be nothing much at all," she said, laughing. "And I should have so liked to have my own carriage, and not an unwanted old thing from Drummoor. Ah well." She went to the looking glass, turning this way and that to admire her emeralds. "It does not matter, for I have all the fortune I need. I have you, Monty dear, and what more could any woman want for?"

He wrapped his arms around her waist and kissed her neck. "And I have you," he murmured. "My sweet, wonderful Melissa."

23: Family

Mary, Lady Hardy married Mr Daniel Merton on a sleety day in early February. No one minded the weather in the slightest, for the ceremony was held in the Drummoor chapel, officiated with aplomb by Monty, and witnessed by some fifty friends, relations and servants. The bride was beautiful, her new husband smiled constantly, and no one could doubt their happiness or the strength of their attachment.

Afterwards, there was a wedding breakfast in the great hall, and when all had eaten their fill and toasted the happy couple sufficiently, a small group of stout-hearted souls donned cloaks and furs and scarves to accompany Mr and Mrs Merton on the short walk to their home through the softly falling snow. Uniformed servants waited on the steps, despite the weather, to welcome their new mistress.

Monty and Melissa walked hand in hand through the spacious rooms of Lake Cottage, each one fitted out with the greatest elegance, and furnished with the newest styles of furniture.

"Now this is how it should be done," Monty murmured. "Mr Merton has ensured that everything is in readiness for his bride. No cast-off furniture, no smell of paint or newly cut wood, and undoubtedly there will be a good dinner on the table this afternoon."

Melissa laughed. "You do like a good dinner, husband dear. This house is beautiful, but I like our way better. Besides, Mr and Mrs Merton had to wait several months to marry, until she was out of mourning, so there was plenty of time to prepare the house. I should not have liked to wait so long."

Monty suspected that the Mertons had been waiting somewhat longer than a few months, but he said nothing of it. If they had fallen in love while she was still married, they had managed the business very discreetly and no one could have found the slightest cause for censure in their behaviour. Monty said only, "It is very pleasing that such patience has met its reward at last."

Although she declared herself content with her half-finished house, Melissa decided to stay at Drummoor a while longer. She and Monty drove over to Kirby Grosswick each Saturday, entertained some half a dozen of the local worthies to dinner, participated in the Sunday offices and returned to Drummoor on Monday. From time to time, Melissa and Monty stayed overnight with Lord and Lady Reggie, or with Lord and Lady Humphrey, and Melissa began to feel as if she belonged to this sprawling Marford family.

Her friends from the past arrived, Patience with her four children, who wept all over Melissa, and hugged her very tight and then wept some more. Lady Carrbridge looked Alice over with a practised eye and then swept her away to spend the afternoon trying on gowns.

"Why did you go to Birmingham?" Melissa asked Patience one day.

"That is where my sister lived," she replied. "She and her husband have no children of their own and a large house to maintain, so they were glad enough to have my modest jointure to help with the expenses. Between us we had just about enough to live upon, so we managed well enough."

"But you are a countess," Monty said, in his gentle way. "There should have been a dower house or some such."

"Oh, the dower house was sold years ago, and there was no money to spare for me or the children. I shall be very thankful for Alice to have her season, though. It was much spoken of when my husband was alive. He always promised that she, at least, would have a proper season, no matter the cost. But Randolph will not do it. Well, he has not the money, poor man. He inherited little but the title, the hall and a mass of debts. No wonder he wanted to keep hold of your allowance, my dear Melissa. And he married very foolishly — a widow, and not a penny to her name, so I heard. It will be down to Cornelius to restore the family's fortunes. And so you are on good terms with them? That surprises me."

"It would be very bad to have it spread about that I spent the night locked into a bed chamber with a man who was not my husband," Melissa said. "And on their side, it would be very bad for Cornelius to be had up in court accused of attempted murder. So it is agreed that we will put it behind us. Randolph has written to me in very conciliatory terms."

"He just wants to keep in with the Marfords," Monty said.

"You are a cynic," Melissa said, smiling fondly at him.

"A realist," he said. "That does not make the approach unwelcome, however. At least now we will not have to decide whether to cut him if we meet in town."

"True, and I do not have to worry about my family any more." She squeezed Patience's hand as she spoke.

"There is always something to worry about with families," Monty said. "You would think that Carrbridge would be happy enough, would you not? He has his fortune restored and is once again one of the richest men in the kingdom, thanks to Merton. Sharp has gone, his little empire returned to its rightful owner, his misappropriated fortune dissipated. His wife — if she is indeed his wife — is behind bars in Northumberland awaiting trial for her crimes. Yet Carrbridge is not happy. He worries about Sharp, and believes he may still be capable of some mischief."

"Is he right? I have never known Mr Sharp so I cannot judge."

"Sharp is too clever to be vindictive. I am certain he still has money secreted away, and if he is sensible, he will take that and slip away quietly. Somewhere abroad, perhaps, where he is not known and cannot be pursued. That would be the course any man of sense would take, and Sharp was ever quick-witted. He will never be seen again. But Carrbridge frets over him. And then there is Gil."

"Is there still no word of him?"

"Nothing, but he was always so, prone to vanish. He is so distractible. There will be a mill somewhere or a curricle race or some such. All we know is that he has left his camp at Dover, heading for London on the first stage of his journey here, and has not been seen or heard from since. But he will turn up. He always does."

~~~~~

One day a huge, antiquated coach drew up outside the door. From it alighted four portly bewigged gentlemen in sombre black.

"Good gracious, who can this be?" Melissa cried, spying them from the library window where she was making use of the daylight to read.

Monty set down his pen, for he had been trying to write his sermon for the next Sunday, and came to the window to look. "I have no idea. I never saw them before in my life. They will be here to see Carrbridge, I expect."

And so it seemed, for they were admitted to the house and led away to some inner fastness. Melissa returned to her book, and

Monty to his sermon. But it was not long before Mr Merton tap-tapped his way across the vast expanse of wooden floor.

"Beg pardon, my lord, but there are four gentlemen from London waiting in the ship room."

"Want do they want of me?" Monty said.

"Actually… it is Lady Montague they wish to see, if you permit," Mr Merton said.

"Who are they, Merton, and what do they want with Lady Montague?"

"The gentlemen are lawyers, my lord, although they have not divulged the purpose of their visit."

"How very mysterious," Monty said. "Are we at home, my dear?"

Melissa was too astonished at the very idea of refusing to see anyone, let alone lawyers who had travelled all the way from London, to formulate a reply. Luckily, Monty saw her difficulty and laughed.

"Well, perhaps that would not be very civil, although it is usual to write and make an appointment on such occasions."

"Indeed it is," said Mr Merton in disapproving tones. "They are fortunate that you are not at Kirby Grosswick or visiting elsewhere. It is not mannerly to call without an invitation."

"Perhaps they wished to surprise us?" Melissa said.

"Then they have succeeded in their objective," Monty said gravely. "Come, let us go and unmask our secretive and unmannerly visitors."

The ship room seemed rather full. The four severe-faced lawyers were arrayed upon a line of chairs, and by the similarity of feature and the gradual increase of roundness from youngest to oldest, Melissa suspected they might be brothers.

"Ah, Monty, Lady Monty," Carrbridge said, with signs of panic in his eyes. "Do come in. These gentlemen are from Cummings, Cummings, Cummings and Cummings, a legal firm London. They are all called Mr Cummings. Gentlemen, Lady Montague Marford, Lord Montague Marford."

"Good day to you, gentlemen," Monty said politely. "You wished to see Lady Montague, I understand?"

The eldest Mr Cummings was the spokesman. "We wish to speak to the lady who was known to the world as Miss Melissa Frost, ward of the Earl of Bentley, of Bentley Hall in the county of Hampshire."

"I am… *was* Melissa Frost," she said, although greatly wondering at what it all meant. What could these four imposing gentlemen have to do with her?

"Then we are very happy to make your acquaintance at last," the lawyer said, and all four of the brothers rose and bowed in unison. "We should have discharged this duty some weeks ago, but when we went to Bentley Hall to find you, we were told only that you had gone away, and no one knew where you might be found. Fortunately, the housekeeper had seen the notice of your marriage to the Lord Montague Marford in the newspaper, and informed us of this fact. We went then to Marford House in London and were directed here. And very glad we are to have found you at last. Will you be seated, my lady?" he added gently.

Mr Merton brought forward a chair for her, and Monty stood beside her, one hand resting lightly on her shoulder. How reassuring that was! Any number of formless fears swirled in her mind, all of them centred on the terrible prospect of losing Monty, but while he was there, and touching her, no matter how lightly, she knew herself to be safe.

"We are here," the lawyer intoned, "to inform you of your parentage, and all the provisions made for you, which now come to fruition. There is much that you do not know of your history which we are here to convey to you. You must be prepared for a great shock, Lady Montague, for your true name, the name of your birth, is not Melissa Frost at all."

"Oh, I know," she said, smiling happily. "I am— I *was* Lady Emily Brockenhurst really. Monty found it all out. I am sorry if you have come all this way to tell me this."

The four lawyers all murmured at once, but the eldest Mr Cummings waved them to silence. "Excellent. Then it is not necessary to explain who your esteemed parents were, nor shall we be needing the smelling salts. Excellent. But there is much that you may not appreciate of all that was done for you over the years, so we shall recite your history as we know it, so that you may understand."

He paused to mop his brow, and Mr Merton took the opportunity to dispense glasses of Madeira to the lawyers, who all nodded their thanks.

The eldest Mr Cummings went on, "You were born at Bentley Hall, and given into the care of a nurse called Martha."

"Yes! I remember her," Melissa cried eagerly.

The lawyers smiled and nodded again. They were very good at nodding. "When you were six months old, your mother... it pains me to say this, but Lady Bentley ran away with a Frenchman, taking you with her. But she did not run far, only to Harpeth village, where you and the nurse were left with the nurse's sister, to be raised as Melissa Frost. Melissa is a corruption of your real name, Emily, and Frost — well, seemingly it was a frosty day when you were born. Her ladyship then came to us in London, and we helped her to establish funds by which you might be supported until such time as she could return to collect you."

"She meant to come back for me?" Melissa said, wide-eyed.

"Why, certainly. But she was going into France, and it was not a fit place to take a baby, not then, so she left you in a place of safety. But in case anything should happen to her, she left with us certain items — a letter certifying your identity, details of where your birth was registered, your baptismal bracelet, her marriage lines, a locket of hers." As he spoke, he laid each item on the desk in front of him. "Enough to identify you beyond doubt, Lady Montague. And we were charged with ensuring that your nurse and foster family were recompensed for your care."

He sipped his Madeira, and Melissa gazed at him in stupefaction, this elderly, plump stranger who knew so much about her. Tentatively, she stretched out a hand to the desk, where lay the small fragments of her life. In wonder, she picked up the locket — her mother's locket! The first possession of hers that she had ever held in her hands.

"When you were not yet six years old, your mother was tragically taken from the world. Her gentleman companion then came to see us. Since your mother would never now have the opportunity to reclaim you, it was your father's duty to take charge of you and raise you as a lady. The French gentleman had been very fond of your mother, and so he wished to make that possible. He was prepared to offer a handsome allowance to Lord Bentley, but only if he agreed to take you into his house, educate you appropriately and find you a suitable marriage partner when the time came. We approached Lord Bentley, but, sad to say, he was not cooperative at first. He had expunged all evidence of his wife and child from his life, and had no wish to acknowledge his daughter. However, he offered a compromise — he would assume his responsibilities towards you but only if you remained as Melissa Frost, and were introduced as his ward. We agreed to it, for we could not force him to recognise you as his daughter. Our only stipulation was that he must use your real birth date, for otherwise proving your heritage would become impossible. And so you left your foster family and moved to Bentley Hall, and we did not see you again. We were forbidden from visiting. Instead, Lord Bentley came to see us in London every year, and gave us his word as a gentleman that you were well and being raised according to the specifications laid down in the agreement. In return, we paid the allowance."

"He treated me well enough," Melissa said. "He was not a generous man, but he was not cruel. Not like his sons."

"Ah, yes," said Mr Cummings. "Everything changed when the fifth earl died. The sixth earl caused us some concerns. But by this time, you were nearing your majority, the moment when we were charged to explain everything to you, so we felt it best not to interfere. But there is one other matter of which we must speak, and that is the wager which took place between the fifth earl and the eighth Marquess of Carrbridge."

"I know all about that," Melissa said. "I had a letter promising me to the marquess's son."

"Indeed. But you may not know how that letter came to you. Lord Carrbridge came to us one day, quite unexpectedly. He knew all about you, that you were a legitimate but unacknowledged daughter, and he explained about the wager. Being himself an honourable man…" He turned here to make a little bow towards the present Lord Carrbridge. "…he wished to do the right thing by you, and therefore pledged you to his son, and wrote that letter to bind himself to the deal. He attempted to give the letter to Lord Bentley, but he would have none of it, insisting it was all nonsense. So Lord

Carrbridge came to us, and asked us to ensure that you received this pledge when you were old enough to understand it. We therefore gave it into the care of your foster family and clearly they succeeded in conveying it to you, for here you are, and married into the family, if not quite to the expected member of it. Still, it is very satisfactory."

"Yes, indeed it is," Melissa said, glancing up at Monty. He smiled down at her. Yes, it was very satisfactory.

"So it remains only for us to obtain a few details from your husband, Lady Montague, so that we may transfer the remainder of your fortune into his care. Now that you have attained your majority, the whole amount is freed from our care."

"My fortune…" she said faintly.

"Oh, yes. Your mother's gentleman friend has left you very well provided for. We do not have the exact sum, for it is scattered about rather, but it will come to at least forty thousand pounds."

There was a long silence. Melissa felt dizzy with shock, hardly aware of what was going on around her. Monty chafed her hands gently, and someone — Mr Merton, she thought — pushed a glass of brandy towards her. Forty thousand pounds! It was an inconceivably vast amount. In the last few days, she had acquired a title, an unexpected array of relations, and now an independent fortune.

"Well, Lady Monty, it seems you may have your new carriage after all," Monty said gravely.

"I grew up thinking I had nothing at all," Melissa whispered. "No family, no fortune, no name. I was just a burden on my guardian, as he told me many times. And now to discover that I am not nobody after all, that I have a name, a family, brothers and sisters, money to call my own... It is too much! I am so blessed."

And she burst into tears.

~~~~~

The day finally came when Melissa deemed the parsonage finished, or at least sufficiently finished for her to live in permanently. Drummoor was a charming house, and the marquess and marchioness made her very welcome, but there was nothing like having one's own home. She had a morning room to work in now, and a music room for entertaining, as well as several guest bedrooms, ready to be occupied by Patience and her children whenever they visited, or Miss Hay, when she held her informal surgeries for the poorest of the villagers. Together, Melissa, her step-mother and her sisters spent their days perusing the advertisements and catalogues, choosing splendid new rugs and chairs and escritoires and clocks with which to enhance the parsonage.

The new carriage arrived, and conveyed Melissa and Monty to Kirby Grosswick, and they walked into their home side by side. Melissa could hardly remember now the bleak days at Bentley Hall, and her desperate flight north to claim a husband in the Earl of Deveron. So long ago it seemed, and yet it was but a few short months.

"Is it not strange how everything has turned out?" she said to Monty, as she curled up beside him in bed that night, her head on his shoulder. "Had it not been for that drunken wager between your father and mine, I should never have met you. I should have been married to the charming Mr Pontefract, I daresay. And you only offered for me from pity, for you did not want to marry me at all."

"I was never unwilling," he said, kissing the top of her head. "There were moments when I wondered if it would ever be within my power to make you happy, for you seemed so... so *angry* sometimes, and at other times merely sad and lonely. But I always wanted to try to reach the warm, affectionate Melissa that was hidden beneath that prickly exterior. Never did I regret my offer, and it was not long before my heart was entirely yours. Darling Melissa. You bring me such joy."

"Oh, Monty!" She rolled over so that she could see his dear face clearly. "My hero. You rescued me twice, you know. Once from the humiliation of discovering that the earl I planned to marry was a child of four, and again from the clutches of Mr Pontefract. And as if that were not sufficient heroism, you also rescued half the village from the floods. What an astonishing man you are. I do not deserve to be so happy, and I shall try very hard to make you happy too."

"An admirable ambition in a wife," he said. "You could perhaps begin by giving me a kiss?"

"You shall have as many kisses as you like," she said.

With a low chuckle, he pulled her towards him, and as her lips settled on his, she closed her eyes and gave herself into the warmth of his loving embrace.

Epilogue

The chambers of Markham, Willerton-Forbes and Browning were enjoying their usual afternoon somnolence. Sir Rathbone Willerton-Forbes had had but one appointment at noon, after which he had dictated one letter to his clerk, Eversley, had read three letters delivered with the mid-day post, and perused the announcements of births, marriages and deaths in the newspaper. He had reached that depressing age when more of his acquaintance were to be found amongst the reports of the deceased than elsewhere. After that, exhausted by his labours, he drank one glass of port and snoozed in his comfortable chair behind the desk until such time as the clock struck the hour appointed for him to make his way home.

A sharp rap on the door announced the arrival of Eversley.

"A package just arrived for you, Sir Rathbone. Delivered by hand this moment. It being addressed to *'The Lawyer Acting for The Most Noble Marquess of Carrbridge'*, I dare presume it is for your eyes."

"Most Noble?" He sighed. "What is the world coming to when a man writes to a marquess without knowing the correct manner of address?"

Eversley had no answer to this rather sweeping question, so he bustled about tidying the discarded newspaper, arranging the pens and inkpot in their stand, straightening the sander and writing mat, placing the fire irons in a neat line.

Sir Rathbone stared at the unassuming package. Wrapped in brown paper and string, it was very light, as if there might be nothing inside it at all. He sighed. He could, of course, lock the package away in a drawer, and deal with it some other time. It was late and he wanted to go home, to enjoy his bath and the ministrations of his very efficient valet, to dress for dinner and stroll round to his club to eat. Then he would spend a quiet evening in pleasant conversation with some of his friends, just as he did every day of his life now, since his wife had inconsiderately died before him, leaving him quite alone in the world.

But duty was a difficult habit to shake off. Reaching for his pocket knife, he snipped the string, unfolded the brown paper and drew forth the single sheet of paper residing within.

"Shall I call you a hackney carriage, sir, or shall you walk home today?" Eversley said, looking up from his tidying.

Sir Rathbone gave a strangled sound.

"Sir? Is you having a seizure, sir? Shall I send for the physician?"

There was a long silence, then Sir Rathbone threw the paper forcefully to the desk. "Oh God!" he cried. "Oh, dear God!"

Eversley, having never heard his employer use such language before, was struck dumb with shock.

"This is a disaster," Sir Rathbone said. "The ramifications— No, it does not bear thinking of."

"Sir?"

"This, Eversley," said Sir Rathbone, picking up the paper and waving it under Eversley's nose, "is a special licence. It proves, beyond a shadow of doubt, that the eighth Marquess of Carrbridge was legally married to Miss Amelia Gartmore several months before he married Miss Adela March. And there was issue, Eversley. There was issue from that marriage. A son. What was the boy's name? Benjamin, I believe. Yes, Ben Gartmore is the true heir, and therefore the present Marquess of Carrbridge is not the legal heir. Is illegitimate, in point of fact. Oh, dear Lord, whatever is to be done?"

He put his head in his hands and groaned in despair.

Thanks for reading!

If you have enjoyed reading this book, please consider writing a short review. You can find out the latest news and sign up for the mailing list at my website: http://marykingswood.co.uk/

A note on historical accuracy - and an apology!: I have endeavoured to stay true to the spirit of Regency times, and have avoided taking too many liberties or imposing modern sensibilities on my characters. The book is not one of historical record, but I've tried to make it reasonably accurate. However, I'm not perfect! If you spot a historical error, I'd very much appreciate knowing about it so that I can correct it and learn from it. Thank you!

One area where I have taken some liberties is geographical. In *The Daughters of Allamont Hall*, I squeezed the mythical county of Brinshire into a non-existent space between Staffordshire and Shropshire. In *Sons of the Marquess*, however, Drummoor is firmly set in the (very real) county of Yorkshire, the West Riding to be precise, and not too far away from York itself. I haven't attempted to place it precisely, to give myself the freedom to add estates and towns and villages of my own invention. In the interests of such creation, several very real towns have been wiped off the map. To the good people of Yorkshire, I apologise.

About *Sons of the Marquess:* *when the ninth Marquess of Carrbridge finds himself short of funds, his five younger brothers have to make a choice: take up a career to support their lavish lifestyle or marry an heiress. But love has a strange way of appearing when it's least expected...*

Book 0: The Earl of Deveron (a novella, free to mailing list subscribers)

Book 1: Lord Reginald

Book 2: Lord Humphrey

Book 3: Lord Augustus

Book 4: Lord Montague

Book 5: Lord Gilbert

About the author

I write traditional Regency romances under the pen name Mary Kingswood, and epic fantasy as Pauline M Ross. I live in the beautiful Highlands of Scotland with my husband. I like chocolate, whisky, my Kindle, massed pipe bands, long leisurely lunches, chocolate, going places in my campervan, eating pizza in Italy, summer nights that never get dark, wood fires in winter, chocolate, the view from the study window looking out over the Moray Firth and the Black Isle to the mountains beyond. And chocolate. I dislike driving on motorways, cooking, shopping, hospitals.

Acknowledgements

Thanks go to:

My mother, who first introduced me to the wonderful world of Jane Austen.

Shayne Rutherford of Darkmoon Graphics for the cover design.

My beta reader: Mary Burnett.

Last, but definitely not least, my first reader: Amy Ross.

Sneak preview of Lord Gilbert: Chapter 1: A Winter Journey

Captain Lord Gilbert Marford was so angry he could barely form the words.

"Sent home like a schoolboy!" he hissed in a low voice. "It is the outside of enough! Who do they think I am, to be treated so? I joined the Hussars to fight the French, not kick my heels in Yorkshire."

"They might let you fight the French if you stopped fighting your fellow officers," Davy, his batman, said, without looking up from his task of folding shirts.

"I never minded being sent home from Eton, it was almost a point of honour to be rusticated once or twice a year, but I am an adult now! How could they do this to me?"

"Daresay you never got rusticated from Eton for bedding someone's wife," Davy said. "Pass me that coat, will you, Gil?"

"Actually, I did, once," Gil said, instantly diverted. "The Latin master was a dry old stick, but he had the most luscious wife whom he neglected shamefully. She had a penchant for activities that would have astonished her husband. A few of them would have astonished the Roman Emperors, I suspect. Well, *some* of the Emperors, anyway."

Davy looked up in amusement. "Did she make you dress up in a toga?"

"Ha! Not quite, but she was the greatest fun imaginable, until her husband caught us in bed one afternoon."

"Really, Gil!" But Davy was laughing. Having grown up with Gil, he was quite unshockable.

"I know, and I was supposed to be in a class with Mr Cornish, the history master. Henry the Eighth. Well, he had six wives, and I never quite saw why I should not, too."

"But at least they were his own wives," Davy said, turning back to his packing.

"Well, where is the fun in that? I am the last sensible one in the family, do you realise that, Davy? All my brothers are married now, even Monty, and I never thought to see *that*. I always liked Monty. At least he never lectured me like Carrbridge does. *You are such a trial to me, Gil. Think of the family honour. Why can you not be more like Reggie... or Humphrey... or Gus... or Monty?* Bah! At least I have been out of his disapproving eye these last few months. Sometimes I wish I were not the brother of a marquess. That is the worst of this business, being sent back to Drummoor. I had rather be flogged."

"Do you have to go? Can't you just head for London and enjoy yourself until the fuss dies down?"

"If only that were possible! But no, Colonel Jefferson has written to Carrbridge and if I fail to turn up, or disappear later, he is to write at once, and I shall be cashiered and that will be the end of it. He will really do it this time, he says. It is so annoying. There is no real harm in what I do, Davy, *you* know that."

"Aye, you get bored, that's all it is, and then you get into mischief, and if it were just a bit of a scuffle with the other officers, no one would mind that. But the Major's wife, Gil! And you really should take care with that leg of yours. Every time you ride too hard or push yourself too far, you damage it. After that horse race with Captain Walters, the sawbones was threatening to cut it off."

"Stuff!" Gil said. "Nothing wrong with my leg now. Just a bit of a limp, no more than that."

"You should take care, that's all I'm saying. There, that's the last box packed. I'll get the carriage brought round."

"Carriage!" Gil said in frustration. "How humiliating to be driven about like a dowager."

"Physician's orders," Davy said firmly. "Got to look after that leg, Gil, or you won't have a leg to worry about."

~~~~~

The first flakes of snow were falling just as they turned in to the inn yard to change horses. The place was in chaos, ostlers rushing hither and thither with teams of horses, dealing with several carriages at once, to a chorus of angry shouts.

"Sorry, nothing to spare just now," a harassed ostler told them. "Everything is out, and not a pair rested enough to put to the traces. Go inside, sir, sit by the fire. Rest for an hour or two."

"Rest!" Gil expostulated, but the man had already gone. "I hardly need rest when I have been sitting on my rear for the last two hours. We will not make London today at this rate."

"It was always unlikely," Davy said. "Specially at this time of year. Look at the weather! If it settles in, we'll be lucky to make it to Sittingbourne."

"Pfft! What is a bit of snow? I have been out in worse. Surely there must be some horses for us."

He strode into the capacious stables, dodging a steaming team of bays being led to stalls. The ostler was right, there were no horses left that were fresh enough to be put to a carriage. But there was one horse...

"You there! This hack of yours... is it for hire?"

The stable boy jumped, looked around as if wondering who was being addressed, then licked his lips nervously. "Aye, sir, but—"

"Saddle him."

"But—"

"Just do as I say. Here—" He pulled out his purse and pushed several silver coins into the boy's hands, and had the satisfaction of seeing his eyes widen. "Now saddle him. And if you get in trouble for it, tell them that it was for Captain Lord Gilbert Marford."

"Aye, milord. At once, milord."

It was the work of a few minutes for the boy to prepare the horse, although the animal danced and blew and side-stepped as if, for some unfathomable reason, he was loathe to leave his warm stable to venture out into the falling snow. Gil swung himself into the saddle, and then, as pain shot through his leg, remembered why he should have used the mounting block. He grimaced, took a deep breath and fought down the nausea that assaulted him. Then he trotted into the yard, the horse dancing about the whole time.

Davy was still standing beside their carriage, chatting amicably to a couple of the tap boys. Gil would have ridden straight past his batman with a cheerful wave had Davy not grabbed the reins, causing the horse to half rear.

"What are you doing, Gil?" he cried, more fear than anger on his face.

"What does it look like? You cannot expect me to sit here like an old woman for hours. With luck, this fellow will get me to London by nightfall."

"With luck? Gil, you're insane! It's snowing hard, you'll never make it, and think of your leg. Gil! For God's sake, Gil!"

With a quick jerk on the reins, the horse was free of Davy's restraint. With a snort, the animal bounded forward and took off through the arch, and then they were on the London road at a fast canter.

Gil laughed aloud in delight, as the snow spat freezing drops into his face. All around him, the snow fell softly, not heavy but steady now, the flakes drifting gently to earth. Already the road had a thin covering, the dark lines of coach tracks fading to invisibility. The horse soon lost its initial enthusiasm and slowed his pace, as Gil settled down for the long ride back to London. They passed a few coaches, the drivers and outside passengers muffled up to their eyebrows, and one small town, its inns beacons of warmth in the white wasteland, but Gil was not minded to stop. That would mean admitting he was wrong to attempt the ride, and that he could never do. So he pressed on.

It was not a comfortable ride. His leg throbbed abominably, and as the snow whirled ever faster around him, it made him feel queer and dizzy. The cold seeped into his very bones. But the horse was a good one, and needed little direction, and after a while Gil stopped noticing the cold. He rode on, although the horse had slowed to a walk. And the snow fell more and more thickly. Perhaps he would stop at the next inn after all, but the thought was hazy, as if his mind were filled with treacle. But he had seen no inn for a while now, and no coaches either. Nothing to do but push on, always onwards. Sooner or later there would be an inn.

The horse stopped. Gil jerked up from his position low to the creature's neck. He had almost fallen asleep! That would never do, not in this bitter weather. He tried to kick the animal forwards but somehow his legs would not move. He flicked the reins instead, and the horse jolted into motion, almost tipping Gil off backwards.

And now that he had begun, the animal seemed to have found a sudden burst of energy for he cantered along in a manner which had Gil screaming from the pain in his leg. Where had this agony come from? And why was he so hot, with an inch of snow on his shoulders? The weather had worsened considerably, for it was almost dark. He could barely see the horse's head in front of him.

An inn… he must find an inn…

There was a light! Like a lighthouse in the gloom, ahead shone a thin golden beam. Gil pulled on the reins, but the horse tossed its head imperiously and moved even faster. Panic swept over Gil. He must stop! If he rode past the light then he might never find another one. He had to stop, at all costs!

He pulled again on the reins, heaving with every last ounce of strength remaining to him. The horse reared, and with a cry of despair, Gil slid sideways.

The ground was hard, knocking the breath out of him. For a moment he lay, too stupefied to move. When he came to himself again, the silence was absolute. Not a creature moved in this white wasteland, not an owl was abroad, nor a fox, not so much as a hedgehog rustling in the undergrowth. Was he dead? He felt neither heat nor cold, only the dull, relentless pain of his leg. He was tired, so tired. If he lay still, if he kept his eyes closed, he would drift off to sleep and he would feel better in the morning, he was sure of it. At Drummoor. He would be home soon.

No.

Something was wrong. If he slept… he must not sleep, somehow he knew that.

The light. There was a light. With a massive effort, he lifted his head. Yes! There it was, shining unwaveringly through the white shroud of the falling snow. He tried to get up, but his legs would not work. But he must reach the light, he must! His head was as thick as soup, but he knew that much. No matter how great the struggle, he must reach the light. Slowly, trembling with the strain, he raised himself a little on his arms and shifted an inch nearer to the light.

~~~~~

Genista rather enjoyed the times when her father went away. It didn't happen often, but maybe once or twice a month he would be summoned to a patient so distant that he would be required to stay overnight, and occasionally, if the patient took a long while to die or the baby was slow to be born, there would be a second night away too. With the snow so thick now, surely this would be one of those occasions.

She checked the roast in the hot oven, and the vegetables in the slow oven. The soup was simmering, and the fruit pie was ready to go into the hot oven as soon as the chicken was out of it. She watched Betty lay the table in the kitchen — another treat, to eat off the plain wooden table, with no ceremony and no need to change her gown. She sighed with pleasure. She loved her father dearly, of course she did, but he did like everything just so. *'We must maintain standards, daughter,'* he always said. *'Your mother would wish it.'* And of course he was absolutely right — Father was always right — but just occasionally, it was lovely not to worry about doing things properly.

She had just closed the door of the oven when she thought she heard a noise, an odd sort of tapping sound.

"What was that? Did you hear something?"

"I didn't hear nothing, Miss Genista. Most likely it's the wind catching the—"

"Hush! There it is again. Did you hear it?"

"No, Miss Genista."

"You don't need to be so formal, Betty. You can call me Genista when Father isn't here."

"That seems disrespectful— Oh! I heard it! It's at the door, Miss Genista."

"This door? Why would anyone come to the kitchen door? Oh, the light, of course. The front of the house is dark."

She went through to the scullery, where a lamp hung on a hook over the sink, shining out through the uncurtained window. There it was again, a definite tapping sound, but faint. Perhaps Betty was right, and it was just a broken branch knocking against the door. But there was no harm in checking. She slid open the bolts and opened the door.

On the doorstep, half covered in snow and just visible in the thin light of the lamp, lay a dark shape. It groaned.

"It's a man," she said. "Quick, Betty, help me get him inside. Heavens, look how wet he is, and cold! His face is frozen. Quick, we must take him through to the kitchen. Can you carry his feet? That's it. One… two… three… lift."

The man screamed, and then silence fell.

"To the rug… in front of… the range…" Genista puffed.

Half carrying and half dragging the unconscious man, they set him down as gently as they could on the rug. Genista began to unfasten his snow-covered greatcoat and loosen his cravat.

"His clothes are soaked through. We must get him out of them at once. Blankets, Betty, and towels — as many as you can carry."

Cautiously, remembering the scream when they had lifted him, she began divesting him of his sodden garments, the greatcoat first, then the top boots, then his coat. He was heavy in her arms as she raised him up, but not unmanageably so.

Betty came back in at a run, her arms full. "How did he get here, Miss Genista? There's little enough traffic on this lane, for it goes from nowhere to nowhere."

"That's a good point. He can't have walked from Elversham, for his boots aren't muddy enough. There must have been a carriage… or a horse! It will die in this weather if we can't get it into the stable. Betty, will you go and look? But don't go too far, just down the path to the lane."

With a quick nod, Betty disappeared, and Genista turned back to her unexpected guest. He lay motionless on the rug, eyes closed, his long lashes resting on his pale cheeks, his breathing rapid. He was young, very young, perhaps three or four and twenty. Tendrils of dark hair clung damply to his forehead. He was beautiful, like an angel fallen to earth, his symmetry unmarred, his nose aquiline, his lips full. Who was he, this vision of perfection?

She touched his forehead again… cold, so cold. He was chilled to the bone. There was heat enough from the range, but the stranger's wet clothes would leach all the warmth from his body if they were not removed. Waistcoat, shirt, breeches. Then whatever lay beneath. Waistcoat, shirt, breeches. Oh Lord. If only Father were there! He would carry the man into the surgery and deal with… whatever lay beneath. But Father was not there, and if Genista didn't do what was needful, then this fallen angel might well die and it would be her fault. She unfastened the waistcoat, and lifted him to slide it off. Then the shirt and undershirt, pulled off all in one movement. She paused, her eyes drawn to his bare skin, so pale in the lamplight. He'd looked so slender when they'd carried him in, but he was neither thin like a boy, nor soft like a woman. There was strength in his arms, and his chest...

A deep breath. How foolishly missish to allow herself to be distracted. She was acting as his physician now, so she must be impassive, and do what she needed to do, and quickly. Another deep breath, and then she unbuttoned the breeches, and began to wriggle them down his legs. And before she could think about it, the undertrousers.

His upper left leg was an angry purple colour, the jagged scar raised and torn. Green matter oozed from one corner. With an exclamation of shock, she quickly wrapped him in blankets, then lit a candle and ran through to the mixing room for the necessary materials. Her expert hands had soon made a poultice.

Betty was in the kitchen when she returned. "No sign of horse nor carriage," she said. "I can just make out hoof marks heading towards Elversham. I guess he fell off and the beast went on by itself."

"Nothing we can do about it now," Genista said briskly. "Hold the bowl, Betty, while I apply the poultice." Lifting a small amount of blanket to reveal the injured part of the leg, she set to work.

"Shouldn't be doing that," Betty said, with a sniff of disapproval. "He's a *man*."

"He's a very sick man, who will likely die if we do nothing," she said sharply.

Betty pointed to the discarded pile of clothes, the undergarments clearly visible. "But he's *nekkid*, Miss Genista. And you a lady an' all."

"I am a physician's daughter, and my conscience won't permit me to refuse to help. Father would wish me to," she said, hoping that was true. Father could be such a stickler for propriety sometimes. Yet he had taught her everything he knew and why else but to help people, just as he did? But she felt uneasily that helping people didn't quite mean stripping handsome young men naked.

END OF SAMPLE CHAPTER OF *Lord Gilbert*

Made in the USA
Coppell, TX
08 July 2022